Golden Eights

The Search For Churchill's Lost Gold Begins Again

Nigel Seed

EMPOWERWORDS

ISBNS
PARENT : 978-1-78215-118-0
EPUB: 978-1-78215-119-7
MOBI: 978-1-78215-120-3
PDF: 978-1-78215-121-0

A CIP catalogue for this book is available from the National Library.

Published by EMPOWERWORDS LTD., Dublin, 2014.

Printed and Bound in the UK by
www.printondemand-worldwide.com

We are all travellers in the wilderness of this world and the best that we can find in our travels is an honest friend.

-Robert Louis Stevenson

I have been blessed with a number of honest friends who have helped me by reading my book at the embryonic stages and giving me useful criticism. You know who you are and thank you all. I have also been privileged to have my book edited by that exceptional author John Gordon Davis and to whom I owe a great debt for his advice and encouragement. The biggest debt though is to my wife who has lived this project with me and been supportive throughout, especially when I was struggling.

The story is a mixture of fact, legend and pure fiction. None of the characters, except one who is acknowledged in the factual chapter, in my story bear more than a passing resemblance to any real people and the names have been conjured from somewhere in my head.

Also by this author.

In the Jim Wilson series (as of 2014).

V4 – Vengeance Delayed

Coming soon:

Two Into One

1579 – The Pacific Ocean

Capitan San Juan de Anton stood on the sunbaked deck of his ship, the *Nuestra Señora de la Concepción*, as she sailed slowly along the coast of Peru on a fine Sunday morning. His masthead lookout had reported the ship sailing slowly behind him an hour ago and now he could just see the sails in the heat haze. He watched idly for a while then returned to the management of his own ship. He felt no alarm. The Pacific Ocean was a Spanish Lake and the only full rig ships operating in these waters were under the auspices of His Christian Majesty.

By nine o'clock that evening the ships were within hailing distance and the Capitan returned to his stern rail to await the first hail. When it came, it was a rude shock as the voice in Spanish informed him that this was an English ship and ordered him to heave-to and surrender. San Juan was no coward and defiantly refused, despite his ship being unarmed. He soon found to his cost that the mystery ship was the heavily armed *Golden Hind* captained by the English Privateer Francis Drake.

Drake's sailors opened fire with their arquebuses and loosed a cloud of arrows from their powerful longbows. The Golden Hind's bow chaser cannon fired a chain-ball shot which brought down the Spanish mizzen mast and caused the sail to trail in the water. A second shot from one of the heavy guns was followed by another order to strike sail. This time the wounded Spanish Captain submitted rather than see his crew slaughtered.

The English sailors swarmed aboard and made the Spaniards prisoner while the Capitan was questioned about his cargo. He was forced to admit that he was carrying a considerable treasure. In the cargo, that was properly registered with the Spanish Authorities, were large quantities of gold and silver. A search revealed that there were at least 1,300 silver bars and 14 chests of gold and silver coins much of which was privately owned and had not been registered. The haul was so big that it took Drake's rapacious crew six days to transfer it to their own ship.

During the transfer Drake sat in the captain's poop cabin rummaging for Spanish maps of this coastline. Opening a heavy chest in the corner of the cabin he found a carved wooden box, polished to a deep lustre with brass reinforcing at each corner. Opening the box revealed a crimson silk lining with recesses for the five Pieces of Eight laying there. A Piece of Eight is made of high grade silver but these were solid gold. Drake removed the top tray and then the rest. Surrounded by twenty solid gold Pieces of Eight he puzzled over their purpose. He stood and went to the cabin door. Calling over one of his crew he sent him to fetch the Spanish captain.

Minutes later San Juan entered what had once been his own cabin to face the English pirate.

"Tell me, Capitan," said Drake in execrable Spanish "what is the meaning of these coins. Pieces of Eight are silver yet these are gold. Why?"

"Ah, Captain," said the Spaniard sadly, "the vanity of kings has always to be managed to gain favour, has it not? The Spanish Empire is founded in great part upon the Piece of Eight as you call it. A coin that is minted of silver so pure it is accepted by all men. These are a personal gift for King Phillip minted especially for him in the moulds of Lima by master craftsmen. A thoughtful gift of this nature, when presented with the gold crucifix you have on my table, should bring a smile to the King's face and gain us his favour for our future enterprises."

Drake looked up from the coins and said "Do not worry Capitan, they will serve your intended purpose but with a different monarch. When we come safe home these will make a fine gift for Queen Elizabeth and persuade her to continue to smile upon my voyages."

Back aboard the Golden Hind, Drake considered his options. His intention had been to return to England around Cape Horn, the way he had originally entered the Pacific. Seizing a treasure of this size would rouse every ship in the Spanish Empire against him and a new way home had to be found. The charts he had seized from this ship and others gave him the information he needed to find his way across the vast Pacific Ocean and from there home to England. The specially minted coins would find favour for him with the Queen especially on top of the share of the treasure she was already owed for partially financing this voyage.

Chapter 1.

Present Day - London

Major Jimmy Wilson, of the Royal Engineers, pushed his way to the door of the overcrowded Jubilee Line tube train and stepped onto the Westminster Underground station platform. He let the crowd carry him though the pedestrian tunnels to the foot of the escalator and he stood on the moving staircase as it carried him upwards once again. He watched the harassed faces of the morning commuters as they rushed to get to their tedious offices. The ones who got off at this station were mostly Civil Servants who worked in Whitehall or the Houses of Parliament. Heaven only knew how they managed to do this day in and day out for a whole career. He had been doing it for nearly six months now and he could feel the frustration building with every week.

He climbed the stairs out of the station and looked across Parliament Square through the drizzle. He turned to the right, away from the river and walked down the slight slope to the large building across the road at the bottom of Whitehall. 100 Parliament Street is the main office for Her Majesty's Revenue and Customs, the taxation people. A strange place to find a serving Army Officer and his small team of only two soldiers. But then that was the idea. Anybody looking for a team like his would be unlikely to look among the tax officers who served in this building.

The building nominally has four working floors but on the side that overlooks Parliament Square there is a small fifth floor annexe where staff of various improvement projects used to sit. They had been cleared out at short notice, amidst considerable grumbling, to make room for the new team and any additional members they might need in the future. Now there were just three of them rattling around in a room that could hold thirty.

Jim swiped through the security gates and took the lift to the fourth floor. He nodded pleasantly to the staff, that looked up from their desks, as he walked through to the doorway at the top of the stairwell. He climbed the narrow staircase. His two soldiers, Sergeant Major Ivan Thomas and Sergeant Geordie Peters were already there. Although both were wearing similar nondescript civilian suits to his own, the sharp creases in their trousers and the highly polished shoes marked them out as different from the Civil Servants they were concealed amongst.

Both men stood as he came in and both said, "Good morning sir". It was the daily ritual of military formality that was then put aside.

"Anything today, Ivan?" said Jim, more in hope than expectation.

"Sorry Boss, nothing at all. It's beginning to look like this was all a waste of time and effort."

Geordie brought the ritual morning coffee across and the three of them sat in the cheap red armchairs in the conference area.

They all sipped the scalding brew and then Geordie said, "So how long do we have to sit here before they let us go back to the Army then, boss? Or have they forgotten all about us?"

Jim nodded, "After all the good intentions following the V4 attacks on New York I must confess I expected this special unit to be more active than this. We'll give it another week, I think. That will be exactly six months since we moved in here. If there is nothing for us then I will ask for us to be posted to a regular unit. OK?"

They both agreed and went back to their daily routine of checking emails, scanning the Internet and then playing solitaire on the computers.

At 10 a.m. they went down to the basement, to the small fitness facility and changed for their daily run. Rain or shine they ran three times around St James' Park every day, dodging the tourists and trying to keep their physical fitness at a reasonable level. Back in the basement they then lifted weights for half an hour before grabbing a coffee each from the ground floor coffee shop before heading back up to the office. It was not a satisfactory routine for three capable and intelligent men.

They had been sitting in the conference seats for a few minutes over their coffee when the door at the end of the room squeaked and a round rosy face peeped in. A young man in a well cut grey suit stepped into the room and walked over to them.

"Major Wilson?" he said, looking round at them.

Jim looked at him. "I'm Wilson."

"How do you do sir? Brian Dickinson, I am from Number 10. I have a message for you from the Prime Minister. He would like to see you and rather oddly he also said '... and tell him to bring his two pirates with him.' Does that make sense to you sir?"

Jim nodded. "It does, Mr Dickinson. When does he want to see us?"

The well-scrubbed young man checked his watch. "In about an hour. Plus he did ask if you could avoid using the front gates of Downing Street as there are rather a lot of press people there today."

"Sounds interesting. How else do we get there? Through the fabled secret tunnels?"

"Oh no, sir. No need for those today, I will take you through the Foreign Office, they have a rather handy back gate that comes out just opposite the Prime Minister's house. If we could go now I can ask you to stay in the waiting room so he can see you as soon as he is free"

Chapter 2.

The four of them stepped out of the front door of 100 Parliament Street and turned left. At the end of the building they turned into King Charles Street and walked along to the staff entrance of the Foreign Office. Security passes were waiting for them and the guard let them through into the central courtyard. As they walked across what is now a car park they looked around at the impressive building. Ivan noticed the heads carved into the wall around the courtyard, each with a name below it.

"Oh wow!" he said. "These are the Foreign Secretaries, going back years. Some of these people worked for Queen Elizabeth the First."

Their guide stopped. "Are you interested in history?"

Jim and Ivan nodded and Ivan said, "Particularly military history of course."

The young man looked at his watch. "We've just got time. There's something in that part of the building you might like." He led the way over to the right and through a door into an office area. Showing them up a staircase and into a meeting room he said, "Did you know that Lord Wellington and Admiral Nelson met only once? That was in 1805 when both of them were waiting to see Lord Castlereagh. The fireplace from that room was recovered when the building was demolished and this is it. It always gives me a little tingle to think that the two of them might have leaned on here during that meeting."

Jim looked across at Geordie who was looking out of the window at the attractive secretaries crossing the courtyard.

"You seem unimpressed, Sergeant."

Geordie hastily turned back into the room.

Ivan grinned at Jim. "The man's got no soul, sir. Doesn't get excited unless you want him crawling around in tight spaces or blowing something up, typical ex-miner."

The young Civil Servant checked his watch again and hurried them back to the courtyard.

They walked under a large archway and found a security guard waiting to swing the ironwork gates open for them. Passing through they found themselves in Downing Street and walked towards the front door of Number 10. As they reached it the door swung silently open and they walked in. They had been left in the waiting room for only a few minutes when their guide returned.

"He can see you now," he said and led them to a pair of impressive wooden doors.

They entered the Cabinet Room with its famous oval table. Half way along on each side sat a single figure. The first was David Orwell, the Prime Minister, but none of them recognized the other man who watched them as they came in.

The Prime Minister rose with a broad smile that they recognised from a thousand newspaper photographs and from their meeting after the V4 attack in the USA.

"Welcome, gentlemen. Nice to see you again. Do sit down. Would you like some tea, coffee, anything?"

They all declined. The door to the room closed and the five of them were alone.

The Prime Minister regained his seat and said, "Well, I suppose some introductions are in order. Gentlemen, this is Sir

Richard Wallace and he is the new Governor of the Bank of England. Richard, these are the three men I mentioned who I think are the people to solve our little problem."

Sir Richard looked uncomfortable. "I would hardly call it a little problem, Prime Minister and to be honest I am unclear how three soldiers are suitable to help?" He turned to the three and said, "No offence intended, gentlemen, but this is a vitally important issue and very delicate."

The Prime Minister looked at Sir Richard. "Richard, you told me that the most important issue was keeping the secret. Is that still correct?"

"It is, Prime Minister. It is crucial if a disaster is to be avoided."

"Then let me give you some background on these three men and you can tell me what you think then. You obviously recall the missile attack on New York six months ago and the huge robbery that it was a cover for?" He looked to Sir Richard for confirmation and then continued. "The story that the press had was incomplete. The perpetrator of the attack was not a mystery as the public was led to believe and the story that the proceeds of the robbery were lost is a lie. I can't tell you exactly what did happen for security reasons but it was far more than the story the press was given. The British part of the team sits beside you and not a word of the secret part of that operation has leaked. Major Wilson and his small team have my absolute confidence and have demonstrated an ability to keep their mouths shut, which seems to be a rare quality these days."

"They were also the ones that initially discovered the whereabouts of the submarines that were used in the attack, so they have the investigative skills we need. They have my total admiration as highly capable people, which is why I recruited them as part of a secret international task force which has yet to begin operations. I imagine they are now bored to tears and would welcome something useful to do."

Jim leaned forwards and said, "You are quite right about the boredom, sir and the ability to avoid running off at the mouth. Whatever task you have for us would be very welcome."

The Prime Minister turned back to the Governor. "Well, Richard?"

Sir Richard seemed to have a talent for looking uncomfortable but smoothed the lapels of his chalk-striped, blue suit and said, "Very well Prime Minister, on your recommendation I accept that these are our team but I would have preferred trained investigators."

The Prime Minister nodded. "That's settled then. Gentlemen, Sir Richard has a strange story to tell you and you may wish to change your mind about the tea while you are listening to it."

The three agreed and the Prime Minister pressed a call button near him and then ordered five mugs of tea and a plate of biscuits. At the mention of mugs, Sir Richard looked uncomfortable again but said nothing.

Chapter 3.

With tea in hand the three soldiers settled down to listen to Sir Richard who coughed, sighed and began. "Well gentlemen I don't know how much you know about the history of World War Two."

Jim said, "I like to think I know a little. I studied at the Royal Military Academy, Sandhurst and was posted there as an instructor when the historian Richard Holmes was lecturing there. I used to sneak into the back of his lectures whenever I could."

Sir Richard was a little taken aback; he cleared his throat and said "Yes well. That's useful, of course, but the story I have to tell you is one of the secrets of that war that has not been publicised at all. In fact, I myself only became aware of it recently. It is a secret that is passed to each Governor of the Bank of England as he or she takes over the post."

The governor took a breath and then continued "You will be aware that in 1940 there was a very real possibility of Britain being invaded and you will recall that the British Army had been virtually destroyed in France. Many of the men got out through Dunkirk in all sorts of ships and private boats but most of their personal weapons and all their heavy weapons and transport were left behind. Luckily for us, Hitler decided he needed command of the sky before he could risk the cross channel invasion and the RAF, with help from some overseas contingents, fought and won the Battle of Britain."

Sir Richard paused and looked at the Prime Minister who nodded for him to continue.

"However, the government of the time had not predicted that the RAF could hold the Luftwaffe back and as a precaution, a major part of this country's gold reserves were spirited away to Canada for safe keeping. That was 'Operation Fish' and it was incredibly successful. Despite the U Boat risks in the North Atlantic, tons of gold were shipped and not a single bar was lost. Most of it was stored in a special vault below the Sun Alliance building in Montreal and the secret never came out until long after the war."

Sir Richard paused and sipped his tea. Jim noticed that even when handling the mug his little finger was cocked out.

"However, what is not known, outside a small group, is that because the Atlantic crossing was so hazardous it was decided that we would not risk all the gold and a large percentage was sent into hiding in this country. This action was even more secret, so much so that it did not even get an operational code name. The gold was entrusted to a secret group that had been set up on Churchill's personal order and they were just known as the 'Auxiliary Units'. Very few records were kept of this Secret Army so that, had the Germans succeeded in landing, there would be no record that they ever existed. Perfect people to hide our gold. Sadly in the rush and panic of those times nobody thought about how to get the gold back. Since there is no record of who it was issued to, we do not know where to look or who to contact. You see our problem?"

There was a silence as the three soldiers absorbed all they had been told. Geordie was the first to speak. "So, maybe a naïve question but, why don't you just put a notice in the papers or on TV asking the people who have it to come forward?"

Sir Richard looked at him. "A few reasons. First the treasure hunters and criminals would be out in force and anything they found would probably get 'lost'. Next we don't have the code word needed to get these people to bring it back and anyway most of the people it was entrusted to are probably dead by now. But the big one is our financial credit in the world. International financial institutions know how much gold we have to back our currency. Or rather they think they do. There are tons of gold less than they think in our vaults. It is in the country, but we don't know where. If that became known outside the UK the pound would crash in value and the country would be in a huge monetary crisis. Basically, we need it back without anybody knowing it was ever lost."

Ivan looked thoughtful. "So how much gold are we talking about here? Enough to fill a back pack or what?"

Sir Richard looked across at the Prime Minister who nodded and said, "They need to know. Go ahead."

Sir Richard swallowed. "Not easy to calculate. We know that there are nearly 12 tons of gold bars, of various sizes, but that is not all. Golden art treasures were passed to the bank for safe keeping during the war and they are out there somewhere as well. All in all there is probably somewhere in the region of 20 tons unaccounted for."

Geordie gave a low whistle. "Bloody hell, that's a lot of metal to shift but with our usual 10% commission that could pay for my wedding rather nicely."

The governor slammed his hands on the table and leapt to his feet "Prime Minister, that is unthinkable!"

The Prime Minister looked at the three soldiers and noticed their shoulders were shaking.

"Sir Richard," he said, "I think you have been the victim of a little Army humour there. I trust these men implicitly and anything they recover will end up in your vaults. Never fear."

Jim managed to regain a straight face and turned to Sir Richard who clearly had the sense of humour of a golf ball.

"Sir Richard, this gold has been missing for more than seventy years and yet only now you want it found. Why? What has changed? And surely this can't be the first time the Bank has tried to find it?"

The Prime Minister leaned forward and rested his elbows on the highly polished table. "I asked the same question and it seems attempts have been made to recover the gold. The first was in 1945 as the war ended. That was when we found out that the officer of the Auxiliary Units who had coordinated the concealment in 1940 had been dropped behind enemy lines in 1944, just after D-Day. That was Captain George Galway of the Loyal North Lancashire Regiment, a brave man but one who keeps his secret to this day. Any more, Sir Richard?"

Sir Richard smoothed his already perfect old school tie. "Yes, in fact in 1954 a Police Inspector called Spelling, from Scotland Yard, was given the task of searching for it. Nothing much happened for months and then one day he told his Sergeant that he had a clue he was following up and would not be back for a week. He was never seen again. Since then we have never had a starting point to begin another search."

"So what has changed?"

Sir Richard was obviously not used to being questioned but recovered his composure and said "I mentioned the gold treasures that were shipped out with the bullion. One of them has turned up in a New York auction house." He slid a glossy brochure along the table opened at the page that showed pictures of each side of a gleaming golden coin on a blue velvet cloth. "If we ask too many questions on an official level or demand it back we will expose the problem and the financial trouble will start."

Jim nodded. "OK, that will give us a start point. But what is this coin and how do we know it's one of ours for sure?"

Sir Richard took a sip from his mug with obvious distaste, then said, "In the time of the Spanish Empire the internationally accepted currency was the Spanish Dollar. These were also known as 'Pieces of Eight' due to the custom of cutting them into eight smaller pieces for smaller purchases. These were minted in various places in the Empire such as Mexico City and Lima in Peru. They were made of high grade silver of which the Spanish had a vast supply. However, as a gift for Phillip II, twenty of these coins were carefully cast in pure gold along with an ornate, solid gold crucifix. This was intended for his personal altar. He was a very devout Catholic. Unfortunately the Spanish galleon carrying these gifts was one of those attacked by English privateers and the cargo of gold and silver, including these gifts for the King, was taken. The privateer in this case was Francis Drake and the ship he took in the Pacific during his famous circumnavigation of the world was the unarmed *Nuestra Señora de la Concepción*. In fact the treasure was the reason he did not come back the way he had sailed out, he did not want the Spanish to catch him. He brought his haul back to England after circumnavigating the globe. His investors, who included Queen Elizabeth, each took a share. Drake kept back the gifts intended for King Phillip and made a present of them to the Queen to ensure he kept her favour. They could well have been one of the reasons he was given a knighthood and why he was honoured on the deck of his ship in Tilbury. The coins were kept in Buckingham Palace until nineteen of them were brought into our vaults for safe keeping in late 1939."

Ivan leaned forward with his big hands flat on the highly polished oval table. "You said nineteen were brought to the bank's vault. What happened to number twenty?"

Sir Richard looked at him. "We don't know. It was sent to the Spanish government as a gift in 1934 but during their Civil War it vanished. We think it may have gone to Russia, as much of the Spanish gold reserves did, to buy weapons for the Republican

Army. But if it did there is no record of it. Equally it may have been looted when Madrid was taken. We just don't know."

"So how do you know the one in New York is one of ours and not the Spanish one?"

"We don't and that is another part of the problem."

The three soldiers leaned back in their chairs. This was a big deal. After all these years trying to track down a highly secret organization, with no starting point, was not going to be easy. Jim looked across the wide table at the Prime Minister who was watching him expectantly.

"How much authority do we have to get this done and what resources can we call on, sir?"

"What do you need?"

Jim shook his head. "At this stage I don't have the faintest idea. If we narrow down the search area we might need a helicopter or possibly even satellite imagery. I won't know until we get into it and we may need things at short notice."

The Prime Minister thought for a moment. "Would a letter from me giving you authority to call on all British Government resources, military and civilian, do the job for you?"

"Yes sir, it would."

"I will have one drawn up and delivered to your office in Parliament Street before the day is out. In addition, you have whatever budget you need for travel and anything else you need. The details of the financial codes to use for that will come with the letter."

There was a pause as the Prime Minister contemplated the three soldiers. He cleared his throat.

"Gentlemen I know that you are used to danger in your profession but I do want to stress the importance of this mission. The need for secrecy is not just for Sir Richard's benefit, I fear that if this task becomes known there is a significant risk, to all of you, from criminal elements who would stop at nothing for this amount of gold. But I have confidence in you. Thank you, gentlemen, please keep me apprised of your progress."

The three men rose and left the Cabinet Room. The pink-cheeked young man was waiting for them and steered them out of Number 10 and back through the Foreign Office to avoid entanglement with any reporters who might be prowling outside the gates of Downing Street. They walked in silence, each of them thinking about their new task and wondering where the devil they were going to start.

Chapter 4.

The three men walked across to the Treasury side of their building for a lunch in the staff restaurant. They were still quiet, absorbing what they had been told. They took their trays to a table away from most of the other diners where they could speak without being overheard.

Ivan was the first to speak "Well it seems to me that the first thing we have to do is find out if this coin in New York is Number 20. If it is, we are out of clues to start with and we can ask to go back to a proper job. If not, we might just have a place to start."

The other two nodded agreement over their Shepherd's Pie.

"Agreed," said Jim, "I think we may need to split up and each take a part of this puzzle. Geordie how long have we got before your wedding and how much time can you spare to be away before it?"

Geordie smiled. "It's just less than two weeks away and to be honest, I think Sam and her Mum would like me out from under foot while they are organising it. All I have to do is turn up on the day and stay vertical during the service."

"That should be plenty of time to identify our starting point at least. After lunch we need to get up to our garret and work up a plan."

Back in their room on the fifth floor they dragged a whiteboard to the conference area and started to work out what they knew and what they needed to know. What they had was pretty thin. The first port of call had to be the auction house in New York. The catalogue listed the sellers of the various items they were offering, but against the coin it just said 'A Private Seller'. It appeared that the present owner did not want to be identified.

There could be any number of reasons for that but it probably only meant that, with this being a reputable auction house, they were going to respect the seller's privacy.

Jim stared at the ceiling. "Who do we know that can persuade a New York auction house to release privileged information?"

Geordie looked round from the whiteboard. "It has to be Raoul."

Ivan shook his head "How can a Lieutenant Commander in the US Navy do that? Even if he is a Navy SEAL."

Geordie sat down and said "Maybe he can't, but the SEALs work with a lot of spooky people in some strange agencies in the US. Maybe one of his contacts owes him a favour? Heaven knows the whole of the USA owes him a favour after the V4 incident, if only they knew about him. If it came to arm twisting he would be ideal but I suspect we need to be a little more subtle."

Jim sat up "That's good thinking. Geordie, you take that angle. Give him a call and find out where he is and if he is in the US go and see him. No mention of this search in phone calls or emails. You can't tell him why we want to know. He should trust us enough for that."

Geordie went to make his phone call and Jim turned to Ivan. "Ivan" he said "if it is not on display in Spain it has either been stolen or it went to Russia. To avoid waiting for the answer from New York I want you to go to Russia and see if you can find it."

Ivan was surprised "Bloody hell, boss! You do know Russia is a big country, don't you? Where would I start?"

Jim smiled. "Not as big as you think in this case. This is a very special piece so it will probably be in one of two places. My thought is that it is either in the Kremlin itself or in the Hermitage Museum in St Petersburg."

Ivan nodded. "I take your point but can't we just get the Embassy people to go and have a look?"

Jim shook his head. "I would guess that they have already done that as far as they can and not seen it. The Hermitage is huge and they cannot display all their items all the time so it could be in storage and if it is in the Kremlin, I doubt they can just walk in for a look round. We need someone to help us."

"Andrei!" said Ivan. "After the big bear hug he got from the Russian President at the end of the V4 incident he must have some really useful influence to get into places others could not go. I'll call him now."

He got up and went to his desk to phone the Russian Police Commander who had nearly died with them during the New York attack.

Jim walked back to his computer. He had decided that his part of the initial search would be to see what information was available about Churchill's Secret Army. The Internet was always a good place to start provided there was not too much conspiracy rubbish surrounding these people. As he sat down, the door opened behind him and the Prime Minister's rosy-cheeked assistant appeared once more, this time holding three envelopes.

"Hello sir," he said, "the Prime Minister has sent these over for you. He thought you might need one each. He says to tell you that if anyone gives you any trouble there is a phone number in there that goes straight through to the Duty Officer in Number 10 who can contact him day or night to back you up."

Jim opened the first envelope and read the letter. It was simple and straight to the point. It should do the trick. He turned to the young man. "Would you thank the Prime Minister for me? These will do very nicely."

He stood as the young man in the nice suit left down the narrow staircase. Then walked across to give Geordie his envelope and sat down at the next desk.

Geordie swiveled round to face him. "Raoul is down in Florida with some of his team. They are engaged in a training exercise and operating out of Eglin Air Force Base. It's a bit of a pain to get there using scheduled airlines but it seems there is an E-3D Sentry AWACS aircraft leaving RAF Waddington first thing in the morning on its way to the US. If that's the Prime Minister's letter I can get them to take me and divert through Eglin on their way."

Jim nodded and handed the letter over. "Good idea. Why is a Sentry going to the US, though?"

"It seems they have been invited to take part in an annual USAF training exercise called 'Red Flag'. It's in the desert just outside Las Vegas."

Ivan turned round at his desk. "Typical RAF. We get to freeze our backsides off training to throw bridges across the rivers of Northern Germany and they get to go to Las Vegas. I think I joined the wrong mob."

Four more phone calls and Geordie was on his way to Kings Cross station to catch the train for Lincoln. The RAF would have a car waiting for him to take him to the air base at Waddington to be ready for his flight the next morning.

Ivan had contacted Andrei and booked a scheduled British Airways flight to Moscow. Leaving at 10.05 the next morning, he had arranged for Andrei to pick him up at Domodedovo airport and not to ask any questions until they met up. He took his copy of the Prime Minister's letter and went home to pack.

Jim topped up his coffee and settled in behind his computer to research one of the most secretive military units the British Army had ever formed.

Chapter 5.

Geordie woke early the next morning in the RAF Waddington Sergeants' Mess. He dressed in casual clothes for the nine hour flight to Florida. An RAF Police Land Rover picked him up from the front of the mess building and carried him across to the 8 Squadron flight line where he was given a flight suit and a short briefing. The briefing officer was clearly not happy about having to make the brief so short and so early. He was equally unhappy when Geordie declined to tell him why they were to take him to Eglin.

He walked out to the large grey aircraft that already had its engines running and the radar dome on its back rotating. He climbed the mobile steps and the door was swung shut behind him. He was led through the main body of the aircraft past the ten mission consoles, with operators sitting at each one. They watched him walk by. At the rear of the banks of consoles were three seats for extra crew or passengers and he strapped himself into one of these as the aircraft started to taxi out to the runway.

The seat next to him held an RAF technician who said, "I hear we are diverting to Eglin in Florida just for you. What's going on there, then?"

Geordie smiled at him. "I just fancied a bit of Florida sunshine and so I booked with Crab airlines."

He turned away from the technician and opened his book. The conversation was obviously over.

Two hours into the flight Geordie was awakened from his doze by a Flight Lieutenant who said, "The skipper wants to see you. Come up to the flight deck."

Geordie roused himself and followed the officer through the cabin and once again the operators watched him go by. He moved into the surprisingly cramped cockpit of the aircraft that was based on the old Boeing 707 airframe. He found three officers and a senior NCO already in there and he was directed to a small fifth seat; he supposed this was what is known as the jump seat. The pilot turned round to him and Geordie was surprised to see the rank badges of a Wing Commander on his shoulders. He had not realised he was being flown by the unit commander.

"Well now, Sergeant Peters isn't it?"

Geordie nodded. "Yes sir, that's correct."

"Well now Sergeant, I think it's about time you told me what this is all about. This aircraft was due in Nevada this evening and my crew was looking forward to an evening in Las Vegas. Instead, because of duty time restrictions, we will be stuck at Eglin overnight. So just what the hell is so important that we are tasked with flying a mere Sergeant so far out of our way?"

Geordie hesitated. The Wing Commander was clearly not a happy man.

"Speak up! I asked you a question."

Geordie cleared his throat. "Sorry sir, I am unable to tell you. It is a security issue and one not for discussion."

The officer flushed. "Sergeant, I fly this surveillance aircraft and I command the squadron that operates them. I have the highest security clearance available. Now, why are we flying to Eglin for you?"

Geordie had not expected this level of aggression. He stood up and said, "With the greatest respect, sir, you are not cleared to be told what my task is and I am afraid that this conversation has to end now."

He turned and left the flight deck to return to his seat. Even over the noise of the engines he could hear the outraged yelling behind him. He reached his seat and was about to sit down when he realised the Wing Commander had followed him. He was red in the face and clearly ready to give Geordie a piece of his mind. Before the shouting started Geordie unzipped his borrowed flight suit and withdrew the Prime Minister's letter from his inside jacket pocket.

"Before you start sir," he said, "and embarrass yourself in front of your team I suggest you read this."

"Don't you dare speak to me like that!"

He read the letter and looked up at Geordie who was standing calmly in front of him. He read the letter again then threw it at Geordie and stormed back to the flight deck.

The technician in the other seat picked up the letter and handed it back to Geordie. "I don't know what you have in that letter but I would have paid good money to watch RFS put back in his box like that."

Geordie sat down and reached for his seat belt. "RFS?"

The technician smiled. "It's the boss's nickname among the technical staff. 'Red Faced and Screaming'. You can see why."

Geordie smiled and settled back to continue his doze. He woke as the engine note changed and looked around.

The technician next to him looked across and said "We are on approach to Eglin now. We should be on the ground in about half an hour."

There were no passenger windows in the Sentry so Geordie tightened his seat belt and picked up his book again to pass the time until the wheels thumped down on the runway. The aircraft taxied to its allocated parking spot and the engines whined down to a stop. Geordie stood up and grabbed his shoulder bag. He walked along the passageway beside the operator's consoles as they were packing up their last bits and pieces ready to disembark. As he reached the main exit he met the flight deck crew coming the other way. He stood back politely to allow them to exit the aircraft first.

As he walked onto the mobile aircraft steps, he saw two vehicles waiting to transport them away from the flight line. In front of the blue grey US Air Force bus was a shiny black Chevrolet Suburban. He could see the Wing Commander striding confidently towards the car while the rest of the flight crew headed for the bus. As he reached for the door handle the driver stepped out and shook his head. He pointed to the crew bus waiting behind. Although he could not hear the conversation, Geordie could see that this was not going down well and the Wing Commander was remonstrating with the driver. The driver pointed to the aircraft steps and when the officer realised the Suburban was for Geordie he stomped away in high dudgeon. Geordie watched him go. RFS indeed. He walked over to the black car and gripped the hand of the driver. It was good to see his friend Raoul Martinez again.

The Suburban accelerated away from the flight line and was heading towards the base accommodation area when Raoul said, "If you are staying in Florida you may want to stop at the Base Exchange to buy some lighter clothes. It gets pretty hot down here even at this time of year."

Geordie said, "I don't intend to be here long. Just time enough to beg a big favour of you. If there is aircon in the bar we'll be fine."

Martinez smiled. "This is Florida, there's always aircon. Now what is so important that you couldn't tell me on the phone?"

"I will talk you through it as soon as I can get a shower and change. That aircraft may be high tech but I have flown more comfortably."

Chapter 6.

Geordie settled into his chair behind a glass of icy cold Sam Adams beer. Martinez waited until they had both worked their way half down their glasses before saying, "OK Geordie, time to 'fess up. Why did you divert a large expensive aircraft here and in the process really irritate a senior Royal Air Force officer who even now is complaining long and loud in the Officer's Mess bar?"

Geordie smiled and looked up at the SEAL officer "Raoul, I have a problem and I am going to need you to trust me. I can't tell you why but I need to get some information from a New York auction house without them knowing who is asking or why. All I can tell you is that it is really important. I am guessing one of your odd agencies could help"

Martinez sat back in his chair and stroked his ear lobe. "OK, before we go anywhere with this I need an assurance that, whatever this is, it is not going to harm the interests of the United States."

Geordie thought for a moment. "If we can't get this information there is a real possibility that at some point in the future the United Kingdom might not be able to fulfil its responsibilities as a reliable ally of the USA."

Martinez sat up. "That sounds a bit melodramatic. Are you sure it's that important?" Geordie just nodded, worried that he had gone too far already.

"OK then. You'd better tell me what you need and I will see if I know anyone who can help."

Geordie pulled the auction brochure from his pocket and passed it across the table. "Page seven. Two pictures of a gold coin. It's a bit special and we need to know where it came from.

To do that we need a name and address for the seller. As you can see the auction house is withholding that information. For reasons that I, again, can't tell you we can't do anything as simple as asking a question."

Martinez said "And you don't want me to ask out in the open, I guess?"

"Correct."

"OK then. Let me think about who I could ask. With the business we are in there are a number of black agencies that we work with."

"Black agencies? What does that mean?"

Martinez took a quick look over his shoulder before saying, "You know that when we are developing secret equipment like the Stealth aircraft we run them as 'Black Projects'? That means that there is no information about them in the public domain and even the funding is hidden from the oversight committees. Well, there are certain agencies that operate the same way. They have limited oversight and don't have to answer for the money they spend."

"And they get away with that? I'm impressed. So who gives them their tasking?"

Martinez smiled. "My turn. That's heavily classified and you don't need to know."

Geordie laughed. "Good one. So can they help us do you think?"

Standing up Martinez said, "I'll find out. Let me make a call and while I'm away you can order dinner. I'll take a steak, medium rare. Oh and by the way, you're paying."

Geordie ordered the food and another couple of cold beers. Before they arrived Martinez returned and sat down again. He was about to speak when the waitress reappeared with the two beers and two excellent steaks with all the trimmings.

Once she was gone Martinez cut into his meat and said, "OK, I've got somebody who will get you the information. Where should they send it?"

Geordie finished chewing a juicy piece of steak. "Nowhere. No emails. No phone calls. They are too easily tracked or intercepted. I need to meet the person doing the job and have him tell me the information."

Martinez looked thoughtful and put down his fork. "Is it really that serious?"

Geordie nodded. "I wouldn't be asking this of you if it was not serious. I wish I could tell you just how serious."

Martinez picked up his fork again. "I think you just did."

They finished their dinner and went to sit out on the veranda of the bar with another couple of cold beers. The time difference was starting to catch up with Geordie, so he was planning to head for bed shortly. The mobile phone in the pocket of Martinez' fatigues started to ring and he fished it out.

Pressing the receive button he held the phone to his ear and said, "Yes". He listened for a moment and then said, "We'll be there in the early hours of tomorrow. Yes, it is that urgent." He ended the call and turned to Geordie. "They've got it, or at least they will have, by the time we get there. Finish your beer; we have a flight to catch."

Geordie gulped the last of his beer and went back into the bar to pay. Through the window he could see Martinez was back on the phone. As he went back outside the American said, "Flight leaves in forty minutes. You can sleep as we go."

"Where are we going? Or shouldn't I ask?"

"Pax River."

"Where the devil is that?"

"You'll see."

A little after midnight, local time, the US Air Force Gulfstream landed at Patuxent River Naval Air Station in Maryland. The inevitable black Chevy Suburban with the tinted windows was waiting for them as they disembarked and within minutes they were on their way. Leaving the base they drove along virtually deserted roads and across the bridge into the small town of Solomons. They left the main highway and pulled up outside a nondescript two story house with a neat garden and a tree with a swing hanging from one of its branches. As they walked up the driveway the front door swung open and they walked in. The hallway and living room were comfortably furnished and a lady in a dressing gown was sitting by the fireplace reading a book. It was only when she put the book down and stood up that Geordie saw the automatic pistol in her hand.

The man who had opened the door turned to Martinez. "You vouch for this man?"

Martinez said, "I do. He has no need to see any more of the building. He just needs the information you have for him."

The man at the door pressed a button on a pad on the wall and after a few seconds a door at the other side of the sitting room swung open to admit a man in a checked shirt and jeans. Geordie had just time to see the bank of mainframe computing equipment behind him before the door closed.

Checked shirt came over to the group. "You're the Brit?"

"That's me" said Geordie and took the small piece of paper that the newcomer thrust towards him.

Geordie looked at the name and address, then looked up to thank the man who was by now disappearing back through the far door.

Martinez took him by the elbow. "Time to go." He steered him back out of the front door. "Where to next Geordie?"

The Englishman looked at the small piece of paper in his hand.

"Now that I have this I need to be in London with it PDQ. Can you get me to an airport? Washington Dulles would probably be best. I can catch a flight from there fairly easily."

Chapter 7.

Ivan's flight to Russia with British Airways was much more comfortable than Geordie's to Florida and the in-flight entertainment was far superior, but he was still tired as he walked out of the arrivals hall in Moscow. Andrei was there to meet him and to speed him through the traffic into the city in a rather nice Mercedes saloon. They spoke of their adventures during the attack on New York and recalled just how cold they had been when marooned in a rubber dinghy in the Atlantic. They didn't mention how close to death they had been but the knowledge made a bond between them.

They didn't speak about why Ivan was there until they were seated comfortably in Andrei's apartment close to Red Square. Andrei made them both a cup of his signature strong black coffee and sat opposite Ivan to sip it.

"Well my friend, how can I help you this fine Russian day?"

Ivan put down his coffee cup. "Andrei, what I am about to ask of you may seem strange but I have to ask you to trust me. I cannot explain why we need to know this but I promise you it is important."

Andrei smiled. "I did not think you came here just to see me and of course I will respect your confidence. Russians are good at keeping secrets, we had a lot of practice during the communist years. Tell me what you need."

Ivan produced a colour photocopy of the page from the auction brochure. "This is a rather special coin that we think was given to the Spanish government in 1934 but it disappeared during their Civil War. We think it might have been brought to Russia with the rest of the Spanish gold to buy arms for the Republicans. Being such a special piece we think it might have ended up in one of your museums, possibly the Hermitage. We need to know if it is still here."

Andrei stared at the pictures on the sheet in his hand. "This is a small coin," he said, "and Russia is a big country but I can try. I will send copies of this to the museum in St Petersburg and they can tell us if they recognise it."

Ivan leaned forward. "Andrei, please don't do that. There must be no record that we even asked the question. No phone calls, no emails, no faxes. We need to ask the right person face to face so there is no trace of us."

Andrei sat back and contemplated Ivan for a moment "This sounds very important to you."

"It is or I wouldn't put you to this much trouble."

"Very well. I owe you much more than this. We take the train to St Petersburg in the morning and ask your questions. My Police Commander's badge will get us in to see the people we need to speak to with little trouble. But now a little vodka and a few reminiscences and then we sleep here. We will book onto the new fast train that can have us there in less than four hours. In the old days we would have been sleeping on the train overnight"

The next morning dawned bright and clear and Ivan was glad of the sunglasses to protect his bloodshot eyes. There had been rather too many vodkas powering the reminiscences and he was not used to the potent Russian brands. Even Andrei was moving a little more slowly than usual.

A police patrol cruiser took them to the station to avoid the risk of leaving the Mercedes in a Moscow parking lot. The tickets had been booked the night before by Andrei and his police rank had acquired them a compartment to themselves. Both of them were glad of the quiet and soon slept to recover from Andrei's vodka. The journey was uneventful and on arrival in St Petersburg they were met by yet another police cruiser that took them straight to the Hermitage.

Avoiding the crowds of tourists from some of the cruise liners docked in the harbour, they slipped through one of the staff entrances. When challenged by a security guard a quick flash of Andrei's identity pass was sufficient to gain them a salute and rapid entrance with directions to the Museum Director's office. A further showing of the police pass propelled a secretary through the door of the Director's private office and an equally rapid invitation in to see the great man. Communism may have died in Russia but old habits die hard and a senior police officer still commands respect and attention.

The two visitors settled into the comfortable chairs in the Director's office and accepted his offer of tea from the antique, silver samovar resting on an ornate sideboard. Once the secretary had delivered the tea they could move on from general small talk to the business at hand. Ivan deferred to Andrei as his own Russian language skills were rusty despite his time at the Army language school in Beaconsfield. He could follow the conversation but it would have taken far longer for him to compose sentences and mentally check his grammar. Andrei explained what they were looking for and showed the Director the photocopy of the coin. He declined to answer the Director's questions about why they wanted to know. A child of the communist era, the Director understood that when officials do not answer questions there is no advantage in pressing the point.

The Director picked up the telephone on his desk and dialled a short number. Ivan assumed it was an internal call and when the Director spoke that proved to be true as he called in the head of the Numismatic Department. A small silver haired man, with remarkably thick glasses, appeared through the door very shortly afterwards and was shown the photocopy.

He peered at it then shook his head and looked at the visitors. "We do not have such a coin in the Hermitage although we have examples of the silver versions," he said in Russian. "But such a special piece leaves a trace for those of us who love the history and magic of coins. There is such a coin in Russia. It was a gift to Stalin from his allies in Spain as a symbol of a special relationship during their difficult time. Because of that it was held in a special display in the Kremlin. It is not normally available to the Russian people or even officials of the Hermitage."

Andrei nodded. "Do you know the name of the man in the Kremlin to speak to in order to ensure this coin is still there?"

The coin specialist looked at his Director, who nodded slightly. Then he turned to Andrei. "For access to the special collection you would need to ask the President personally. I doubt even a policeman of your seniority would have such access."

Ivan recalled the bear hug that the President and Andrei had shared when they had recovered the gleaming religious icon at the end of the attack on New York. The President had gained a lot of political credit with the Russian people by bringing that home to Moscow and Andrei had stayed in the background to let him. That felt like a favour that could be called in.

Andrei and Ivan rose to their feet and expressing their thanks, made their exit. Ivan would have liked the chance to visit this superb collection but his mission was clearly in Moscow as soon as possible. After a surprisingly good meal at the station they caught the train back to Moscow. Andrei pressed a little to try to find out the significance of the coin but gave in with good grace when Ivan stonewalled him. Once back in Moscow, it took an hour or so on the phone to finally get through to the President's personal assistant.

Ivan listened as Andrei said, "Tell the President that Andrei Popov and one of the others from Florida need to see him for a few minutes only. He will understand the significance." He paused, listening and then Ivan heard him say, "There is no need for you to understand the significance. This is for the President only. Ring me back on this number when you have passed on my message."

He put down the phone and shrugged. 'Every functionary builds his ego by being as difficult as he can be. It is the curse of bureaucracy. But how they change when they screw up and need a friend in the police." Andrei went to make coffee but before they could drink it the phone rang. Andrei picked it up and listened "Agreed," was all he said. He put the phone down and said to Ivan, "Better grab your jacket. The President's car will be here in a few minutes. It seems he does not forget a debt of honour."

They left the apartment and went down the stairs to the entrance hallway of the building. A large and well maintained limousine was waiting outside. The driver sat behind the wheel while the escort officer held the rear door open for them. The drive to the Kremlin did not take long and the car swept through the impressive gates without slowing. The escort was out of the car as soon as it stopped and had the door open for them as a tall, slim young man came down the man steps to meet them.

Andrei nudged Ivan. "And what do you bet our functionary here is much more polite now?"

"No bet" said Ivan.

The greetings were brief and the tall man in the excessively tidy suit ushered them inside and led them rapidly through the various corridors and straight into the President's large and impressive office. The President was sitting behind a massive desk and rose as they came in without any of the customary pretence of signing papers. He stepped to Andrei and clasped his shoulders.

He then turned to Ivan and held out his hand. "A long way from the sunshine of Florida, Mr Thomas. How can I help you?"

Ivan said "Mr President your English is better than my Russian as ever. If you will permit us we would like to take a look at the private museum collection of artefacts concerning the time of Stalin."

The President looked surprised. "Is that all? Should I ask why?"

"I wish you wouldn't, sir."

"Very well, I certainly owe you that much, but one day you must tell me what this is all about over a vodka or two. Come this way," he said leading them into an adjoining room.

Around the walls were arrays of display cases with huge impressive paintings in ornate frames on the walls. They walked slowly around the cases until, at the bottom end of the room, they came to the case that contained items from Spain. The gold coin rested in its red silk display setting in the centre of the case. Ivan stared for a few seconds. In reality it was a beautiful piece of craftsmanship. The pictures in the auction brochure did not do it justice.

Ivan turned to the President. "Thank you sir. That has answered my question. Now if you do not mind I need to get back to London as quickly as possible."

The President of Russia was nothing if not a gracious host and showed them back to the limousine himself. As they climbed into the car, he said, "Remember, Mr Thomas one day you owe me an explanation."

"One day, sir and I hope your vodka is smoother than Andrei's."

Chapter 8.

Back in London Jim Wilson had not been idle and had spent hours trawling the Internet for any details he could find about the Auxiliary Units. He had visited the National Army Museum and with the help of the highly knowledgeable staff had trawled through their extensive supply of documents. He had called up and watched the few TV programmes that had been made about the Secret Army when their existence had first become public knowledge. Despite his efforts the information he had come up with was still very thin and did not seem liable to lead them readily to any remaining gold stores.

What he had found was fascinating to a military man. The task of organising and setting up the Secret Army had been given to Colonel Colin McVean Gubbins and he had selected Coleshill House as his Headquarters. The men had been recruited from many walks of life all over the country. Most had jobs that would give them a reason to be wandering about the countryside at all hours of the day and night. Farmers, Game Keepers, Doctors, Vets and Clergymen had all been recruited and sent secretly to Coleshill to be trained in the skills of reconnaissance, sabotage and assassination. Training and coordination had been provided by experienced Army personnel. They had been formed into small teams of six or less and had been taught how to construct hidden small team bases in such a way that nobody was likely to stumble across them by accident and they were unlikely to be found, even by a dedicated search. When the invasion came they were to retire to their hides to allow the attacking forces to pass by before starting their operations. Their life expectancy once they started to operate was short, very short, but they could have caused considerable disruption behind enemy lines.

Jim could see why these dedicated people would be the ideal types to have the country's gold entrusted to them. People with that kind of commitment had to have a certain special mind-set that would make them totally trustworthy and they already had secret hiding places that could be used. But, now that the secret was emerging, surely any of the surviving old men who had been part of the Auxiliary Units who knew about the gold would have come forward by now. There was something else here that he was not finding. He needed to speak to any of the survivors he could find before their voices were stilled for ever. During his researches he had found that there was a group of amateur historians based around Coleshill House who were researching the Auxiliary Units and gathering any records and artefacts about them that they could find. Even after seventy or more years the amount they were finding was small; the security need for these units had been intense and had been carefully maintained.

His visit to Coleshill to speak with the researchers was helpful and the bunker they had showed him in the grounds was illuminating. These were no foxholes in the woods. The walls were of concrete and they had been equipped with up to six bunks. Weapon racks were hung on the walls and there was sufficient storage for food to last the six occupants for the three weeks of their expected survival time once operation began. There was an entrance way and an emergency exit, should they be discovered. One of the most amazing things to Jim was that, even after more than seventy years, the base was still dry. The location had been selected well and the construction had been careful and competent. Judging by the Coleshill base there was every possibility that the hides he was looking for would still exist and their contents might be undamaged.

Chapter 9.

Jim returned to London and was using the whiteboard in the office to marshal his thoughts when Geordie and Ivan came through the door. They had met in the arrivals hall at Heathrow airport and travelled in to the city together. The constant crowds around them had prevented them speaking about the task in hand so they were delighted to find Jim in the office and working on the problem.

"Well boss," started Geordie, "we appear to be out of a job. Raoul and his spooky friends got us the information from the auction house."

"Hang on a minute," Jim said, "how did they do it? Will there be any trace of the query?"

"No problem there, boss, the people finding the information were even spookier than the SEALs. They didn't tell me how they got it but my best guess is that they hacked into the auction house computer system and picked up the name and address of the seller from there. In any case it's all over. The coin came from Spain so it must be number twenty. The trail has gone cold before we properly got started. Does that mean we can ask to go back to the Army now?"

Jim sat down feeling deflated. "Well, that's a shame, I was just starting to enjoy this. Oh well, I suppose I'd better go and tell the Prime Minister he's still broke. I nearly forgot, Ivan, how was Andrei?"

Ivan was quietly rubbing his earlobe with a small smile on his face.

"Oh he was fine, boss, enjoying the authority his new police rank gives him. He seemed to quite enjoy throwing his weight about a little, with the government stiffs, to get us in to see the President."

"You saw the President?"

"Of course," said Ivan still maintaining his secret smile, "how else would I know that the twentieth coin is still in Russia in a very impressive display case in the Kremlin?"

Jim sat back in his chair. "Are you sure?" he said. "Sorry, that's a stupid question. Of course you're sure. Geordie, let's have a look at the details you got on our mysterious seller."

Geordie fished into his shirt pocket and produced the note he had been handed in Maryland. He handed it across the coffee table to Jim.

"There you go boss, I was quite looking forward to getting back to something real."

Jim looked at the note in his hand. He looked up. "Either of you ever heard of a place called Benidoleig? I know about Benidorm but I've never heard of this one."

Geordie stood up. "I'll go and Google Map it."

Ivan watched Geordie walk back to his desk and leaned across to Jim. "Not long to his wedding, are we going to chase this lead before or after?"

"Good thought. We have no idea how long it will take in Spain. It can wait until after the weekend and that will give you all the next day to sleep off your hangover. Do we have the arrival times for Andrei and Raoul? I take it Geordie still doesn't know they're coming?"

"Nah! He's out of the loop. Only Sam and her Mum know. They've booked them rooms in the same hotel we're staying at. All we have to do is pick them up on Friday morning. Sam made me promise that once they arrive we are not to let Geordie get too 'happy'. She wants him vertical and looking presentable at the ceremony."

They stopped talking as Geordie came back from his computer. "Turns out there are buckets of villages north of Benidorm that start with 'Beni'. I've got Benidoleig, Beniarbeig, Benissa and loads more. They must have run out of ideas back in the day. So how many tickets do you want me to book to go and see this guy?"

Jim smiled. "Just book us two for Monday afternoon, will you? Ivan and I will handle this one."

"Are you sure boss? I like Spain, I could show you round."

"Geordie, you have other things to do next week," said Ivan, "or have you forgotten you are getting married on Saturday?"

Geordie's jaw dropped. "Oh hell! I had forgotten. Do me a favour and don't tell Sam, I don't think she would be understanding about that."

Chapter 10.

Friday morning arrived and the two overseas guests for Geordie's wedding arrived within half an hour of each other to be met by Jim and Ivan. Getting the car through the crowded roads around Heathrow Terminal Three was a trial but once clear they joined the M25 Motorway and it became a little better, although the roads was still extremely crowded with the usual crush of commuters and delivery vans. Eventually they left London's circular motorway and joined the road network heading for Huntingdon in Cambridgeshire. Ivan turned round to the two guests in the back seat to start pointing out the landmarks of interest as they drove. He could save his breath, they were both fast asleep.

As they turned off the Great North Road and through the village of Brampton the two visitors woke up and started to look around. They cleared Brampton and turned towards Huntingdon.

After a little over a mile they came alongside a tall brick wall and Ivan turned to say "Behind that wall is Hinchingbrooke House. That's where we're having the wedding reception tomorrow. It's an old manor house that used to be owned by Oliver Cromwell's family. During the week it's part of one of the local schools."

They carried on past the railway station and into the town. As they joined the ring road they swung into the small car park of the George Hotel.

"Here you go, gents," said Jim, "this is where we are staying. It used to be an old coaching inn many years ago and there are stories that Dick Turpin, the famous Highwayman, stayed here. And if you have a word with the folk at the reception desk they can tell you the story about the ghost they have in the upstairs ballroom."

The four friends retrieved their baggage from the car and walked into the hotel to check in.

That evening Geordie arrived to take up residence for the evening before his marriage. Jim and Ivan met him as he came through from the hotel courtyard. They arranged to meet in the bar at seven o'clock that evening for a quiet dinner in the hotel restaurant and Geordie went off to his room to shower and change. Ivan and Jim took the chance to walk along the high street, remarkable only for the Cromwell Museum in the old school building that Oliver Cromwell had attended as a child. They took a look at the old church across the road from the George Hotel where the wedding was to take place next morning. It was an interesting building but lost in amongst the modern shops and buildings around it.

As Geordie came down the staircase to the bar area that evening he looked to his left and saw four friends sitting at a table by the bar smiling up at him. The last time they had all been together had been at the end of the incident following the attack on New York. Geordie went to the table and shook hands with Andrei and Raoul.

"Thanks for coming, guys" he said, "it wouldn't be the same without you." He turned to Jim and Ivan who were sitting at the table grinning like two Cheshire Cats "I take it you two set this up? Thanks guys. This is special."

"Not just us, mate," said Ivan, "Sam gave us our instructions two months ago."

Geordie turned back to Andrei and Raoul. "So have you two ever tried a proper beer? Not that insect urine they sell in America, the good stuff."

It turned out that jet lag and strong English beer are not a good mix and an hour or so later Raoul Martinez was on the verge of sleep. Andrei was also finding that long working hours and Russian vodka were not good training for heavy English beer. By a little after ten that night the party had ground to a halt and the five men decided to head for bed.

Geordie paused at the top of the staircase. "I guess this means I am getting old. Still capable of walking on the night before my wedding. Promise you won't tell my mates when we get back to the Army?"

The wedding ceremony the next morning went smoothly with a full church. Quite a few of the guests on Sam's side of the church were from the theatre world she worked in and the suits and dresses were that little bit over the top. The sensible suits and smattering of military dress uniforms of Geordie's side of the church made a distinct contrast. Even Andrei had managed to bring his police uniform, though it was a little drab compared to the other uniforms with their shiny buttons and medal ribbons.

Jim watched Geordie turn as the bride entered the church, noticing his jaw drop just a little. He turned to look at Sam coming down the aisle on her father's arm. She was an extremely attractive girl but today she was transformed and looked absolutely gorgeous. For a second or two he let his mind drift back to his own wedding. She had been a vision that day too. Hopefully this marriage would last better than his had done.

After the ceremony the guests filed out of the church to climb aboard the motor coaches that were waiting to take them to the wedding reception. The surprisingly attractive school building and its well-manicured gardens were ideal for the wedding photographs and the guests took full advantage of this with personal cameras clicking away and getting in the way of the official photographer. Many of the younger guests retired to the bar and were finding that drinking on an empty stomach is a quick route to 'happiness'. The five friends in their dark blue dress uniforms waited until just before the meal before heading to the bar for a pre-lunch glass. As they left the bar a young man, obviously the worse for wear, wandered up to them.

"My, what a band of heroes we have here," he said, rocking gently.

Geordie cleared his throat. "Gentlemen, may I present my brand new brother-in-law, Michael Lanton, the actor. Michael these are my friends and colleagues."

He was about to name them when Michael said "Ooh and who is this one with more ribbons than a ladies hat stall?" and poked Raoul in the chest.

Geordie cleared his throat again. "That is Lieutenant Commander Raoul Martinez of the US Navy."

Michael immediately started an over the top imitation of gay behaviour and cooed, "Hello Sailor! You must let me climb your mast sometime."

Geordie looked embarrassed. "Michael, these are my friends."

"So what?" said Michael "Are you and your military friends going to beat me up then? Just about all you are good for."

He turned as he was tapped on the shoulder and just had time to register the approaching fist before it struck him painfully in the nose and knocked him to the floor. He looked up to see his sister in her wedding dress rubbing her knuckles.

"What did you do that for?" he whined.

"Two reasons," Sam said. "First, nobody is going to make trouble at my wedding, least of all you and secondly you don't know who you are dealing with here. I have just made sure you make it to the lunch table. Now come on."

She turned, grabbed Geordie by the arm and marched him into the dining room. Geordie looked over his shoulder at the group with his widest smile.

Ivan turned to the others. "Now there is a young lady who will make a fine soldier's wife." He leaned down, pulled Michael to his feet and dusted him down. "Come on, son," he said, "no harm done" and led him through to the dining room as well.

The meal finished with the usual toasts and speeches including a rather amusing one from the bride's father. But then, Jim thought, as a professional actor a good speech should be expected. The tables were moved back and the dancing began. Never much of a dancer, Jim sat with his back against the wall cradling a very pleasant glass of wine. He was remembering his own wedding day. That had been a rush job in a Registry Office because his deployment to Iraq had been extended and had prevented them booking the church wedding his wife had dreamed about for years. Janet would have liked a day like this one. He roused himself from his day dream as an old man sat down heavily next to him. The old man leaned his walking stick against the table; put down his glass on the white table cloth and held out his hand.

"James Lanton," he said. "I'm Samantha's grandfather, just about the only one in the family who isn't a ruddy actor." Jim shook his hand, surprised at the firmness of the grip from such an old person.

"Pleased to meet you, sir. I'm Jim Wilson a friend of the groom."

"Oh, I know who you are Major. Sam has spoken about you. You seem to have had some sort of adventure in America that she won't talk about, but I respect that, I had to keep a secret for many years too." Jim nodded and looked back to the dance floor. He was only half listening when the old man said "Nice array of medal ribbons you have there. They never gave me a medal for my wartime service. None of us got one. We weren't supposed to exist."

Jim nodded absently, then the penny dropped and his mind clicked back into gear. He sat up straighter and turned to the hunched old man by his side.

"Which war was that, sir?" he said quietly.

The old man looked at him through clear blue eyes.

"The big one, '39 to '45. At my age which did you think it would be? Although I did get sent to the one in Korea as well a bit later"

Jim looked at him. "Do you fancy some fresh air? I think we have something in common I would like to ask you about."

They stood and walked out into the garden with the old man leaning on Jim's arm until they sat down on a bench at the edge of the lawn.

"Now then" Jim said "I have been doing a little research into the war and I only know of one unit that was never acknowledged with a Defence Medal because they were so secret. Were you by any chance part of the Auxiliary Units?"

Out of habit the old man looked around before answering.

"I was," he said. "I was 13 when it started. I had left school and was working as a Baker's Boy delivering fresh bread on my bicycle. Looking back it was big heavy horrible thing but I loved that bike. Anyway, because I had a reason to move about the place they made me a messenger between the teams in our area. I think we had more of the hidden bases than other places because it is such a great place to land parachute troops."

"So where were you then?"

"I was delivering to villages on Salisbury Plain. There were three bases out there, including the special one. You must know the Plain from your time in the Army, big rolling open grasslands with woods and copses scattered about. Nice in the summer but really cold in the winter when the wind is whistling."

Jim looked at him. "I know a little about the Auxiliary Units hidden bases but what do you mean by a 'special one'?"

The old man thought for a moment. "I don't really know," he said. "The other two would let me inside on a cold day for a cup of tea and to get warm, but the people at the special one never would. They would come and sit in the wood with me and give me a mug of something hot out of a thermos flask but even if it was pouring down I was never allowed to even see where it was."

"Do you know why it was special?"

The old man shook his head. "No. They never said although one of them did let slip that there were other special hides spread all over the country. But what they were for I never knew. They didn't get many messages so I didn't go up to them much."

Jim looked around. "This could be very important. Can you tell me where the special base was?"

"After all this time I don't see why not," said Sam's grandfather. "After all the story is out now, though still not well known. I used to meet them up by Stonehenge but I'm not sure their base was actually there. The Druids picked a good place for their temple, you get a good view across the plain from there so maybe they were an observation unit, I really don't know."

"Mr Lanton you have no idea how valuable that information may be. But tell me, did you do your training at Coleshill?"

The old man nodded slowly. "I did. They laid on a special training course for lads like me who were going to be passing messages. Looking back now it's surprising what they taught boys of my age. They even issued us with combat knives in case we were caught and had a couple of ex-Shanghai Police Officers teaching us unarmed combat. They were the ones who had designed the knife too."

Jim looked at the old man. "I don't suppose you are still in touch with any of the boys who were on that course are you?"

The old man looked wistful. "I was," he said, "but most of them are dead now of course. The only one I know who might still be alive is Cyril Davies. Last I heard his mind was going and they had him in a home near Derby. The rest are gone or I just lost touch."

"Is granddad boring you with his old stories?"

Jim turned to see Michael walking towards them. The blood had stopped dripping from his nose but his shirt was stained. The punch seemed to have sobered him up.

"I have been sent to rescue you and to tell you the cake is about to be cut."

"No rescue needed,' Jim said. "I will bring Mr Lanton in. No need to hang around and miss your cake." Michael shrugged and turned away. Jim waited until he was out of earshot and offered his arm to the old man for the walk back inside. "Mr Lanton," he said, "you may just have done your country another service.

If it works out I'll let you know and if you remember anything else I really would appreciate you contacting me."

Chapter 11.

Having dropped Raoul and Andrei back at Heathrow, Jim and Ivan drove the hire car back up to the airport at Stansted and handed it in to the Avis desk. They headed to the security gate to catch the last economy airline flight of the day to Alicante. Just over two and a half hours later they were climbing into yet another hire car in Spain.

Leaving the airport they were on the coastal motorway in just a few minutes. Neither of them had been to Spain before and the superb condition of the almost empty motorway and the rugged mountains were a surprise to both of them. The drive to Benidoleig took just over the hour and they arrived in the centre of the village with no idea where to find the hotel they were staying in. Finding a small café with chairs and tables set out under the trees they sat and ordered a coffee. The young waiter spoke no English but they managed to ask him where they could find 'El Cid' where they were booked for two nights. The waiter indicated by waving his arms that they should drive another 50 metres to the traffic island and turn left. How far along that road they should drive was unclear but it was a small village so they decided to give it a try.

They headed out in the direction the waiter had waved. The village petered out after about 200 metres and they were back among the orange groves. The sign they were looking for appeared. They pulled the car into the small car park and shouldering their bags they climbed the rough stone stairs and found themselves on a wide open terrace with a very inviting pool. They turned into a very comfortable bar area and checked in. They were taken up to their rooms by Charlie, the manager. Having emptied their bags the two met up in the bar to discuss their next move. Ivan brought over a couple of beers and sat down at the terrace table.

"Well boss, do we just go and bang on this guy's door or are we going to be more subtle?"

Jim thought. "It might be a good idea to see if anyone around here knows this man and try and get an introduction. We want him to help us, not be upset and uncooperative. Maybe we could ask Charlie?" He stood and went to the bar.

"Charlie, can we have a word?"

She came round the end of the bar and joined them at the table.

"How can I help?"

Jim sat forward. "We have come to try and meet up with a man who lives in the village. He's English so we wondered if you know him, Martin Crowther?"

"Martin? Yes I know him; he's a member of the bowls club that plays here."

"Is there any chance you could ask him to meet us? We don't want to just turn up on his doorstep like a couple of bailiffs."

Charlie nodded. "I've probably got his number in the membership lists. Can I tell him what it's all about?"

"Could you tell him it's a private matter but important."

She nodded and went to make the call. In a few minutes she was back. "They are on their way out right now but he says you are welcome to go round in the morning about ten o'clock."

Charlie went back behind the bar and the two men sat over their beer looking across the orange groves to the rugged mountains on the other side of the valley.

Jim cleared his throat. "Ivan, a friend of mine lives somewhere around here and I would like to go and see her. Do you mind if I leave you here and take the car?"

Ivan was surprised. "No problem, boss, there's a game on this evening and they have cold beer and a good TV here."

"Thanks, it's important to me." Jim stood and went inside to get directions from Charlie. He came back and said "Ivan I don't know how long this will take. I may be back for dinner or I may be late. I'll see you for breakfast, whatever happens."

Following the directions Charlie had given him he was soon driving under the archway that led to the hillside housing development known as Monte Pego. A quick visit to the bar at the foot of the hill got him further directions to the address he was looking for and he set off up the slope, following the steep winding road. In a few minutes he was outside a neat white villa with a wrought iron gate. He stepped out of the car and opened the gate, walked through the small garden and around the villa. As he came to the pool terrace he could see the end of a sun lounger and a pair of feet. He walked around the corner and looked down on the woman dozing in the shade.

"Hello Janet" he said.

Janet started awake. "Stupid man! You could have given me a heart attack. What the hell are you doing here?"

Jim sat down on the next lounger and sighed. "You're looking well. How have you been?"

"I've been fine. What are you doing here?"

Jim sat back. "Nice view," he said, "how did you find this place?"

Janet sat up. "Enough of the chat. You walk back into my life three years after the divorce without any warning. Now, why are you here?"

Jim smiled. "Three years, two months and one week but who's counting? Anyway, I have a job to do in the next valley. I was surprised to see Monte Pego was so near when I looked up where Benidoleig was on Google. I couldn't very well ignore you when I was so close."

She looked at him. "I'm ready for a cup of tea. Would you like one?" They went inside and she put the kettle on.

"So how long have you been here then?"

"Just over two years. I came out when the house sale went through in the UK."

He nodded. "I was surprised when you sold the house. I thought you liked it? Your lawyer worked hard enough to get it for you."

"And you didn't try very hard to keep it."

He smiled. "I thought you deserved that much after putting up with me for eight years."

"Jim, it was never about putting up with you." She turned to pour the boiling water on the tea bags. "It was always the separations and the uncertainty I couldn't handle. It was good when you were home but that was so seldom with all the deployments overseas."

"I know," he said. "I always knew that was why and I never blamed you. I think that's why I came today. I never actually said that it wasn't your fault and I do understand. So how do you keep yourself occupied when you get bored with looking at that view off your terrace?"

Janet paused, staring at his face "That was a really nice thing to say Jimmy, thank you." She smiled. "Anyway, when I can tear myself away from the view I write children's books. I've had three published and the fourth is going through the editing process now."

Jim smiled back. "I'm really pleased for you. I'm glad things are working for you."

They walked back out onto the terrace and looked down on the valley with its rice fields glistening in the sun and across to the glittering blue Mediterranean.

Janet leaned against the metal railings around her pool and said, "So what have you been doing since ....?"

Jim looked into the distant heat haze. "Oh, nothing very special, just more of the same."

He could not tell her about the attack on New York or about the search for the Secret Army.

"So then" she said "what are you doing in Benidoleig?"

"Nothing much, there's just someone there who might be able to help with a project I am working on."

"That's it? That's all I get from you?"

He looked at her sideways "Sorry. That's all there is, or at least all I can tell you."

"So nothing really has changed?" she said. "Just for a moment I thought there was a chance you had turned human inside that khaki suit of yours. Well, it was nice to see you're alright. Keep in touch."

Jim shook his head and smiled. "Well, as dismissals go that was short and sweet." He put down his still full tea cup and looked at her for a second or two. "Goodbye Janet, I hope the books go well."

Chapter 12.

The next morning, after a leisurely breakfast by the pool, Jim and Ivan left 'El Cid's' and drove the short distance to the village following another set of Charlie's directions. They took the left fork up the steep road towards the church. Then pulled over and parked close to the village farmacia. They walked up the narrow street to the church and turned left, they turned right at the small restaurant on the corner and found the house they were looking for just after it. They knocked at an ornate wooden door which opened almost immediately.

"Very prompt, gentlemen. Come on in."

They stepped through the door into the cool, dark hallway. "Mr Crowther? I'm Jim Wilson and this is Ivan Thomas, we have a couple of questions for you if we may."

"Come on in to the yard, the coffee has just brewed." Crowther led them through the surprisingly large house to a small courtyard with a set of garden chairs and then brought a coffee pot and a trio of cups. "Right then, how can I help you?"

"Mr Crowther, we are aware that you put a gold coin into an auction in New York. What we would like to know is where did you get that coin?"

"How the hell did you know about that? The auction house agreed to keep my name out of it. That's really irritating. Anyway what the hell has it got to do with you?"

Jim looked at Ivan then handed the Prime Minister's letter to Crowther. He let him read it and then continued.

"As you can see we are carrying out a task for the Prime Minister personally, so I would appreciate your help. Firstly why the secrecy? But more importantly, where did the coin come from?"

Crowther sat back in his chair and looked up at the square of sky above him.

"Oh well," he said, "why not? The coin was in my father's effects when he died. He had shown it to me when I was about fifteen and told me then that there was a big secret attached to it. He told me that when the time came and he was too old to carry on, he would hand the secret on to me. But then a massive heart attack took him and I never found out what the secret was. But because there was some mystery attached to it I decided to keep my association with it quiet. Or I thought I did." He looked at Ivan and Jim "So why do you care? It may be a valuable coin but why are you so interested?"

Jim sat forward. "It's not just a valuable coin it's also a very rare one and it's part of a small batch of coins that we need to find. Unfortunately we can't tell you why. But where did your father live and what did he do for a living?"

"We lived just outside Morecambe in Lancashire. Nice little farm overlooking the bay. You could see right across to Barrow in Furness on a clear day. That farm has been in the family for five generations but it wasn't making any money, at least not enough for all of us to live on, so I went and got a job in London. Then, when the old man died, I rented it out, took early retirement and came here for the sun and the lifestyle. The rent adds nicely to my pension."

Ivan said, "I went to Morecambe for a holiday with my Mum and Dad when I was quite young. I remember my Dad getting quite nostalgic about seeing a steam train running round the end of the bay when he was a lad."

"That's right," said Crowther. "The track runs across the bottom of our land."

"Just a thought," said Jim. "When you were a boy was there anywhere on the farm you were not allowed to go? Or were there any people who visited your Dad for no apparent reason?"

"What? Why would you ask that?"

Ivan looked just as puzzled as Crowther but said nothing.

"Humour me," said Jim, "it's just an idea that struck me."

Crowther thought about it, Jim could almost see the memories being called up as he cast his mind back.

"Well yes," he said. "My sisters and I were banned from ever going into the storage barn down near the railway line. It wasn't in very good repair and both Granddad and Dad said it was dangerous."

Jim nodded slowly. "And did they ever repair it while you were growing up?"

"No. There was no need, it was just a place to store old equipment we didn't need anymore."

"And did they ever go in there? Maybe with visitors?"

Crowther looked at Jim and Ivan and slowly said, "They did now I come to think of it. There were a couple of people who would visit and then they would go to that barn together about once a month. I never asked why. It was just something that happened. Why, is that relevant?"

Jim shrugged. "I have no idea. It's just something that occurred to me. So who were these visitors to your farm?"

"There was the local vicar, although we never went to church except at Christmas. Then there was the vet and the postman. Strangely, they kept visiting even after they retired but we never visited them. I am confused, why do you care?"

"Mr Crowther," said Jim, "you have been more helpful than I am able to tell you. I would appreciate it if you could refrain from mentioning this conversation. Could you also give us the address of your family farm and the name of your tenant?"

Crowther stood. "I can do better than that. I have a letter from him that has his letterhead on it. You can take it if you like."

When he came back Jim and Ivan were standing in the cool dark hallway waiting for him and admiring the carved Spanish woodwork. Jim took the letter and then both shook his hand, thanked him and stepped out into the bright sunshine of the narrow street.

"Boss, what ...?"

Jim held up his hand. "Let's get back in the car first."

They walked in silence down the hill to the car, admiring the neat, brightly coloured houses as they went. The inside of the car was very hot in the Spanish sunshine so they started it then stood outside to give the air conditioning time to do its work before getting in and weaving their way through the narrow village streets down to the main road and back to 'El Cid'. Jim went to the bar and came back with two ice cold beers with the condensation already running down the outside of the glasses.

Ivan took a swallow, sighed appreciatively and said, "OK boss, what did I miss?"

"Not much I suspect. Young boys are inquisitive creatures, if Crowther had been allowed in the barn he might just have stumbled across something. The people who visited are exactly the type of people who were recruited to the Auxiliary Units, people with an excuse for travelling about at odd times. At first glance putting a base on Morecambe Bay would seem like the place to monitor an invasion fleet but the tides in the bay are savage and there are wide areas of quicksand, so not a good place to have troops wading ashore. So why put the secret base there? At Geordie's wedding I found out that among the secret bases of the Auxiliary Units were others that were special and even more secret. I think we have the clues to one of those. Plus, I have a possible lead on a second one and with just a little bit of luck we may find a trail to a third. Problem is I don't know how many we are looking for. It could be dozens."

Ivan nodded "I think we need to talk to the Governor again, boss."

"Why's that then?"

"It seems to me that they would want as few people as possible to touch this stuff and it's pretty heavy. So my guess is it was loaded and unloaded just once. If the bank made it up into loads we should be able to nail down how many special bases we are looking for."

Jim thought about that and smiled slowly. "Good thinking" he said. "Time to go back to London. There is nothing here for me, at least not anymore."

Chapter 13.

Back in the office in Parliament Street Jim put a call through to the Bank of England switchboard who refused point blank to put him through to the Governor. Next he rang the number on the letter of authority he carried. The duty officer in Number 10 answered at the second ring. Jim asked to speak to the Prime Minister. There was no hesitation; the duty officer was clearly well briefed. The Prime Minister was on the line within five minutes.

"Ah Jim, nice to hear from you. How's the holiday going?"

Jim picked up on the language immediately; it was obvious that the Prime Minister was somewhere he could not speak freely and where he might be overheard.

"Well, David," he said, "we are having a fine time, we only need a few things to make it perfect. It's a shame we can't get together with Richard, he would love this."

"I'm sure he would, Jim. You must bring your holiday photos round to show me when you get back. I'm afraid I have to cut this short, I am just going in to lunch. Goodbye, Jim."

Half an hour later the phone rang and Jim picked it up to hear Sir Richard on the line.

"Major," he said, "I am told you wish to speak to me. My car will be at your building in about five minutes, it will bring you to my house."

Before Jim could reply the phone went down. Sir Richard was obviously not at all happy with being disturbed out of the office.

Ivan and Jim stepped out of the front door of the building in time to see a highly polished black Daimler pull up at the kerb. They walked across the wide pavement dodging the crush of over excited tourists and reached the limousine as the chauffeur opened the back door for them. They slid across the tan leather seat and settled themselves for the drive through the city. The driver was skilled at weaving his way through the chaos of London's traffic and in short order, they found themselves pulling in to a tree-shaded driveway that led to a Queen Anne style house set in beautifully manicured gardens. Climbing out of the car they crunched across the weed free gravel to the front door to be met by a shirt sleeved, cravat-wearing Sir Richard. Without speaking he gestured for them to follow him and turned back into the house. Jim looked at Ivan, shrugged and followed the governor into the wide hallway and then into a book lined study. Sir Richard settled behind a wide walnut desk and indicated two green leather seats facing him.

"Have you made any progress?"

Jim looked him in the eye and said "Good morning to you, too. Yes we have, but before we go much further we need more information from you."

Sir Richard grunted, making it very clear he did not appreciate his private time being disturbed.

"What do you need to know?"

Jim leaned back in his chair. "We need the details of how the gold was handed over to the Auxiliary Units back in 1940. What trucks were used, how many, how was the load distributed, in fact everything you can give us."

Sir Richard leaned forward with his elbows on the highly polished desk.

"We do not have that kind of information in our records. However, after our meeting in Number 10 I did some further research. I found that we are still paying a pension to one of the people who was involved in the transfer. He was a very junior clerk back then and was effectively used as a labourer on those nights we were moving the gold. I have checked and he lives with his granddaughter down in West Sussex. I have his address here." He handed it over. "It is in Henfield, not far from Brighton. Now since you are here, tell me what progress you have made."

Jim took the address and read it before slipping it into his shirt pocket.

He looked up at Sir Richard. "We know that the coin in the auction came from Spain, but we also know that the coin sent to the Spanish government in 1934 is still in Moscow. We identified the seller and Ivan and I have spoken to him. We know where he got it from and established that he does not know its significance or where the rest of them are. From certain conversations we believe that within the Secret Army, or more properly the Auxiliary Units, there was a small cadre of specially selected units that were even more security conscious. We think they may be the ones holding the gold."

"That is progress. It seems I may have been wrong to doubt your abilities. I will be back in the office next week." He handed over a business card. "If I can be of any more help my direct phone number is on there. My driver will take you back to your office."

Sir Richard rose from behind the desk and showed them to the front door. As they were about to leave, he shook both their hands. "My apologies for my earlier brusqueness" he said "I was convinced you were wasting my time. It seems I was wrong."

Chapter 14.

The drive down to Henfield the next morning put them into the village by just after 10 a.m. They had phoned the day before to request an interview with the Bank of England pensioner, Harold Greenly and been told by his granddaughter that this would be a good time as he was normally awake by now and was normally lucid in the mornings. The half-timbered houses along the high street gave way to a modern housing estate as they followed the directions the granddaughter had given them. A turn to the left brought them into a street of well-maintained bungalows with neatly tended gardens. They cruised slowly along checking the numbers and attracting the attention of the local neighbourhood watch, judging by the twitching of the net curtains as they passed. They parked outside number 38 and climbed out of the car. Ivan couldn't resist waving to the old couple peering at them from the front window of number 36 and was rewarded with a rapid adjustment of the curtains.

The front door of number 38 opened as they approached and a tall, slim woman in her early thirties, with long auburn hair waited for them, with one hand still holding the highly polished brass door handle.

"Right on time. I'm Harold's granddaughter, Helen Jennings. Granddad has just had his breakfast so it's time for his morning tea, would you like one?"

Jim shook her hand. "It's been a long trip so that would be welcome, Miss Jennings. Thank you."

She let go of his hand as he stepped into the hall way and briefly grasped Ivan's.

"It's Mrs. Go through into the lounge and I'll bring your tea. Granddad is expecting you and he is reasonably alert this morning, so you're in luck."

They walked into a neat and cosy lounge. The old man was sitting by the fireplace. He raised his head slowly as they came in. It seemed to take a second or two for his eyes to focus and he stared for a few seconds more before he spoke.

"So, you must be the people the Bank called about. I think that's the first time I have spoken to the Governor of the Bank of England since 1940 and then he only told me to hurry up."

Jim smiled. "Hello Mr Greenly, it's good of you to agree to see us at such short notice."

Greenly looked at them both again. "Sit down, please. Not short notice at all really. In fact I have been waiting for someone to ask me about those days for many years now. You are the first people who have been interested."

His granddaughter appeared from the kitchen bearing a tray of steaming mugs with a sugar bowl and a small milk jug.

She set it down on the coffee table between the chairs and said, "Help yourselves to sugar and milk. I forgot to ask you how you take it."

She carefully handed a mug to her grandfather and Jim noted that her hands hovered near the mug until she was sure he had got a firm hold of it. She then took a mug for herself and sat down to listen.

Jim cleared his throat. "Erm, this is a little difficult, Mrs Jennings, but what we are about to ask Mr Greenly concerns something highly classified and I am not sure you ought to be here for that."

She smiled. "I have been hearing my Granddad's tales for years and years and when he forgets some of the details I can fill them in for you, from the days when his memory was sharper and he was telling a little girl his magic stories about gold. And by the way, it's Helen."

Jim thought for a second or two. "Alright then, Helen, but please keep the conversation between just us four. It might turn out to be very important." He turned to face the old man. "Mr Greenly, Sir Robert tells us that you are the last of the people who were involved in 'Operation Fish' back at the start of the war. Do you remember that and can you tell us what you know about it?"

The old man's eyes seemed to lose focus as he stared across the room.

There was a quiet, then Mr Greenly, his voice stronger now, said, "It was cold that winter, and wet. The trucks used to come to the bank in the early hours of the morning. We could still see the fires from the bombing raids. In a way they were quite helpful because all the street lights were turned out so the bombers could not use them as aiming marks. They were Army trucks at first with security from one of the Guards regiments. Tall men, very smart with highly pressed battle dress uniforms and shiny boots. They had armed men at each end of the street while we worked and even the police were kept away. The trucks used to load up and then drive away long before dawn with a truck full of armed men in front and rear. Usually five trucks to a convoy. We used to send a bank employee with them to sign the boxes over at the ship. I went once and we drove all through the next day to Liverpool to meet the ship. Liverpool docks were a mess, I remember. They had been bombed hard a day or so earlier but the ship we were going to was untouched. Some of the others told me they went to Glasgow or Holyhead with their cargoes. We did that a few times in 1939 and 1940. I found out later that the cargo went to Canada and was stored under an insurance building, it was very secret. I seem to recall being told that we never lost a single bar."

Ivan had been making notes, while the old man spoke. There was nothing new here, they knew about Operation Fish.

He was about to speak when Jim said, "You said they were Army trucks at first. What about later? Were there other trucks?"

The old man nodded slowly. "Yes. There was one night. The last night in fact, when four household removal vans came. The bombing raid was still going on and we could hear the bombs pounding the east end of London around the docks. I think it must have been a bad one since it went on for so long. The anti-aircraft guns were working overtime and there were pieces of shrapnel from the airbursts dropping on the roof and in the street. You could hear the hot metal sizzling in the puddles. We were expecting the Brigade of Guards soldiers to turn up as usual but these four removal vans came instead. The men were in uniform but they were from the Home Guard. Strange though, they were all young men and they were wearing pistol belts even though they weren't officers. You probably know that the Home Guard were usually men who were too old for normal Army service. Anyway the senior managers were there and told us to start the loading. The men in uniform helped but they didn't say much. When they did speak they had accents though. They weren't from London that's for sure. We split the bullion boxes evenly between the trucks and then we loaded the special boxes. Those were split up as well. As soon as we had finished the loading they shut the doors in the back of the trucks, jumped in and drove off. They didn't sign any paperwork and this time none of the bank employees went with them. We went back into the bank and were given tea and biscuits."

Ivan looked at his notes, then said "Just a thought, did you by any chance see any company names on the removal trucks or anything else to show where they had come from?"

Jim nodded at Ivan. After all these years it was a long shot but a damned good question. He said nothing but sat back in his chair to let the old man think. He could almost feel the old man travelling back, in his mind, to that rainy night so many years before with the bombs falling and the aircraft engines passing above him. The pause in the conversation stretched and as he sat there he felt he was being watched. His eyes flicked to the left to find a pair of deep brown eyes contemplating him. She didn't look away. They looked at each other for what seemed a long time, until Harold Greenly returned from his mental time travelling. As he leaned forward in his chair, the three younger people switched their attention to him and waited. The old man put his face in his shaking hands and covered his eyes as he remembered.

His voice was distant as he said, "The red van came from Lancashire, it may have been from Lancaster. There was a green one from Salisbury. The black one was from Derby. There was another one but I don't think there was an address on it. There was a painting on the van side I seem to recall. I think it was a painting of a horse pulling an open cart." The old man sat back. He looked exhausted. "Isn't it strange?" he said "I can't remember what happened yesterday but I can recall the names of towns on a vehicle side after more than seventy years. But then travel was not as easy in those days and those town names were almost exotic. I had never been further from home than a trip to the seaside at Southend."

He slumped in his chair and his granddaughter stood. "I think that's all you are going to get from him today. He's tired out. If he says anything else I could give you a call."

She ushered them back to the front door. As they entered the hallway they could hear the quiet snoring from beside the fireplace. Ivan made his goodbyes and headed for the car.

Jim paused in the doorway. "When he wakes would you please tell him how much we appreciate his help." He checked his watch. "We seem to have taken quite a lot of your time. I hope that won't make Mr Jennings' lunch too late?"

She smiled and shook her head.

"Nicely done" she said. "Mr Jennings is long gone. I just have my granddad to look after now."

Jim flushed slightly. "So much for my attempts at subtlety. OK then, in with both feet. Do you ever come up to London and if you do can I buy you lunch next time?"

She looked him over. "Good recovery. Yes I do and yes, you can."

He handed over his business card. "I'll look forward to it. My mobile phone number is on there. Let me know when you are coming and I'll book somewhere nice."

He walked back down the driveway and climbed into the car. They waved and Ivan drove away. Jim couldn't resist checking and she was still standing in the doorway watching them leave.

"Stop smiling, Ivan. It's just lunch."

Ivan nodded. "Yes sir. And about time too."

Chapter 15.

Jim spent the weekend sailing on a friend's boat on Rutland Water. The two day regatta was very pleasant although the competition was a little too skilled for them. They clapped politely at the prize giving all the same. On Monday morning Jim fought his way through the crowds on the London underground and got back into the office in time to climb the stairs with Geordie who was now back from his brief honeymoon. The three man team assembled in their over large office and sipped their morning coffee, assembling everything they now knew about the special units of the Secret Army.

They had a good indication that the gold that did not go to Canada during Operation Fish was entrusted to four special units. These units had been spread around the country and as far as they could tell, they were in Lancashire, Wiltshire and Derbyshire with one in an unknown area.

Jim sucked his teeth. "Right, gents, we need to find an old man called Cyril Davies. I want both of you to work on it. We may end up having to check all the nursing homes around Derby to see if we can find him."

Ivan and Geordie stood up to go back to their desk to start the search.

"Any idea how many homes there are around Derby, boss? By the way, just who is Cyril Davies?"

"No idea at all, but before you get into that you might see if the Department for Work and Pensions can help you. Cyril used to be a friend of Sam's grandfather, in the Auxiliary Units, a long time ago so at his age he must be getting an Old Age Pension and to pay that I guess they have to have an address."

"Fair enough boss, but DWP is a huge department. Who the hell do I talk to?"

Jim smiled. "That's an easy one. Take your copy of the Prime Minister's letter and go and see the Permanent Secretary. Despite the strange job title, he or she is the permanent head of the department and all you have to do is give them the problem. They should be able to task someone in their staff to get you the information in double time. The trick is not to take 'no' for an answer."

Geordie nodded. "This could be a lot of fun."

Ivan and Geordie grabbed their jackets and headed out of the office, both wearing broad grins. Jim shook his head, he hoped the Civil Servants in the DWP were not too difficult with his two men or they might find their bubbles well and truly popped.

Twenty minutes later the two soldiers walked through the front door of the DWP headquarters building and presented themselves at the security desk. They showed their military identity cards and asked very politely to see the Permanent Secretary. Naturally the security staff wanted to know if they had an appointment and told them that without one they would have no luck getting in to see their boss. Ivan and Geordie remained polite and asked the security people to call for the Personal Assistant to the Permanent Secretary to come and collect them. They reluctantly agreed and shortly a very attractive and smartly dressed middle aged lady appeared to see them.

She looked over her glasses at the two men and said, "I'm sorry, but you can't just walk in off the street and expect a very busy senior official to drop everything to see you."

Ivan smiled sweetly. "But what if we said please?"

The woman sniffed. "Don't be ridiculous!" and turned to leave.

Geordie spoke up. "It really is important. Honest! We really would like to see him."

"Then you need to book an appointment and state your business."

"OK," said Ivan, "who do we book it with?"

"Me."

"Perfect. We would like an appointment please and the business is classified."

"Send me an email or a letter and I will see if I can fit you in sometime next week."

Ivan was tired of the game by now. "Oh, we have a letter already" and handed over the authority letter from the Prime Minister, "and of course we are prepared to wait. Anytime in the next ten minutes would do."

The Prime Minister's letter worked its magic and in a little over ten minutes they were explaining to the Permanent Secretary that they wanted him to find a pensioner somewhere near Derby. After the customary bluster expected of a senior official, a more junior official was called in and instructed to find the person they were looking for. As they left the office the official explained that a request of this kind would take time and they should call back next week. Ivan took the man by the elbow, turned him around and steered him straight back into the Permanent Secretary's office. They walked in without knocking.

"OK if I use your phone?"

The Permanent Secretary was startled. "Why mine? Can't you use one out in the main office?"

"Of course I can," said Ivan, "but I thought it would be more convenient for you when I pass the Prime Minister on to you so you can explain why your department with all its expensive computer systems will take a week to find an old age pensioner that you are paying."

He paused while the two officials absorbed that and said, "We're going for lunch now. We will be back in an hour and I think you'll find that you want to give me the address as we walk into the building."

Chapter 16

The two soldiers reported back to Jim in their office with the address of the nursing home they needed. Jim looked at the two of them suspiciously "What have you two been up to?"

"Oh nothing much, boss," said Geordie, "Ivan has just been spreading a little of his innate joy and kindness to some Civil Servants."

Jim let it go by. No doubt he could deal with any complaints that came his way. But now they had more serious business and a clue to follow up. They needed to speak to Cyril Davies if his mind was still sharp enough to recall those far off days.

"Right gents, time for us to start to earn our pay I think," said Jim standing up, "get your gear ready, tomorrow we are going on a road trip. Geordie, will you book us a car for the morning. We'll set off from here at about 9 a.m. Derby seems like the best place to start with Mr Cyril Davies. Oh and pack your working uniforms, I think we may need them at some point."

The drive the next morning was long and tedious with delay after delay on the motorway heading north. Eventually they joined the trunk road called "Brian Clough Way" into Derby. The nursing home was easy for the satnav to find and they pulled into the drive way and up to the imposing building in the early afternoon. While Geordie parked the car, Jim and Ivan went through the large front door and into the reception area. They were met by a harassed nurse who demanded to know their business. Jim explained that they had driven up from London to see Cyril Davies.

The nurse seemed puzzled. "Cyril? I can't remember the last time he had a visitor. Are you relatives? "

"No," said Jim, "we are from the Army and we need to see him to ask him a few questions. Is he available? "

"Well, the patients usually have their afternoon nap around now but I will check for you." She bustled away through an inner door while the two men stood and looked at the chipped and peeling plasterwork around the walls. "This must have been quite something when it was a private house," said Ivan, "but it is well overdue a coat of paint now."

Jim nodded "Hopefully all the money is saved for patient care, rather than making the building look pretty."

The nurse returned. "You're in luck. He is awake and seems to be making sense for a change. Now listen, he's very frail, so treat him gently. If he starts to get upset stop asking questions. Got it?"

"Yes ma'am," said Ivan, "are you sure you weren't a Drill Sergeant Major in a previous life?"

The nurse turned and looked at him, "As a matter of fact I was an Army nurse and did two tours in Afghanistan. So I was a Captain and don't you forget it."

"That told you, Sergeant Major," said Geordie who had just come through the front door.

Jim said, "If you're worried he will become upset, I can see him on my own if that will help? These two characters can take a walk round the garden."

Jim followed the nurse through the inner doors and along a wide corridor past a couple of sitting rooms where old people sat and stared at dusty television sets. They climbed a staircase with a threadbare carpet, up to the first floor. She led Jim into a clean functional room where an old man lay in bed, propped up on pillows

"Cyril," she said, "this is your visitor. Use the button to call me if you need me." She turned to go, then stopped and said to Jim, "And you remember what I told you."

Jim sat down on the upright chair next to the bed.

"Hello, Mr Davies," he said "I'm Major James Wilson of the Royal Engineers and I need to speak to you about your wartime service. James Lanton said you might be able to help me."

The old man stirred. "Jamie? I haven't spoken to him in quite a while. Did he tell you we used to do the same job during the war?"

"He did and that's why I need to speak to you. You were one of the young lads who carried messages for the Auxiliary Units, weren't you?"

"I was, until late 1944 when I was drafted into the Army. For some reason they put me into a Lancashire regiment and I ended up guarding Belsen concentration camp after we liberated it from the Germans. I still have dreams about that place. Not nice ones either."

"Mr Davies, it's important that you tell me about the Auxiliary Units. You know that they have been declassified, don't you? But there are still many things about them that have been lost as the people have moved on."

"I think you mean died, Major. You don't have to soft pedal around me. We have a lot of time to think about death in this place. It's no stranger to me. What do you need to know?"

"OK then. Can you tell me about the hidden bases around your area and in particular was there a base that was a bit different to the rest?"

The old man lay back on his pillows and his eyes went up to the ceiling as he remembered. "I was a delivery boy back then. I used to take the groceries out to the old folks who couldn't get about too well anymore. It seems strange that I am one of them now. Anyway that was my cover for riding about the area. If anybody asked me I was to say I was going to some of the outlying sheep farms with something they'd forgotten. I used to hide messages inside the frame of my bicycle. They were good days, except in the really bad parts of winter."

Jim waited for him to continue but he seemed to have got lost in his own memory "And was there anything different about any of the bases you supported?"

"Oh, what? Oh yes. Sorry, I was just remembering. There was one base where they called themselves the 'Blue John Fusiliers'. I used to meet them in one of the caves outside Castleton but I never saw their base."

"Which cave was it?"

"I always met them in Peak Cavern, the one the locals used to call the Devil's Arse; they changed the name when Queen Victoria came to visit. We used to meet in the old rope working area. I think their actual base must have been somewhere else but I never saw it."

"Is there a road up to that cave? And did they ever give you a clue that they were going to do anything different to the other teams?"

"There was a track for the old rope wagons and after the war they made a better roadway for the tourists. But no, they never spoke much to me. They weren't nasty but they weren't friendly either. They always seemed very serious."

Jim sat back to think about what he had heard. He looked out of the window to see his two men sitting on a bench in the garden talking and enjoying the sunshine. He turned back to the old man in the bed. His face had changed, it seemed to have sagged and his eyes were unfocused.

"Mr Davies, are you alright?"

"What? Who are you?" The old man seemed confused and was starting to become frightened. Jim stood quietly and left the room. As he entered the corridor he saw the nurse who had led him in.

"I think Mr Davies needs you," he said, "he seems to be having a problem." She stepped past him into the room and settled the old man down. She came back to Jim.

"Not your fault," she said, "he has periods of lucidity but then he lapses like that when he gets tired. He'll sleep now."

"OK, that's a relief. Can you give him my thanks when he wakes, please?"

"He's unlikely to remember you and it might confuse him more if I tell him about you."

Back outside Jim walked around to the garden at the rear of the building to find his two men. They saw him coming and rose to walk towards him.

"Any luck boss?" said Ivan.

"Possibly. We might have a lead on the consignment that went to Derbyshire. So, do we follow that lead first or would you like a trip to the seaside?"

Chapter 17

The team found their way to the village of Castleton in the hills of Derbyshire. Having booked into the small bed and breakfast hotel, in the village centre, they walked the short distance to Peak Cavern at the edge of the village. They bought their tickets to enter the show cave and joined one of the guided tours. The guide was knowledgeable and attractive so they paid close attention to her talk on the history and geology of the cavern. These caves had not been spoiled by being excessively 'improved' for the tourists and were impressive, in their own right.

At the end of the tour the three men sat on the dry stone wall outside the cavern and stared up at the overhanging mountain.

Jim was the first to speak. "Well, Geordie, with your mining background you're our underground expert. So what do you think?"

"Well boss, I picked up a couple of brochures in the hotel before we came out and with them and the story that guide just told us I think we have a big problem."

"Go on."

"That cavern has been a tourist attraction since before the time of Queen Victoria so Lord only knows how many people have walked through there. Plus, people who explore caves for a hobby come here frequently and there is still mining going on in the passages that lead to the remaining seams of Blue John stone."

Ivan turned to look at him. "We know all that but so what?"

"Seems to me that if thousands of people have been through here for well over a hundred years and found nothing, then we would have to be incredibly lucky to find anything hidden in there."

Jim and Ivan both nodded slowly and Jim said "That's assuming that the hide is in the cave at all. We know that they met the messenger in there but that's all. They could have come from anywhere to get here."

"So realistically we are no closer?" said Ivan

Geordie shook his head. "Not sure that's true. We know there are at least four big caves in this valley and we know they go a long way into the hill and have lots of passages within some of them. Plus, we know that this place has been mined since at least Roman times. Now unless miners have changed recently they don't like to carry spoil and debris out of the mine if they don't have to. What we did, when I was working in the mines, was when a gallery was worked out we would dump the earth and rocks from a new gallery in there. It seems unlikely they would just dig in the four big caves and not try to find other seams."

Ivan was puzzled. "Yeah, but so what? Where does that take us?"

"What it means is we have two new avenues to explore. Are there any blocked passages that aren't really blocked but just seem to be? Or and this seems more likely to me, they may have used one of the ancient test pits somewhere close by."

Jim said. "Logical, but where the hell do we start? It's a big valley and we have no other clues."

Geordie shrugged and they sat in silence, each searching for a way forward. Ivan broke the silence. "I've never asked you but do you believe in extra sensory perception?"

Jim looked at him. "ESP? No. Why do you ask?"

"Because there is a beer in that pub down there that is calling out to me."

"I think I can hear it too," said Geordie, slipping down off the wall. "A pie and a pint might help with the thinking process."

The three men walked back down the track into the village and along the main street to the pub close to the hotel they were staying in. They sat around the scarred and stained oak table at the back of the public bar and sipped their pints of local beer.

"Mmm, not bad," said Ivan, "nearly as good as Welsh beer."

While they waited for the lunch, they had ordered, to be brought out to them, Jim pulled out a note pad and pen. "So, what do we know?"

"We know that there are likely to be holes all over these hillsides and some of them might have passageways that lead into Peak Cavern, or might have once," said Geordie.

"How do we know that?"

"Those brochures from the reception desk. They say there are connections between Peak Cavern and Speedwell Cavern, one of the other show caves. So after all these years of use there must be others somewhere too."

Jim made a note. "What else?"

Ivan rested his elbows on the table. "We know the gold is bloody heavy and would be very awkward to handle over a rough cave floor. So we know there must be a decent track for the truck to get fairly close."

"Good point! We might be able to see something like that from the air or maybe even on the computer using Google Earth." Geordie was quite excited.

Jim shook his head. "If these guys were as good as we think they were, they will have picked somewhere that was not too obvious from the air. They would not want the Luftwaffe to have been able to find it. We need something a bit more sensitive than Google."

"I'll buy that boss but what have we got available?" said Ivan.

"I think we need the people from JARIC to help us on this one."

"JARIC boss? Give us a clue."

"Joint Air Reconnaissance Intelligence Centre. They are based down in Cambridgeshire, at RAF Wyton, I think. They should be able to call on any assets we need to survey the valley in quite a lot of detail."

"OK, so do we try and find something ourselves first or do we wait for them?" said Ivan.

"I think we leave this place for the time being and take a trip to the seaside. We have pretty good clues about the location that the golden coin came from and it would be nice to be able to report at least a partial success to the Prime Minister."

Chapter 18

The journey from Derbyshire though the Pennine hills was uneventful and quiet with most traffic seeking out the motorways and avoiding the older winding roads. The team drove into Lancaster and crossed the River Lune towards Morecambe. Reaching the sea front they turned north and followed the instructions from the Satnav until they were parked at the gate of the farm. They climbed out of the car and looked over the five bar gate and across the field to the wide expanse of sand and mud that is Morecambe Bay when the tide is out.

"That takes me back," said Ivan. "Dad used to tell me tales about the quicksand out there. We got hold of a special guide who led us cross the sands. I was bloody terrified the whole way. Especially when he had me feel in the sand with my feet. It started to move and I thought I was going under, but it was just a flatfish that had buried itself."

"That would have made it a difficult place to stage an amphibious invasion then?" said Geordie.

"Especially with the tides out there. They can sweep in or out faster than you can run. There are people drowned here every year who don't heed the warnings."

Jim had been quiet looking over the farm and its buildings. "From the description we got in Spain I think that old barn at the far end must be what we are looking for. Have you got your building passes with you?"

They both nodded and Jim said, "OK, put them on. It will make us look more official. Our story for the farmer is that we are from the Lancaster City Council engineer's department. Just follow my lead and try to look official and annoyed."

They walked down the farm track to the house at the left. As they neared the door it opened and the man who stepped out said, "And what do you want?"

"Good morning, sir," said Jim "we are from the Lancaster City Council works and engineering department and we need to speak to you about your barn."

"What about my barn?"

"I understand you are the tenant on this farm? How long have you been here now?"

"Three years. Now what about my barn?"

"That barn was condemned a little over seven years ago and the owner was instructed to demolish it. We have just found out that the demolition never took place. Can you explain why not?"

"No, I can't. The barn was fenced off with notices telling people not to enter when I got here. There was no mention of demolition."

"I'm afraid we will have to inspect the building to decide what steps are needed. Is there a gate in the fencing around it?"

"Yes. I'll get the key and take you down there."

"No need for that. Actually, I would prefer you not to come with us in case there is an accident. You would not be covered by the council's liability insurance."

The farmer stepped back into the house. He was back a moment later with the key. Handing it over he said, "I'll be in the top field, over there beyond that hedge, if you need me."

Jim thanked him and the three men walked around the house and across the field to the old barn. Once they were clear of the house Ivan looked back over his shoulder. "Boss, you've been around Civil Servants too long. You lie beautifully."

They reached the barn, being careful to step around the cow dung in the field. They found the gate. The padlock was overdue lubrication but they managed to open it.

"Geordie, make sure we are not interrupted will you. Slip the chain and lock back on that gate."

While the gate was being locked behind them Jim and Ivan went to the main door of the barn and pulled it open. They found themselves in a typical disused barn. Dusty farm machinery and broken tools were dumped everywhere with pride of place going to a trio of old and battered tractors in the middle of the floor. A Morris Oxford car, that had once been green, stood to one side on deflated tyres, half covered with a dirty tarpaulin. The walls were hung with more rusty and broken tools and they could see the farm house through the gaps in the wall planking. There were old metal advertising signs nailed to the wall.

They split up and walked around, looking for any anomaly that might show them the location of the secret hide. After fifteen minutes of careful scrutiny they had seen nothing out of the ordinary. Ivan climbed up onto the seat of one of the tractors and sat looking around. Jim and Geordie wandered back to stand by him.

"Any ideas?" said Jim.

"Are we sure this is the right place?" said Geordie. "I don't know what that guy in Spain told you but I can see damn all in here of interest."

"This was the place he indicated. Don't you agree Ivan?"

Ivan looked down "Yeah, I guess so. Nothing else here fits the bill."

They walked around the barn again and then Ivan said, "Either of you read the Sharpe books?

"I have" said Jim "there was a pile of them left by the previous tenant of my billet in Afghanistan during my last tour there. Damned good stories. So what?"

"Do you remember that the author, Cornwell I think, tells about how the French army used to live by plundering the farms and villages as they moved? The people used to hide their food and grain but the French got really good at finding it."

"Sorry, I still don't see the relevance."

"Well, we can see there is nothing here above ground, right? And they used to pour water on the floor of the huts to see if it drained away. If it did, they could tell there was a void below. Worth a try here eh?"

"Damn me, that might just be worth a try," said Jim. "Is there a supply of water here?"

Geordie headed for the door. "There's a cattle trough outside and they must have had a way of filling that." He was back moments later pulling a dirty black hosepipe. "It's hooked up to a tap near the trough and the water is still connected."

Jim picked up the end of the hose and told Geordie to turn on the tap. Ivan climbed back up on the tractor and watched as the water started to soak the hard packed earth floor of the barn. Jim spread the water around and puddles formed around him. After a few minutes he called to Geordie to shut the water off.

There was slight sag to his shoulders. "Nice idea, Ivan, but looks like it's a bust."

Ivan grinned. "Not sure about that boss. Step up here and look."

Jim stepped up beside him on the tractor and Ivan said, "Look over there in front of the Morris. The water is pooling in straight narrow lines. That could be some kind of a trapdoor into the floor."

They dropped down from the tractor and walked across the barn as Geordie joined them.

"Any spades around?" said Jim.

"Some over in the corner" said Geordie turning away.

He was back in seconds with an armful of old, dirty but serviceable spades and picks. Ivan took a pick and dragged the tip along the straight narrow puddles to define the edge of the area. Geordie and Jim started to shovel the dirt between those lines and after a very few moments a metal door began to appear.

"Well, we seem to have something but I can't see any way of opening it," said Ivan.

"That's because they hid the mechanism" said a voice from behind them.

They spun round to find themselves looking down the barrel of a large military issue revolver held in a very steady hand.

Chapter 19.

Jim tore his eyes away from the barrel of the weapon and looked up into a pair of steady blue eyes. He took in the sober suit and the clerical collar of the old man who stood before them.

"Good morning, Reverend," he said "do you always carry a Webley .38 when you visit your flock?"

"Not always. But I do when people come into this barn and search for things they have no business with."

"I see. So what do you intend to do about us? If you report us to the police then the story of what is hidden here will come out, instead of it being returned to its rightful owners."

"Nice try. But if you came from the rightful owners as you call them you would have used the proper code word by now and my task would be over."

"Task?"

"My father was a very young curate when the war started and he was recruited to the group who built this hide. He passed the task of guarding it to me just after I was ordained and took over his Parish. I had hoped this day would never come because of what I have to do."

"I think the task you were given is a little out of date," said Jim. "If you let me go into my jacket over there I can show you that we are legitimate."

The vicar's eyes darted towards the jacket for just a second but that was enough. Ivan flung his spade at the priest and then launched himself after it. The weapon came up and to Ivan, the barrel of the big pistol looked like the top of a rain barrel as he closed with it. He heard the hammer fall as he struck the man's chest. Both of them fell to the floor in a cloud of dust from the earth floor and Ivan grabbed the man's wrist and held it out to one side. The priest struggled to bring the weapon round to fire but Ivan's powerful hand prevented him. Geordie darted forward and gently prised the pistol from his grip, then handed it to Jim.

"Let him up, Ivan. I think we owe the good Reverend an explanation before we go any further."

Ivan rolled to one side before he stood up, then he and Geordie helped the old man to his feet. His face was flushed and his eyes were brimming with tears as he brushed the dirt from his torn suit.

He looked at Jim and said "So what happens now?"

Jim smiled as kindly as he could. "Now we explain who we are and relieve you of the task you have carried for so many years. I suspect you haven't changed the ammunition in this pistol since your father gave it to you. Is that right?"

"Yes. With the gun laws in this country and the secrecy of this place we had to save the ammunition for this task."

"Well, luckily ammunition deteriorates with time and it looks like these bullets have failed. But we won't test the rest just now. Sit down, vicar and let me tell you a story."

Geordie pulled a box across and the old man sat down wearily. Jim sat opposite him on the tow bar of an old plough and explained who they were and why they were there. He handed over the Prime Minister's letter and waited while the old man read it.

The old man looked up from the paper and said, "But why didn't you just use the code word? It would have saved all this unpleasantness and my suit would not be torn."

"The code word has been forgotten," said Jim. "All that wartime secrecy was too effective and has backfired a little. What code word should we have used?"

"Cromwell. Rather apt to use the name of the Lord Protector, don't you think?"

"Is that the same code word for all the special groups?"

The old man looked puzzled "All the special groups? There are more?"

"Yes. We are pretty sure there are four groups entrusted with protecting material such as you have here."

"What material do I have here? My father impressed its importance on me from the age of about eight but he said I was never to open the door and look, so I haven't. Not once in all these years. I just check now and then to make sure it has not been disturbed, I can see this barn from my front window, which is why I came over when I saw you."

"If you will show us how the hatch opens we can show you what you have been guarding. Your father didn't lie to you, it is incredibly important."

The old man stood slowly and walked to the corner of the barn, waving Geordie to follow him.

As they reached the corner he pointed and said "If you move that flat stone you will find a metal ring. When you pull on that it tensions a cable under the floor and that pulls out a bolt that secures the hatch."

Geordie bent down and heaved the stone aside to reveal a recess in the floor with a metal ring in it. He looked to Jim for confirmation and when he nodded, the big ex-miner pulled at the ring. There was a creaking from below them and the floor area they had been clearing lifted at one end. Only an inch or two, but there was a definite movement.

Ivan moved towards it, picking up a pick axe as he went.

"Stop!" said the old man. "My father made me promise never to open it but he also said if I ever found it open I should disconnect the wire inside before I lifted it. I think it may be booby trapped."

Ivan lowered himself to the ground and looked through the gap between the hatch and the frame. "Bloody hell! He's right, there is a wire here. It looks like we can lift this a couple of more inches and then it will go tight and do something nasty." He rolled onto his back and looked at the vicar "I think I owe you one, Padre."

They searched in a box of rusty tools until they found a large pair of old and very stiff pliers. Ivan returned to the hatch and lowered himself down again. He slid the pliers into the gap and prepared to cut the wire.

"You three might want to stand behind that tractor just in case I screw this up," he said.

Discretion being the better part of valour the three men retired behind the tractor and waited. Ivan closed the jaws of the pliers and after three or four cuts managed to sever the wire. He raised himself from the floor again and wiped the sweat from his brow, no point letting the others know how nervous he had been. He fetched a length of old rope from the barn wall and looped it around the corner of the hatch, then he went and stood behind the hinge end and started to pull. The door rose slowly, then toppled back onto the old Morris Oxford and stopped with a loud reverberating clang.

"OK, guys, come and take a look!"

The three men came from behind the tractor and joined Ivan at the edge of the hole.

Jim rested his hand on Ivan's shoulder and said quietly "You OK?"

"Yes boss, no problem."

They looked down into the hole and found themselves staring at a concrete lined void about four feet deep that turned into a low passageway that disappeared out of sight.

"OK. Who wants to be first?" Jim said.

Chapter 20.

"Has to be my turn to go first this time," said Geordie, stepping forward and dropping into the hole. He ducked down and looked along the passageway. "Black as a shopkeeper's heart in here, boss. We're going to need flashlights."

He turned to the side of the hole and removed a grenade, which had been linked to the entry hatch, from a recess. He held the striker arm down on the old grenade very carefully until he had found the safety pin. He worked the pin back into place, pushing out the dirt of seventy years. He handed the, now safe, weapon up to Ivan and drew a deep breath.

"I can help you with the light," said the old man, "it's the least I can do after trying to shoot you."

He felt in his pocket and brought out a small silver coloured flashlight and handed it down to Geordie.

"Take it slow, Geordie. That first booby trap might not have been the only one," said Jim. He turned to the old man "Thanks for that. I feel I really ought to know your name. I am Major James Wilson, by the way." He held out his hand.

"Formally, I am the Reverend Thomas Roundhay, Vicar of this Parish. But I prefer to be just Tom when I am not in the pulpit. Who are your two companions?"

"The one down the hole who made the first explosive safe is Sergeant Geordie Peters and the gentleman you wrestled with is Sergeant Major Ivan Thomas."

"All serving soldiers then? So how did you get this job?"

"We are all Royal Engineers and the Prime Minister asked us to do this. We completed another job a while ago and he seems to have been impressed by that."

After making a thorough inspection of the passageway Geordie started to move slowly forward. Ivan dropped in behind him and bobbed down to watch his progress.

"I've come to a corner here," said the muffled voice of Geordie, "just having a look for nasty surprises before I go round it. It's a bit tight in here."

Ivan leaned forward and tapped Geordie on the back. "Take it slow. Don't ignore anything and remember your training."

Geordie didn't answer but shuffled slowly forward, checking carefully for any wires of anything that looked as though it did not belong. He made it around the corner and followed the passageway until the ground dropped away to the floor of a larger room. As he shone the light around he could see four bunks mounted on the walls, a gun rack with weapons still standing in it, rusty tinned food on the shelves and ammunition boxes below the lower bunks. At the end of the room there was a further doorway. He stepped carefully in and continued to check for booby traps. Finding nothing, he called Ivan forward.

Ivan slid along the tunnel and entered the bunkroom. They checked again for any explosive traps without moving anything. Geordie stepped into the doorway at the end of the room. He shone the flashlight into the next chamber and looked back over his shoulder at Ivan.

"Better call the Major down here," he said, "he's going to want to see this. Tell him he might want to bring the vicar too."

Ivan returned to the tunnel and called back to Jim "Boss, Geordie has found something he thinks you both want to see."

"OK, on our way."

"Can I go too?" said Tom "That's very kind of you."

Jim helped the old man climb down into the hole and watched as he slowly crawled out of sight along the passageway. He was about to follow him when his mobile phone rang. He slipped it out of his pocket and said "Jim Wilson."

"Hello Jim, it's Helen. I know its short notice but I'm just catching the train to London and wondered if the lunch invitation was still open?"

"Helen, nice to hear from you. Of course the invitation is open and I would love to see you but I'm afraid the timing is a little difficult. I'm in the North of England at the moment in the middle of a job. I hope you don't mind. Maybe I can come down to your neck of the woods when I get back?"

"That would be nice. My train is here. Call me when you can."

Jim smiled and put the phone back in his pocket then followed the vicar into the bunkroom. The other three were standing waiting for him.

"Ready boss?" said Geordie.

"Go ahead."

"I think the Reverend will want to see this first. Come on Padre, come and see what you have been guarding all these years."

Geordie moved back to allow the old man to walk into the doorway. As he saw what the flashlight was pointing at his jaw dropped.

"I never imagined anything like that."

He stared at the ornate but dusty golden crucifix standing on top of a pile of small wooden crates. It was filthy but the gorgeous craftsmanship was immediately obvious. This had been made with considerable care and skill by a master craftsman.

"This is wonderful. Where did it come from and why is it here?"

From the doorway Jim said "It's quite a story. We'll tell you all about it over a brew of tea after we've had a further look round."

Tom smiled. "I guess that is a subtle hint that you would like me out of your way?"

"Afraid so, sir," said Ivan, "let me help you back into the barn."

Ivan and Tom left as Jim and Geordie started to look carefully at the second room. Two walls were stacked high with the small wooden crates. A shelf had been created with these boxes for the crucifix to stand on. Along the third wall were larger boxes held closed with rusty padlocks.

Geordie tried the weight of one of the small crates and then one of the larger ones. "Hell's teeth, these are heavy for their size. It's going to be hard labour getting this lot out through that passage."

"When I went down to Coleshill House they told me that these hides were always made with an entrance and an exit so they could make an escape, if one was found. If there is a second way in it might be easier."

Geordie looked around "If there is a second way out then it can only be behind this lot. I´ll heave a few out of the way and see what I can find. In this small space it's probably better if you let me do it on my own, boss."

"OK. Mind your back when you are heaving. I´ll go and see if Tom knows about another way in."

As Jim left the chamber and headed through the bunkroom to the passage he could hear Geordie grunting as he started to shift the heavy boxes. Once through the passage he reached the entrance way and stood up. Tom and Ivan were sitting on the trailer arm of a plough talking quietly.

"Tom, did your Dad ever tell you about another entrance to this place? It probably comes out somewhere that can´t be seen from the barn."

The old vicar thought for a moment, his faced creased in concentration. He shook his head slowly. "I don't think so. But we could ask one of the other Guardians."

"Other Guardians?"

"Yes boss," said Ivan "the Padre here has been telling me about the people who have been looking after this place. They call themselves 'The Guardians'."

"Go on."

"Originally there were four members of this special auxiliary unit. They were people who had an excuse for being out at odd times so they would not arouse the German´s suspicions if the invasion had ever happened. There was the vicar you know about, a vet, the farmer whose land it was and the local postman. As they got too old to carry on they passed the task on to their children as some kind of sacred trust. Did I get that right, Tom?"

The old man nodded "Pretty well, yes. My father passed it on to me and helped me join this parish as the vicar. Dan, the farmer, passed it on to his boy who was supposed to pass it on to his son but had a heart attack and died before he could. The boy moved to Spain some years ago."

Jim did not mention that they knew about the grandson living in Spain. "And the other two?"

"David the vet never had children and did not have any other people he trusted enough before he died. But Patrick the postman passed it on to his boy who is as old as me now. He runs a village shop and his boy in turn is in on the secret."

"So there are just three people in this area who know about this?"

"That's right and unless my eyes deceive me, if you look through the gaps in the barn wall behind you I think you are about to meet the other two."

Chapter 21

The barn door creaked open as the two newcomers entered. The older of the two leant heavily on his walking stick and eyed Ivan and Jim.

"Everything OK, Tom?" he said without looking at him. The younger man held back and was clearly nervous or ready to act.

"Everything is fine, Pat. These men and another one down there are from the Prime Minister himself. I think you had better show him your letter, Major."

Jim retrieved the letter from his pocket and stepped forward.

"That's far enough," said the younger man at the door.

Jim saw he had produced another heavy duty Webley revolver and was ready to use it. He stopped and slowly held the letter out towards the older man.

"I'm just going to drop this and move back," he said, "no need for that hand cannon today."

The letter fluttered to the floor of the barn and the old man learned down painfully to pick it up. He groaned slightly as he stood back up, then walked across to sit down on an old box as he opened the envelope. He read slowly and looked up at Jim.

"You sure about this, Tom?" he said.

The vicar nodded. "Yes. They had plenty of time to kill me and get at the stuff in the hide after that big one disarmed me" he said, indicating Ivan.

Ivan smiled and said a little too loudly, "And that daft lad in the doorway can put his gun down too unless he wants me to take it away from him."

The younger man stiffened and stared hard at Ivan. He didn't notice Geordie step in behind him and grab the barrel of the pistol with one hand while gripping the pressure point in his neck with the other.

"I think I'll have that. Thank you kindly," said Geordie as he removed the pistol from the man's slackened grip. He released the neck hold and the younger man sagged to the ground. "Don't worry the neck pinch wears off in a few minutes. Just sit quietly till it does."

"Coming from that direction I take it you found the other exit?" said Jim, retrieving the letter from the old man's trembling fingers. "Nothing to worry about, sir. We're serving soldiers, here on the orders of the Prime Minister. We aren't stealing the material down there."

"How do we know that?"

"Simple really. You lot have waved guns at us twice and tried to shoot us at least once but we have not harmed you." He looked at the younger man in the doorway. "At least not permanently. If we were thieves do you really think you would still be alive now with what is at stake here?"

The old man looked at him with watery eyes, then looked across at the Tom who nodded encouragement. "I suppose not," he said, "but you could have just used the code word."

"You didn't give me much chance to do that before the gun started swinging around."

"Yes. Oh, well, sorry about that. Martin, stop moaning and come over here."

Martin rose from the doorway and came to sit down next to his father on the box. "What happens now" he said.

Jim looked down at the two of them. "Tom didn't know what you were the Guardians of. Do you know?"

They both shook their heads. "We were never told," said Patrick, "all we knew was that it was important and had to be guarded."

"Ivan, will you take our two friends down and show them what this is all about please. Geordie, would you like to show Tom and me the new way in?"

"Certainly would, boss. Right this way, Padre"

He led the way out of the barn and out of the open gate in the safety fence. He walked slowly to allow Tom to keep up and led the way across the field, behind the barn and towards the sea.

"Mind the cow dung," he said, "whatever these animals were eating had way too much fibre in it by the look of this field. Not far now, just where the ground dips down towards the railway line by that hedge boundary."

They walked to the point where the land started to drop away and looked down the slope. Below them, they could now see another hatch that opened almost under the hedge line. The soil and grass on top of it showed how it had been hidden all these years.

"This entrance leads to a better passage than the other one. It will be a lot easier to shift the boxes out this way and we can get a truck down here, right to the doorway. The inner entrance was right behind the stack of bigger boxes. Oh! And hold your hand out, boss."

Jim extended his hand as Geordie fished in his pocket, held his closed fist over Jim's hand and then dropped something into it. As Geordie's hand moved away Jim saw the gold coin laying there.

"Number eighteen, eh? And the rest of those are in one of the boxes inside. That should cheer somebody up next time we see him."

Tom stared at the coin "Who will it cheer up?"

"The Governor of the Bank of England. All this material in your hide is his responsibility and he really wants it back."

They walked down the slope and entered the hidden doorway. The passageway inside was concrete lined but higher than the first one they had found. As they went inside Geordie pointed out the hand grenade mounted in a recess in the wall. The safety pin was now in place but it had been linked to the door to catch the unwary, or the hurried. They moved in until they came to the storage room. Patrick and his son were already there, with Ivan, staring in open mouthed wonder at the gold in the boxes that had been opened. None of them could guess the value of this small room below a rotting barn.

Ivan looked across at Jim. "Well boss, what the hell do we do with this now we have found it?"

"Good question" said Jim contemplating the size and weight of the material they needed to move. "If we try and move this ourselves we are going to be here for days and we are going to get noticed. Then we have the problem of how to move it. Army trucks would be good but they will need armed guards. We need to increase the level of security here to start with."

He turned to the three Guardians. "No offence gents. You and your families have done a superb job for many years but that relied heavily on secrecy and that is going to be lost very shortly. We have to get some help to back you up."

"Who are you thinking of, boss?" said Geordie.

"If we want covert observation I think we want the Hereford Hooligans. Start making a list of everything we have found and I'll make the call. I warned the Downing Street people to put them on standby before we came up here in case we needed some muscle."

Tom looked at Jim quizzically "Hooligans?"

"Not to worry, Tom, it's just the nickname for Special Forces. Rather useful people for a job like this."

Chapter 22.

Jim came back into the hide to find that the Guardians had left and his two men had listed all the boxes they had found but had not opened any more. The wooden case with the brass corner plates that contained the special pieces of eight was sitting on one of the bunks next to Ivan as he thumbed through a yellowed notebook with a cracked leather cover. Geordie was sitting on the opposite bunk examining the Thompson submachine gun across his lap. They looked up as Jim came in.

"Made the call," he said, "the people in Downing Street are quite efficient. It took them about ten minutes to get me through to the Operations Officer at the SAS HQ and they had already briefed him to give us whatever we asked for. It took a while to explain things without saying anything understandable across an open phone line but he got the message."

"So how long before they get here?" said Ivan. "I don't know about you but I'm getting hungry."

"Good thought," said Jim. "The Hooligans will be airborne in about twenty minutes, they have a team on standby at all times it seems. They should be here a little before dark. I've told them to land a couple of fields over. So we have time for something to eat while we wait. I saw a Fish and Chip shop in the village we passed through. I'll stay here if you two want a break to go and get some."

They both stood. "OK. boss. You want anything special?"

"No. Just fish and chips plus a tub of mushy peas if they have them."

Geordie smiled "It's Lancashire, boss, of course they'll have them. See you shortly."

"See you later then. Oh and Geordie."

"Yes boss?"

"Don't call me shorty." He had been waiting for ages to use that old joke on Geordie, ever since he had been caught by it during their voyage across the Atlantic in that old submarine.

As Ivan turned to follow Geordie he passed Jim the notebook. "That was under a jacket on one of the bunks, seems like someone was making notes about things that went on. He describes the night they picked up the gold in London and he also tried his hand at some bloody awful poetry. Other than that, some interesting stuff."

Jim sat down on the bunk and started to read. The pages were old and yellow but the hand writing was clear and legible. He read about the night of the collection. The air raid had made quite an impression on the writer. A big raid like that would have seemed quite something to someone from this quiet part of Northern England. The other trucks in the collection party were described and were just as Harold Greenly had described them in Henfield. But the description of the black van was different. There was a horse and cart, as Harold had said, but on the side of the painting of the cart was a flower. That really might have been interesting if the writer had said what kind.

He carried on turning the pages until he came to the attempt at poetry. Ivan was right, it was awful. His old English teacher would probably have called it doggerel. He was just about to turn the page when the words struck him as odd. He looked again.

In a Barn by the Bonniest Bay

We hide our treasure away

Near the deepest Hole

We live by the Bowl

By the Standing Stones

Where there are no Bones

Another Cave, no?

Where the rich folk go

He thought back to the metal advertising signs he had seen on the barn wall. One of them was a railway company poster picture of an overly jolly fisherman dancing across the sand. The wording had struck him as odd. It said "Morecambe – Britain's Bonniest Bay". Could these be clues to the locations of the four special hides? Surely it couldn't be that much of a gift? He slipped the notebook into his jacket pocket as his two men came back carrying their paper wrapped meal.

They sat on the two lower bunks eating the fish and chips with their fingers and using the plastic spoons to eat the mushy peas from the plastic tubs. The banquet over, they wrapped up the paper and Jim took it out to the barn while the other two carried on looking around the hide. As he returned he could not help but notice the musty smell had been overtaken by that of chips and vinegar. His team was examining the weapons. Ivan looked up.

"It may be fairly dry in here but I'm not sure I would take a chance on firing these, some really heavy pitting around the chamber and up the barrel. I think the vicar was lucky that Webley didn't take his hand off."

"I think we were luckier that the ammunition was so old. Could have been a nasty moment."

Chapter 23

The pounding of helicopter blades echoed within the bunkroom and they went outside to see the bright yellow and white helicopter flying low across the bay. It flared into a landing in a nearby field and seconds later was on its way again, snaking up a shallow valley to the north.

"Was that them do you think?" said Geordie. "I didn't expect a bright yellow aircraft. Bit obvious isn't it?"

"That's the point. Who would expect a covert team to arrive in a yellow helicopter? It's made to look like a civilian commercial one, hiding in plain sight, eh?"

Their speculation was interrupted by a young man walking through the hedge below the barn and approaching them. He was tall and slim with a small backpack slung over one shoulder of his distressed leather jacket. He pushed his overlong hair back off his forehead as he reached them. "Major Wilson?"

"That's me and who are you?"

"Your helpers from Hereford. Do you want to give me a rundown of the job you need doing?"

"No names, no pack drill?"

"That's right, sir. Just point us at the job and you can be on your way."

"Us?"

"My team are having a little look round, I'll brief them once you are gone."

Jim took the newcomer to show him the two access points to the hide. "Let's be clear here. Nobody goes in and nothing is touched inside until I or one of these two men come back here to relieve you. Your team may not withdraw except on my authority. Is that clear?"

"Well, I can't promise that. If we get called back by HQ we have to go."

Jim pulled the Prime Minister's authority letter from his pocket and handed it over.

"I am trumping any instructions from your HQ. On my authority you will not withdraw from here without a direct order from me. You need to understand that this is a career stopper."

"OK. So how much force are we allowed to use to keep this hole in the ground secure?"

"You will not use any force that might attract any attention if you can possibly manage it. This place must remain a secret at all costs. Just persuade people to bugger off and that includes the guy who farms here. He has no reason to go into that barn. If anybody pushes the point, stop them."

"Got it. We'll keep your hidey hole secret and secure."

"Good. Now I am going to lie to the farmer and hopefully scare him enough so he stays away. You have control of this site. Is there anything you need before we go?"

"No, we have everything we need."

With that the younger man turned and walked away towards the hedge line. Jim watched him leave, then shrugged and turned back to his own men.

"Time we weren't here. We need to speak to the farmer on the way out, he should be back down from his top field by now. Try and look seriously fed up with the state of the building."

A short visit to the farmhouse and a series of dire warnings about imminent collapse later, the three men were back in their car and heading for the motorway. Six hours later they crunched across the gravelled driveway of Sir Richard's house. Geordie gave a low whistle.

"Nice place. Maybe I should have gone into banking."

"No mate, you're way too honest for anything like that."

As they approached the door it swung open and the Governor of the Bank of England ushered them into the wide hallway of his house.

"Come through into the study, we can be more private in there."

They followed him into the book-lined room and each took one of the green leather chairs while the Governor seated himself behind the impressive desk.

"Do you have news for me?"

Jim leaned forward and deposited the gold coin in the middle of the writing pad that lay on the desk. Sir Richard picked it up almost reverently and held it up to the light, turning it over slowly as he gazed at it.

"My God! You've found it. I hardly dared to hope. Where's the rest of it?"

"It's still where we found it. We need to know how you want to transport it. I assume you want your own people to pick it up rather than have me hire a security truck?"

"But what if someone finds it while you are here. That could be a disaster!"

"It has been a well-kept secret for more than seventy years and now it has armed guards sitting by it full time. And before you ask they are completely trustworthy. We have a team from the Special Forces watching over it."

Sir Richard picked up the phone and dialled. He waited for an answer then said "I want a security truck organised at once, ready to move at a moment's notice." He paused as Jim held up a hand.

"Better make that two trucks," he said, "modern security trucks are smaller than removal vans and there is a lot of stuff to shift. Plus you will need armed guards."

The Governor nodded and continued speaking into the phone. "Make that two trucks and set up a special escort from the Police." He put the phone down and looked at Jim "Special Escort is the term we use for armed police. Not used very often nowadays but this one is important enough. Where should I send them?"

"Not that simple. Unless we are with them to clear the way the guard team are under orders to stop anyone entering. It could get messy."

"Alright, where should they meet you?"

"It's Tuesday today so we will be at the Forton Service area on the M6 Motorway at 0900 on Friday morning. Have your people park up there and we will make ourselves known to them."

"That seems a long delay. What are you going to do in the meantime?"

"Oh we have a couple of things to arrange. We won't be bored."

As they drove away from the imposing house Ivan said, "So what are we going to be doing until Friday?"

"Well Geordie here is going to go home and see his new wife for a short while. I am going down to Henfield to see if Mr Greenly has remembered anything else since we saw him. And you are going to Cambridgeshire to see the people in JARIC to see what they can do for us by way of an aerial survey of the valley around Castleton. Tell them we are looking for a disused track up to a bowl in the ground."

"Bowl, what bowl? Where did you pull that one from, boss?"

Jim tapped the side of his nose. "I have my sources."

"OK, be mysterious and give my regards to Mrs Jennings, won't you?"

"Who's Mrs Jennings?" said Geordie from the back seat.

"Oh, nobody special" said Ivan, settling back into his seat with a small smile on his face.

Chapter 24

Jim pulled up outside the bungalow in Henfield a little before lunchtime. He felt like a teenager on his first date. In all the years since the divorce he had never even thought about trying again but there was something about Helen Jennings that drew him in a way he had not felt before. He swallowed and opened the car door. As he climbed out he saw that she was standing in the doorway waiting for him, in a simple but elegant, blue dress. He also saw that the net curtains were twitching in the windows of the houses either side. Helen noticed him looking at them and smiled.

"Don't mind them. It makes us all feel safe. They are more effective than a burglar alarm."

As he reached the step she gave him a light peck on the cheek.

"Nice to see you too," he said, "is your grandfather awake?"

"He's not here. Today is his day at the physiotherapy clinic and then he plays chess with his friends at the community centre. He won't be home until after seven."

"Oh. I was hoping to have a word with him to see if he has recalled anything else of use."

"Oh really?" She gave him what his mother used to call 'an old fashioned look'.

"OK. I confess. That was an excuse to take you to lunch. You might at least have pretended to believe me."

She looked him straight in the eyes. "I don't have time for pretence. Not in anything."

"Nice to know. Where would you like to go for lunch then?"

"How about the 'Cat and Canary', that's not far away?"

"The what?"

"It's a pub at the back end of the village. No false roof beams or copper warming pans just good food and cold beer. Unless you want something different?"

"Good food and cold beer will always do for me as long as the company is attractive."

"Nice one. You're getting back into the swing of this," she smiled.

"Is it so obvious that I'm out of practice?"

She lifted a light jacket down from behind the front door, looked at him closely and said "If you're paying attention then, yes, it's obvious. And by the way, before you ask, yes I am paying attention."

He reached for the car keys from his pocket while he absorbed the implications of that statement. But she said "It's a nice day for a walk through the village and the neighbours would be very disappointed if they didn't get a look at you on the way by."

"Do you parade all your callers for inspection?"

"Another good one. A little joke to cover a serious inquiry? At least I think it's serious. Is it?"

"Not sure yet, but I have a feeling it might be. So what's the answer to the question I didn't ask?"

They walked along in silence for a moment or two. She linked arms with him "OK. The history of Helen Jennings. The short version so we don't spoil lunch. Now where to start?"

"How far to the pub?"

"Only about a five minute walk."

"Then let's just have the highlight reel for now. With a Q and A session later."

He tried to keep it light hearted but was finding that he really did want to know about this tall, elegant woman with her arm linked through his.

"Alright. I am thirty three, divorced; no children, no job and getting a little bored being stuck in this village. Enough?"

"Not really. I'd like to know more."

"OK I met my husband at University. He was doing a Law degree and I was doing one in Biology. Nothing in common at all but they say opposites attract. We married the summer after we both graduated. He left me for another lawyer in his firm just after I miscarried for the second time. That was just after my parents were killed in a car crash. I have no brothers or sisters so I moved in here to look after granddad. To be honest I had nowhere else to go. But it has worked out well. He is no great trouble but he does need a little help and I am able to study for my Doctorate in Biomedical Science at Brighton University. And you are the first one I have paraded for the neighbours since I was divorced." She paused, waiting for a reaction, then said, "No questions from the floor so that makes it your turn."

"Ah well, maybe I should invoke the Official Secrets Act and remain a mystery?" He looked at her. She didn't reply, just waited for him to go on. "No way out, then?"

"No and hurry up or we will be in the pub and you have no idea how nosy villagers are in this part of Sussex."

"Thirty-seven years old. I have been divorced for a little over three years after eight years of marriage. There was nobody else involved, she just couldn't stand the constant separations and I couldn't tell her about what I was doing most of the time. She lives in Spain now, writing children's books. No kids. No entanglements. NFTR."

"NFTR?"

"Nothing Further To Report. Sorry, not much of a joke."

"OK. Now what about Ivan? What's the story on your minder?"

"Well he's not my minder, he's my Sergeant Major. He's unmarried and one of the finest soldiers I have ever served with."

"Strange that a big handsome man like that isn't married."

"He's had some problems in that way. He was stationed at the weapon trials range in the Hebrides, some years ago, when a missile they were testing went rogue. It landed on his house and his wife was killed. They never found a trace of her so he has had difficulty coming to terms with it. It will have to be a very special kind of woman to get him to open up again."

"That's so sad. Did they have children?"

"Two. They live with their grandparents in Florida. Sorry; that was a depressing story."

"True but it got us to the pub. So how about one of those beers I was telling you about?"

Chapter 25

Ivan's military ID card got him into the RAF base without difficulty. He found the JARIC compound and parked his hire car across the road. Walking up to the front door he noticed that there was a key card entry pad on the right hand side and a call button above it. He pressed the button and waited until the distorted voice said, "Yes?"

"Good morning. I am CSM Thomas and I have an appointment to see your Commanding Officer."

"Just a moment." There was a pause while the intercom box hummed to itself quietly. "OK Mr Thomas, I have your appointment in the diary, please push the door and turn right as you enter."

The electronic door lock buzzed and he pushed it open. He walked into an empty hallway with the customary display cases on the walls showing the sporting trophies the unit had won, with a couple of cheap, military issue chairs next to them. He turned right as instructed and found himself facing an office with a half door and a small counter top. The RAF corporal stood up from his desk and approached.

"Can I see your ID please, sir?"

Ivan produced his photo ID and passed it over. The corporal fed it into a machine on a side table and waited patiently until it beeped.

"That's fine, sir. The CO's PA will be down to collect you in a few seconds if you could just wait in the reception area."

Ivan walked back and was just about to sit when a voice behind him said, "Right this way, sir."

He turned to find a very attractive Army Sergeant holding open the door to the corridor off the reception area. He followed her down the corridor admiring the view as he went. Too soon they arrived at the end door and the Sergeant knocked and opened it.

"Mr Thomas to see you, sir."

Ivan walked into a well appointed office to meet the officer who was approaching him hand outstretched. They shook hands and the officer waved him to the small conference table in the corner.

"Well Sgt Major," he said as they sat down, "your message was intriguing. So what can JARIC do for the Royal Engineers this fine day?"

"Well sir, first thing is that this task is highly classified."

"We are used to that around here."

"No, I don't think you are, sir. There is no standard classification for this; we are way above 'Top Secret'. There is to be no written record that this meeting took place and there is to be no record kept of the task we need your people to carry out."

"I'm not sure we can do that. You'll have to give me a pretty damn good justification."

"I can do just that sir."

Ivan brought out the Prime Minister's authorisation letter and handed it across the table. He watched as the officer read it and smiled as his expression changed. The officer looked up.

"This is pretty heavy-duty stuff. I assume you want something special from us?"

"I need a valley in Derbyshire fully surveyed by all necessary assets to try and find a trackway that probably hasn't been used in over seventy years and was probably not obvious even then."

"I take it I can't ask why?"

"It would be better if you didn't."

The officer thought for a moment or two while looking over Ivan's shoulder.

"OK. We can do this but it means deploying or diverting some expensive assets and calling in some favours from our American cousins. I can work up a cover story for that part, but before I do anything I am going to have to verify that this letter is genuine. Don't be offended but this is not something trivial you are asking for."

He walked to his desk while Ivan watched him. He lifted the hand set on the desk phone and dialled the number in the letter. The call was answered quickly and the officer stiffened as he listened to the reply to his query. He came back to the table and sat down.

"Bloody hell! I didn't expect to be put through to the PM in person. He was remarkably direct for a politician. It appears I am to 'stop playing silly buggers' and to do what you tell me. I think I need my technical specialists in here so we can work out what we need."

"Fine by me, sir, but you will need to make sure they speak to nobody they don't have to about this."

"No problem. I will give them the Witch's Warning about security, but you will need to explain exactly what you are looking for so we know what kit to deploy."

"I can do that but could we also make this anonymous, they don't need to know who I am and they don't need to know who is tasking me."

The Commanding Officer nodded and left the room. He was back moments later.

"The team we need is being rounded up now and my PA is sorting out the coffee."

There was a knock on the door as the first of the specialist team arrived, to be followed shortly by the other four. They all looked quizzically at Ivan who sat quietly at the table and just looked back. The coffee arrived as they were all finding their seats. The CO waited until they had all filled their cups and grabbed a biscuit before he spoke.

"Alright gents. This gentleman has a task for us and I want it completed as quickly as possible. It is to take priority over all the jobs you are currently running including, your survey of nude sunbathers on Brighton beach, John."

"Oh, come on boss, I apologised for that one."

"Just twisting your tail John, you've been forgiven for that episode. I think it's probably best if I let our guest tell you what he needs but first I have to tell you this is highly classified. Do not mention it to anyone who has no need to know and there are to be no records kept at the end of the task. Is that clear?"

They all nodded and looked at Ivan expectantly.

"Good morning," Ivan said. "What I need you to do is to carry out a very detailed survey of the area immediately around the village of Castleton in Derbyshire. We are looking for a trackway that has probably not been used in over seventy years; it may end at a depression or bowl in the ground or possibly at some kind of structure. When it was in use it was wide enough for a removal van to drive up and probably turn round at the end to get out again. We have no idea how old the track is but we do know that the Romans were mining there 2000 years ago. We know that archaeologists can spot ancient settlements from the air so we are hoping you can do a little better."

"No introductions then?" said a young Flight Lieutenant. "A bit of context would be nice, like why do you need this and when do you want this survey concluded."

Ivan looked across at the Commanding Officer who said, "You have the floor."

Ivan nodded and said "Sorry to be abrupt but you do not need to know why I want it and I need it as soon as you reasonably can. Any other questions?"

He paused and the team around the table looked around at each other. The CO at the head of the small table spoke.

"In which case gentlemen what are you doing here? Let's get this done. I want you back here with your first reports by 1700 hours today."

The team filed out of the office, leaving their unfinished coffee. A couple of them glanced at Ivan as they left, but said nothing. Ivan stood and held out his hand to the CO.

"Thank you, sir. I would appreciate a call as soon as you have something useful. I will leave my number with your PA on the way out."

Chapter 26

Geordie had already collected Ivan by the time he parked the car outside Jim's block of flats in Pimlico. Jim came out carrying his overnight bag before Geordie had time to call him.

"Morning, both."

"Morning, boss. How was Mrs Jennings?"

"Very helpful. Her old granddad had remembered another detail about the fourth van. Apparently the mention of the flower triggered his memory and he now says he saw the horse that was pulling the cart was white and there was a box on the bed of the cart. He can't remember anything else so far." He craned round to look at Ivan in the back seat "How did you get on with JARIC?"

"Fine. They were helpful but a bit unhappy that we won't tell them why we want the survey. The CO will call me as soon as he has some results."

"Good. OK Geordie, off to Lancaster. Did you book us a hotel for tonight?"

"I did, but I booked it just outside Preston so we can join the motorway before the Forton service area. It's a hotel just off the motorway so we can have an easy start in the morning."

The drive to the hotel north of Preston passed without incident, despite the heavy traffic and the awful driving standards. The team retired to sleep after a good dinner and a few quiet beers. As they pulled out of the car park, the next morning and onto the motorway entry slip road Jim noticed Geordie checking his mirror more than usual.

"What's up? Have we got somebody attractive in the car behind?"

"No boss, but I have a feeling we are not alone. We had a car behind us yesterday on the motorway, a BMW with a dirty mark on his forward bumper. I thought it was just coincidence but he pulled out of the car park behind us and he is right there again."

Jim and Ivan made a point of not turning to look out of the back window. Jim lowered the sun visor to look in the vanity mirror.

"Are you talking about the silver one?"

"Yep! That's the one. Look just to the side of his number plate and you can see the dirty mark. Looks like he clipped a post or something."

"How sure are you?"

"Not certain but pretty sure. I wasn't looking for a tail so I don't know how long he was with us."

"Ivan can you wave your arm or something so I have a reason to turn round."

Ivan fished in the bag next to him on the seat and pulled out a file folder. He held it up and Jim turned around to take it from him. He turned back to the front.

"Four people in the car which is unusual to start with and they are all looking at us. Nobody dozing or gazing at the scenery. I think you're right, we have company."

Jim felt a light tap on his elbow and looked down between the front seats to find a black automatic pistol being handed to him by Ivan.

"I started to worry about what might happen at the next site we find. That pistol of the vicar's could have been a big problem if he had cared for his ammunition."

"Where did you get these?"

"Chelsea Barracks. I called in the see the Guards battalion yesterday afternoon. Three pistols and two full spare magazines for each one. That one's loaded by the way and here are your spare mags. Geordie, yours is on the back seat behind you."

"When is the next turn off, Geordie?"

"Not till after the service area. Can't we just pull alongside the truck full of armed coppers and let them deal with it?"

"Don't think so. It would take too long to explain what is going on by which time our friends will be away down the motorway and gone. We need to get their attention and ask them a couple of questions. Ivan, are you ready?"

"Insulted you would ask boss. What would you like?"

"Geordie, as you pull into the service area there is going to be a short time when we are out of sight of the tail car. As soon as we are, stop quickly. Ivan and I will get out and take cover. You go on into the car park and stop as close to us as you can."

"OK, boss, here's the turn. Indicating now."

Geordie moved the car into the slip lane for the service area but did not slow. The tailing car dropped back not expecting them to drive so recklessly. The car slid slightly as Geordie took the corner at the head of the slip road far too fast. He turned into the car park and brought the vehicle to a sliding stop. Jim and Ivan were out in a second and sprinted into the cover of a large tree on the banking as Geordie moved forward and parked about fifty metres from them.

Jim and Ivan stood still and watched the BMW enter the car park and slow down to park. Nobody got out. The occupants sat still, all focused on the car with Geordie in it. The soldiers, with the large black pistols held down by their sides, walked to the BMW. They moved to either side and then at a signal from Jim they grabbed the front door handles and wrenched the doors open. The two front seat occupants stared into the barrels of the pistols, eyes wide.

"Good morning gentlemen and what brings you out on a fine day like this? Going somewhere nice? Oh and before you decide to drive off take a look in front of you."

The two men's eyes swivelled forward and took in the sight of Geordie with his legs braced slightly apart, knees slightly bent and his pistol held in two hands pointing very steadily at the driver.

Ivan leaned in and took the keys from the ignition while resting the barrel of his gun in the driver's ear.

"Now then" said Jim "I think it's time we were introduced don't you? Who are you and why are you following us?"

The driver started to bluster about how they knew nothing about following them and it was all a mistake. He shut up quickly when Ivan tapped his forehead with the barrel of the heavy pistol.

"Don't tell lies or you won't go the heaven. Now answer my friend's question before we get cross with you. And if your hand moves one more inch towards me," he said looking at the men in the back seat, "the inside of this car will take a week to clean."

The two in the back moved their hands slowly to rest in their laps and Ivan turned his attention back to the driver.

"Well? Worked out a story yet?"

"We are from the Bank of England security department. Sir Richard instructed us to keep an eye on you to make sure you didn't run into trouble."

Jim looked at Ivan across the top of the car. His face reflected the irritation he felt.

"Geordie, come over here, will you."

The big sergeant strolled to the passenger side door and trained his weapon on the front seat occupant's lap.

"Could you point that somewhere different?"

"Not really, bonny lad. If I point it at your head and have to fire, the round could go through and hit my friend. After all there is not much in there to stop it, is there?"

Jim retrieved the mobile phone from his pocket and dialled Sir Richard's private number. It was answered quickly and Sir Richard confirmed that the four men were acting on his instructions. Jim explained very clearly that the Bank of England had just risked the lives of four of its employees. After a few choice words he walked back to the car and handed the phone to the driver. The conversation was short and one sided. The driver hung up and handed the phone back to Jim.

"It appears we are now under your orders, sir. What would you like us to do?"

Jim nodded to his two men who made their weapons safe and slipped them into their pockets. Ivan tossed the car key to the driver and turned away. Jim looked at the four security officers.

"Follow us and park next to us when we stop."

He turned and walked to his own car. He climbed into the front passenger seat and said "OK, Geordie, can you drive around and try and find a couple of security vans."

"No need boss. They are parked over there by the door to the café with a white police van next to them."

He put the car into gear and drove across the car park to stop next to the first security van.

Geordie looked across at the driver of the security vehicle and said, "I think they've been here a while, boss. This one has a face like a yard of unmade road."

"Never mind" said Jim as he got out of the car "we'll have them on the move in a couple of minutes." He walked across to the police van and waited as the driver rolled down the window. "Ready to move?" he said as he showed his ID card.

The police driver nodded. "Yes sir, whenever you like."

Jim walked to the two security trucks and instructed them to follow Geordie. Then got back into the car and watched as the convoy formed up behind them as they re-joined the motorway.

Chapter 27

Jim called ahead to the team guarding the hidden base and the five barred farm gate was wide open as they arrived. The convoy swung into the farm and drove down to the condemned barn. Ivan directed the two security vans to back up so that their rear doors were close to the exit from the base near the hedge line. Jim assembled the group and was about to give them their tasks when the young man from Hereford ambled up.

"Morning, Major. Anything we need to know?"

"Good morning. Where are your people and our friend the farmer?"

"Depends. Are we finished here?"

"You will be in a few hours. These people will be removing the goodies. Why?"

"Didn't want to expose our hidey holes if we were carrying on doing this."

He put his fingers in his mouth and blew a shrill whistle. Three men stood up from unexpected places all around, each of them carrying a MP5 sub-machine gun. The one approaching from the hedge line was carrying two, one of which he handed to the team leader as he arrived.

"Have you had any trouble?" Jim asked.

"Nothing really. The vicar came down to see if we needed anything but we persuaded him he was drawing attention to us and he has stayed away since. The farmer got a bit nosey but we had a word and he stays well away now."

"OK, will you brief our police colleagues here and establish a cordon around the site while we work. Keep it as low key as you can."

The young team leader waved for the police team to follow him as he walked towards the farmhouse.

Jim watched them go, then turned back to the bank security team and his own people.

"OK, gents, we are going to form a human chain and pass boxes out of the hide under this barn and into the security vans. With armed police and Special Forces watching over us there should be no distractions and we can get the job done quickly."

In the event it took far longer than expected. The boxes were heavy and the tunnel was narrow making it awkward to handle them. Even once they had settled into the routine of heaving the boxes it was still a slow job. Night was falling as they finished and slammed the doors of the security vans. Everyone was tired and slumped to the ground. Jim looked around and realised these people were in no fit state to drive for six hours on busy motorways.

"Ivan, Geordie, come for a walk."

The three strolled towards the rail line at the bottom end of the farm and Jim said, "We need somewhere to park these vehicles that is very secure and out of the public eye. Any ideas?"

"There was a castle on the hill as we came through Lancaster." Geordie said "Would that be any good?"

Ivan laughed. "Oh yes, that would be a perfect place to hide a fortune in gold, mate. That castle is Her Majesty's Prison Lancaster, it's full of crooks who would be sure to tell their mates about us."

"Hmm, maybe not the best place then. How do you know about it?"

"I thought about joining the Prison Service when I left the Army so I did a bit of research."

"OK gents, that one is not really suitable." said Jim "What else have we got?"

"It's not too far to Preston. We could park up in Fulwood Barracks. It's an old Victorian barracks with high walls around it so we won't be seen from the outside and there is an infantry battalion stationed there who could help with security."

"Sounds like that could do nicely. You two go and round up our security people. We'll have two SAS people in the back of each security van and the police van can run at the back of the convoy. The bank security people can lead while we go ahead and make arrangements at Fulwood. Plus, we can drop those old weapons you found into the armoury there. OK, let's get moving."

Chapter 28

On Saturday night the streets around the Bank of England were quiet which made manoeuvring the convoy that much easier. Jim and his small team pulled up outside the bank and were met by a smiling Sir Richard.

"I never dared hope you would pull this off. An amazing achievement."

They watched as the heavy security vans drove around to the vehicle entrance to the vault area.

"Quite remarkable, Major. Do you have any hope of finding the rest?"

"We do. We've been remarkably lucky and have stumbled across various clues that we need to follow up. Once we found the first base there were more clues there so, yes, we have high hopes of finding the rest."

"Any idea when that might be?"

"We are off to get the results of an aerial survey on Monday morning. If they are useful we will be on the trail of the next hiding place straight after. And speaking of trailing, I appreciate the gesture but I don't need your bloodhounds following us, it draws too much attention. If I need them I will call you. OK?"

"Fair enough. You seem to know what you are doing; I just hope you don't regret the lack of extra security."

With the first batch of gold safely locked away in the safest vault in England, the team decided they deserved a day off. Geordie slept late then went to watch the rehearsal of his wife's new play which they were hoping to take to Broadway; Jim drove down to Sussex to see Helen and Ivan caught up on his sleep before walking along the Thames embankment in the all too rare sunshine.

On the Monday morning the three drove to RAF Wyton to meet the JARIC analysts to be briefed on what they had found in the Hope Valley near Castleton. Their military ID Cards once again got them past the security gate and into the JARIC headquarters building where the Commanding Officer was waiting for them.

"Come on in gentlemen. This has been a useful training exercise for us, so even if we have not found what you need it has not been wasted effort."

He led them into a small lecture theatre where more of his team were waiting. "Sit please" he said "the coffee will be here in a couple of minutes." He walked to the dais set next to the large wall screen. "I am guessing that you do not care how we conducted the survey? So unless you object I will skip that part of the briefing and go straight to the results?"

"That would be just fine, sir," said Jim, "we don't want to take up any more of your time than we have to."

"Good! OK. Well here's the coffee. If you could put it down on the side table Corporal we will sort ourselves out as we go." He waited for the Corporal to put the tray of mugs down and leave the room. "Lights if you please." One of the briefing team stood at the back of the room to lower the lights. "OK John, first slide."

The room lit up as the first slide was projected onto the large wall screen. The picture showed a simple overhead view of the Hope Valley around Castleton. With a long red line encircling the area.

"What you are seeing here is obviously the standard aerial photograph of the search area. The red line shows the limits we imposed to contain the detailed search. As you can see we have gone somewhat wider than the valley itself to give us a little leeway for error. The following pictures will come up in all sorts of odd colours due to the different methods we have used. Next slide."

The next slide came up on the screen with a distinct green tinge. The buildings of Castleton and surrounding farms were a much brighter green. Even the caves showed up although they were much less distinct than the buildings.

"What you are seeing here is effectively a heat map. We were quite surprised at how much heat we picked up from the caves. We are assuming that comes from the illumination inside and the body heat of the visitors. I will draw your attention to five very small lighter spots that you can see on the hillsides above the caves. We have a theory about that which I will come back to."

The slides marched across the screen. Colours changed, angles changed, magnification changed and they learned more about the topography of the Hope Valley than the people who had lived there all their lives.

"This next batch is my favourite. These are simple photographs taken at low level in the very early morning with the sunlight striking the ground at a shallow angle."

The first picture of the next set came up and suddenly they could see shapes and patterns that had not been visible before. As each of the series of six photographs appeared the laser pointer highlighted the five depressions in the ground that could be described as a 'bowl'. Tracks that had not been visible on previous slides now led to each of them.

"The interesting thing about these five bowls is that they correspond exactly with the five low heat signatures that we found on the early slide. Initially that did not make sense. Since hot air rises the bottom of the bowls should have been cold, but they aren't. We puzzled over that one for quite a while until we remembered that you had said there had been mine workings in this valley for the best part of two thousand years. We think that is what we are seeing here. The bowls are the remains of very old surface mining."

Geordie sat up and said, "I'll buy the bowls being the old mine's surface traces, but why the heat? A mine that is being worked is hot, but not once the working finishes."

"We puzzled over that too. Our best guess is that the very old tunnels link up with later shafts and eventually they link to the show caves where the tourists visit. What we think we are seeing is the warmth from body heat and breath that has crept up the old shafts and is just enough to show a temperature difference on our very sensitive equipment. We did think about putting in a 'TA-DA!' at that point but suffice it to say we think we have found you five viable targets for further investigation."

The three engineers stared at the screen with the five locations highlighted. Jim was the first to speak.

"Geordie, you worked in the mines before you joined the Army, does that theory make sense to you?"

"It does. A blind gallery at the top end of a mine can get bloody hot even if the working areas are on levels far below. The depression in the ground makes sense too. If they were mining by hand they would not want to waste effort creating spoil heaps. The earth and rock they dug out would be chucked into shafts they had finished with. I think we might be there, boss."

Jim stood and walked across to the JARIC Commanding Officer who was still standing at the dais. He reached him and shook his hand.

"Thank you, sir. That is a remarkable piece of work by you and your team. We may never be able to tell you what this is all about but I can tell you it's important at a national level."

"You're very welcome, we quite enjoyed the challenge. We have a pack of information for you with all those slides produced as 8x10 glossies and a detailed map with the locations marked. The only drawback is that I think your coffee is cold by now."

They left the building with the information pack and headed along the neat pathways back to the car.

"Looks like Castleton is our next stop then, boss," said Ivan. "Do we need to book a hotel?"

"We do. Maybe we can use the computers in the Education section over there?"

As they turned towards the drab flat roofed building with the Education Centre sign outside it Jim's mobile phone rang. He looked at the caller ID and said, "You go on. I'll join you in a minute."

His two companions went on to the Education section and were soon set up at an internet terminal searching for accommodation in Castleton. They were about to confirm the booking when Jim walked in.

"Can you order another room? We're having company."

Chapter 29

As they walked into the old coaching inn on the main street in Castleton they were greeted by the sight of polished horse brasses against the old oak beams. The carpet was worn in places where the regular drinkers usually stood but the log fire burned in the grate and the whole room had a welcoming air. They walked to the bar that doubled as a reception desk and announced themselves. The landlord checked the computer behind the bar and returned looking worried.

"I'm sorry, there seems to have been a mix up. I've only got two rooms available, a double and a twin."

"I don't think that's going to work" Jim said "we need a minimum of three, even if these two share the twin room."

"Oh you are old fashioned, Mr Wilson," said the voice from behind him.

He turned and looked into the steady brown eyes of Helen Jennings. He swallowed and turned back to the landlord.

"It seems that will be fine."

Ivan and Geordie stood at the bar trying hard not to grin and failing miserably.

"Hello, Mrs Jennings," said Ivan, "I don't think you've met the third member of our little band of hope. This is Geordie."

Helen greeted Geordie with a sunny smile and the three of them turned to continue enjoying Jim's discomfort. The booking-in completed, they moved to a table near the open fire. They ordered drinks while they studied the menu on the blackboard above the fireplace. Selections made they placed their orders and settled back to wait for their meals.

"I suppose I should have mentioned that Mrs Jennings would be the person joining us," said Jim, "since she already knows what we are looking for there is no added security risk and an extra pair of eyes might help."

"Yes of course, boss. Sound thinking. Don't know why I didn't suggest it myself," said Ivan, struggling not to grin.

Lunch came and saved Jim from more gentle ribbing from his team. The food was substantial and tasty as it is in most pubs in the north of England, where the weather lends itself to good, no nonsense food. They exchanged a few pleasantries as they ate but did not discuss their objective for fear of being overheard. As the rest of the diners finished their meals and drifted away they were left in peace near the fire. Jim produced the folder they had been given at JARIC. He spun the map round to face Helen and explained briefly the five targets they were going to examine. She looked at the map for a few moments before speaking.

"Judging by these contour lines, all of them are at the end of fairly steep tracks and if they haven't been maintained they could be quite rough."

"You understand maps?" said Geordie "You're the first woman I've met who could even follow the roads in the right direction."

"Ivan, thump the sexist will you? Geordie, I've been hiking the mountains since I was eighteen and you don't do that without being able to read a map properly. The point I was making is that unless you have the right equipment, even close to the village, it's going to be uncomfortable. I took a walk round before you arrived and there is a good hiking shop at the back of the village, unless you brought your kit with you?"

"Sounds like a plan, boss. The weather does look a bit dicey for wandering the hills."

"OK, let's drop the bags in the rooms and go and see what they have in this hiking shop."

They went out and grabbed their bags from the boot of the car and brought them back into the Inn. Helen was standing at the foot of the stairs waiting for them with her overnight bag over one shoulder. They climbed the stairs and found their rooms. As he opened the door Jim paused and looked at Helen.

"Are you sure about this?"

"I told you back in Henfield I don't have time for pretence in anything. So, yes, I'm sure. How about you?"

"I think I feel very comfortable with you and yes, I'm sure. Unless of course you snore?"

"We'll find out, won't we? Hurry up or your two reprobates will start thinking we have become distracted."

She slung her bag on the bed and waited for Jim to do the same. As he headed for the door she stopped him with a hand on his chest. Stepping forward she planted a gentle kiss on his lips. His hands slid naturally around to the small of her back and then slid down to cup her firm buttocks as he pulled her into a more serious kiss.

"Whoa, steady Tiger! We have some other things to find first."

She gently disentangled herself and pushed against his chest. Jim stood stunned for a moment. It was a long time since a woman had generated this urgency in him. He pulled himself together and followed her out of the room.

As they walked down the stairs back to the bar he took her hand and it felt the most natural thing in the world. They met up with the other two and together they walked through the narrow streets of the village between the stone cottages and gift shops to the hiking shop that Helen had found.

The shop turned out to be well stocked with good quality equipment suitable for hiking and even had some for caving. Jim paid for all of it on his credit card and made sure to take the receipts to claim the costs back later.

"Glad he took my sort of credit card, I need to build up my air miles for my summer holiday."

Helen said quietly, "Where are we going then?"

"I'm thinking of going off to see a couple of old friends just outside Boston. You'll certainly like him and his wife can guide you round the shops."

"For a second I wasn't sure you were inviting me along."

"Oh, if I go, you're invited never fear. I'm sure they'll like you."

They wandered slowly back towards the pub with their bags of purchases. Jim felt Helen's hand slip into his again. He felt a lightness that had been missing for a long time. He saw his two men look back at them and grin but he just didn't care.

Chapter 30

The full English breakfast the next morning was exceptional, with all the trimmings and pots of hot tea. The four of them ate together and Jim and Helen studiously ignored the small jokes being made by the other two.

Breakfast over, they moved to a clean table and studied the detailed map again.

"We have five possible sites, where do we start looking?"

"Well boss, Mrs Jennings here was brought along as a fresh pair of eyes so why not let her pick? We don't have any special leads so any one of them could be right," said Ivan looking across the table

"It's Helen, not Mrs Jennings and I pick that one." She put her finger on the site furthest from the village.

"Why that one?"

"Because I have just had an enormous fried breakfast and I need to walk it off. That one is the furthest away. Plus, of course, it means we can call in at that other one if we have time on the way back."

"Good logic. Any objections? No? Then that's a plan. Back at the foot of the stairs in about ten minutes. Booted, spurred and ready to go."

They retired to their rooms to put on the clothes needed for the gentle drizzle falling through the mist and returned to the foot of the stairs.

Ivan smiled and said "Er, boss, you might want to wipe your cheek a little."

Helen turned round and giggled a little as she wiped the smudge of lipstick from his cheek.

"Have to be more careful with your eagle-eyed companions along."

They stepped out of the door and each of them shrugged their jacket up and lifted the collar to avoid the drizzle as it reached their necks. The walk along the high street took only minutes before they were clear of the village and walking along the main road beside the 'dry stone walls' that had stood there for centuries despite being built without cement. Helen had never looked properly at boundaries built using the 'dry stone wall' technique and Geordie explained it to her as they walked.

"How do you know so much about it, Geordie?"

"Well, I used to be a miner and like a lot of people who work in the pits I used to get out into the country on my days off. I got friendly with a farmer who let me help him around the farm in return for a home cooked dinner. He taught me the technique with the walls and how to look after sheep. Made a nice change from the noise and dust of working underground."

"Did you join the Army to get away from the mines?"

"Not really, the mines closed down around my home town and the Army was a way to avoid being unemployed. Worked out well for me, it's given me a good life and the chance to walk along this road in the rain."

The map told them that they were now coming up to where the aerial survey had spotted the old trackway. At ground level there was nothing to show that a track had ever been there until Geordie went to the other side of the road and looked back with his head tilted to one side.

"It's there," he said, pointing, "that piece of the wall was put up later than the rest. You can see it was another person who did it, the technique is different."

The other three stood and looked at the wall but could see no difference. Then again Geordie was the only one of them who had ever built one of these walls and he agreed with the map they had been given by JARIC, so they climbed over and headed across the field to where the edge of the valley rose up the hillside. Ivan knelt on one knee and looked upwards towards the top of the hill.

"You know what? Those photo recon people know their business. If you look up here you can just make out that there is a flattened part of the land. It's the trackway they showed on their pictures."

Now they had found the old track it was relatively simple to follow it up the hillside until it turned away from the valley and they found themselves looking down on a jumble of stones that had once been a hut. It had once stood next to the shallow depression in the ground that stretched away to their right. They walked slowly, scanning the ground for any indication that this was a very important site.

After the initial walk across the bowl and back Ivan and Geordie set to work rolling over the stones of the ancient hut while Jim and Helen continued to criss-cross the depression alongside it.

After half an hour of fruitless search they assembled at the old hut site.

"Anything?" said Jim.

"No sign that this was used in the last couple of hundred years," said Ivan, wiping his face with the back of his hand, "but there are a couple of nice fossils on those stones over there."

"And we found nothing by tracking backwards and forwards out there. So the initial look is a bust on this one. I think we still have some bacon and eggs to work off, so let's head for the next one."

They walked back over the brow of the hill and down the remains of the old track, with Helen making a point of walking as close to Jim as possible. They walked across the flat valley bottom and turned back towards the village along the road. Ivan was following the map very carefully until he stopped and checked his bearings from the landmarks around the valley.

"According to the map we should turn off and head that way." He pointed.

They climbed over the wall and walked in the direction Ivan had indicated. There was no sign of any track but years of farming in this field could explain that.

"So, Ivan," said Helen, "why is it always you or Geordie with the map?"

Ivan cleared his throat and looked at Jim before answering. "You see," he said, "it is a well-known fact in almost all Armies that the most dangerous creature on a battlefield is an officer with a map. So we try to keep the boss out of trouble by doing the map reading for him."

Helen looked at Jim. "I take it that is some kind of Army joke?"

"Nearly," he said.

They climbed the side of the hill as it rose out of the valley bottom. This slope was steeper and they all leaned forward as they moved. The brow of the hill appeared without any sign of the track, as far as they could see. They stopped at the top to draw breath and to look around. Once again the stones showed where a hut had been.

"What do you make of this, Geordie?"

"Well, boss, if I was guessing I would say that this is the remains of a very old mine. The Romans probably had people up here digging by hand and the huts were for shelter when the weather got bad. They may even have lived up here for part of the time."

"You really think these ruins could be that old?"

"Why not? Dry stone walling has been around for a very long time and rocks don't rot away."

"OK then. Same search technique as the last one."

They spread out and started scanning the ground. All they got for their trouble was more tired and wetter. As Jim straightened from searching through the wet grass he looked at a higher part of the hill and saw a figure standing very still and watching them. As he looked, the man turned slowly and walked away. Jim shrugged.

"That's enough for me for this morning. That log fire back at the pub needs a bit of company and I could certainly do with drying my trouser legs."

Chapter 31

Geordie was the last to reluctantly pull himself away from the log fire and to slip back into his waterproof jacket as they set out for the next of the possible sites. He stepped out of the front door of the pub to find the three others waiting for him in the watery sunshine. The drizzle had stopped and the street was glistening as they walked.

They walked in a different direction as this site was on the hillside above the famous Peak Cavern. Secretly, Jim thought this one to be the most likely of the identified possibles.

They walked past the entrance to Peak Cavern as the few tourists turned in.

"If it's still open when we get back I'd like to go and have a look around that," said Helen.

"If we don't find anything on this hill top I don't see why we shouldn't do just that to end the day."

They trudged on in silence until they found the spot indicated on the map where they should turn off. They stood in the lane and stared at the area where the track was supposed to be, but saw nothing. Geordie cast about looking at the wall and at the small ditch that ran alongside it with silvery rain water trickling through the grass at the bottom. Ivan climbed over the wall and walked across the small field. The few sheep scattered as he passed. He stood under a tree and looked up the slope.

He waved the others towards him. "Those JARIC people were right again. Once you get over here you can see the slightly flattened shape of the land alongside the hill."

They followed his pointing arm and saw the faint trace of where a track had once been.

"Come on," said Jim, "onward and upward."

This track was not as steep as the two they had climbed in the morning and seemed a little wider.

"You know something, boss," said Geordie, "I reckon I could get a truck up this pathway. Might be a bit tight but it's certainly possible."

Jim looked back the way they had come. Geordie was right. A four wheel drive truck could make it up here with care. If it continued like this it might well be the track they were looking for.

They crested the hill and the village dropped out of sight behind them as they approached a stone hut. The roof was gone and the door was a gap in the sturdy stone wall but it was certainly a hut, or at least it used to be. The depression in the earth left by the old excavations and framed by rock outcroppings was just visible as they stood and looked around.

As usual, Geordie and Ivan started to check for evidence in and around the hut while Helen and Jim tracked across the bowl searching for any signs of activity. Jim looked up to see Ivan walking towards him holding something in his hand.

"Little bit of interest for you here, boss." He held his hand out and on his palm lay a brass cartridge case, blackened with age. "Unless I miss my guess that's a .303, the calibre the Army was using back in the 1940s."

"Where did you find it?"

"Just outside the hut doorway, sunk into the mud under a stone."

They walked towards the hut with Helen in the lead. There was a sharp crack as something struck the ground in front of them. Ivan and Jim broke into a run towards the stone walls of the hut. Ivan was the first to reach Helen. He grabbed her around the middle, lifted her off the ground and ran into the hut carrying her. He put her down, none too gently, in a corner and flopped beside her. Jim dropped to the ground inside the door next to Geordie.

"Why, Mr Thomas, this is so sudden," Helen said with a smile. "What was that about?"

Ivan moved to get more comfortable and said, "Well, you see, despite what Hollywood would have you believe, a bullet doesn't whistle as it travels. A high powered round going past you makes a loud crack. We have just been shot at."

"Are you sure?"

"Oh yes and he wasn't a bad shot either. He's winged me."

Ivan moved his right hand from his left upper arm and examined the wound. The bullet had skimmed across his arm taking a deep gouge out of the flesh. Blood was flowing freely down his sleeve.

"Damn, that's a nice new jacket ruined. And this is going to really start stinging soon."

"Oh my Lord! And you carried me after that had hit you? I feel a bit of a fool for making a joke."

Helen moved to try and help Ivan but he pushed her back.

"Try to stay under cover. Whoever put that round down is still out there and believe me, it would ruin your day to get hit."

Jim looked across the hut at Helen and smiled to reassure her. "He's right, just stay down. Ivan can patch that up for himself, at least on a temporary basis. Its messy and it's going to hurt but it won't kill him."

"Thanks for the sympathy, boss."

Jim pulled a small transmitter from his pocket. "Did either of you spot where he is firing from?"

"Not exactly, but judging from the way the round clipped me I would guess he is along the ridgeline away from the village."

"Geordie?"

"The sound was a bit distorted inside these stone walls but I would guess Ivan is right. Trouble is, that means he has a clear field of fire and he has the doorway covered. Going out over the wall would mean being caught with your bum in the air too, so I think we are stuck till he gets bored."

"I think you're both right. So I'd better start earning my salt, then, eh?" Jim lifted the transmitter to his mouth and pressing the button on the side said, "Blue 2, Blue 2 this is Blue 1 Sunray. Target is somewhere along the ridge away from the village and about 200 meters eastward away from position 3." He laid the transmitter on his thigh and they all waited until a tinny voice replied.

"Blue 2 copies. Wait out."

The two soldiers nodded and settled back against the stone walls. Ivan busied himself with dressing his wound and Geordie closed his eyes to rest.

"I don't understand, what is happening and why aren't you doing something?"

"It's OK, Helen, we are doing something. Ivan is getting himself sorted out and Geordie is resting. It's all in hand and you wouldn't want me to spoil the surprise, would you?"

Geordie opened one eye and said, "There's an old Army saying 'never stand when you can sit, never sit when you can lie and never stay awake when you can kip'. There's no telling how long this will go on and since I am the only sergeant around here I need to be rested and ready to sort it all out if something goes wrong."

Helen sank back against the wall, still looking worried. Time passed and nothing happened. The birds sang in the trees and ants wandered around them on the fallen stones. Nobody from the village seemed to have heard the shot and wondered about it.

"How's the arm, Ivan?"

"Frankly, boss, it's bloody painful. If we get the chance I'd like to have a quiet word with the shooter when we meet him."

Jim laughed. "I'll see what I can do for you."

Chapter 32

The small radio crackled to life and a tinny voice said, "Blue 1 this is Blue 2. All clear, moving to your location. Out"

"OK, folks, we can go and meet our new friend now." Jim stood and walked across to Helen, extending a hand to help her up.

"That's it? What just happened?"

"I had a little insurance policy in place just in case something like this happened. At the last hide we were threatened with a gun but luckily that one didn't go off, so I had some friends here just in case."

They stepped out of the ruined hut and Helen looked along the ridge to see five men walking towards her. "Who are they?"

"Four of them are people we have worked with before and I suspect number five is the person Ivan wants to speak to."

The group approached with one of them clearly dazed, walking unsteadily with his hand to a nose that was running blood. They reached the depression in the ground and the dazed one was instructed to sit by one of the escorts, who had the air of a person not to argue with. The team leader they had met at the barn on Morecambe Bay walked over to them and handed Jim a rifle.

"Our friend here was ready to fire again as soon as one of you showed yourselves. He seems to have known his business, the weapon is in perfect condition despite its age."

Jim took the rifle and looked it over. "He's a good shot, too. Managed to wing my Sergeant Major with his first round. Not bad at that distance."

Ivan walked across still holding his upper arm and failing to stop the bleeding. He looked down at the rifle in Jim's hands, then at the shooter.

"I don't suppose one of your team is carrying field dressing?"

"I can do better than that. John over there is a field medic and I have to say rather a good one." He waved to one of the men sitting on his haunches at the edge of the bowl. "John! Customer for you."

Helen looked at the rifle and said "It doesn't look much when you hold it like that."

"Don't be fooled. This is the .303 Short Model Lee Enfield, arguably one of the finest bolt action rifles in the world. The British Army used these for decades when we had an empire and they did a lot of damage. I think Ivan has used up a lot of luck today."

Jim walked over to the dejected man slumped on the ground.

"How did he manage to acquire the nose bleed?"

"That would be my fault," said the fourth member of the team. "He was lying in a depression on the ridge and I saw he was ready to fire again when I came up behind him. So I tapped him on the back of the head and he head-butted poor old Mother Earth. I don't think the Sergeant Major over there will give me a hard time about it."

"Probably not." Jim turned to the prisoner. "I think I should explain. The code word is 'Cromwell'. We are friends."

The man looked over the top of the bloodied hand he still held to his nose. "What bloody code word? What the hell is Cromwell? And you're no friend of mine."

Jim knelt down and looked the man in the eye. "We know what this site is and we know you are one of the Guardians."

The man's eyes widened. "How did you know that? The Guardians are a secret, my Dad told me all about it."

"Not quite all about it if you didn't get told the code word. Let me show you something and then we can get properly introduced." He took the Prime Minister's letter from the inside pocket of his jacket and held it so the prisoner could read it. He made a point of not handing it over to avoid getting it soaked in blood. "Then can we speak to your Dad?"

Helen said very quietly, "Why do you want to speak to his father?"

"Take a look at his eyes. I don't think he is very bright. I'm guessing his Dad didn't mean him to do this. It's all got out of hand. Plus, his Dad is the one who can probably tell us what we want to know."

Jim turned back to the rest of the team. He handed the rifle to Geordie and then spoke to the prisoner.

"Come on, son. Up you get, we need to see your Dad."

He held out his hand and helped the young man to his feet.

"Now then, you and I will lead the way and these rough types won't hurt you as long as you are with me. OK?"

The walk back down into the village was colder now that the fine rain had started again. By the time they reached the first of the grey stone houses their hair was soaked. Jim noticed that Helen paid no attention to it. He smiled to himself.

"So, what's your name? Have you lived here long and what do you do for a living when you aren't shooting at people?"

The man looked sideways at him and after a pause said, "I'm Peter Duckworth and I look after my Dad's sheep. Have done for as long as I can remember." They walked on for another hundred paces in silence, then the young man said "This is the place."

He pointed at a neat stone cottage with a small front garden surrounded by a waist high stone wall, like most of the other houses in the street. Jim opened the wooden gate and paused to let the prisoner go through first. As they approached the cottage door it swung open and Jim found himself being regarded by a pair of misty blue eyes set in a weather beaten and wrinkled face.

"What's this about? What's he done this time?"

"Oh, nothing serious," said Jim, "just tried to kill my Sergeant Major and it seems he wanted to do the same to the rest of us. I think we need to talk. May we come in?"

"Why should I let you in? I don't know you."

"Cromwell."

The old man's jaw dropped slightly but he recovered quickly.

"I have been waiting for someone to come here and say that for bloody years. What kept you?"

He motioned them to enter. The small cottage would have been standing room only with the whole team inside so Jim sent their four saviours and the young man to find a doctor to have his broken nose reset. As they left Jim called the team leader to one side. "Once you've got him cleaned up, go and buy him a sandwich in the pub. I'll meet you there later and remember he is one of the good guys."

Jim re-entered the cottage with Geordie and Ivan close behind him. The old man returned to his chair next to the stone fireplace and motioned them to the other chairs. The old man turned his watery eyes to Jim and said, "You're the one in charge, then?"

"That's me, Major Jim Wilson, Royal Engineers. This is my team and we are on a personal mission from the Prime Minister to recover the material you have been guarding all these years."

"Been a stone hanging round the neck of this family and others since 1940. The others all died off or moved away. Only me and my boy to look after it now and I don't have long with the heart playing up the way it is. Not sure the boy could do it on his own; he's good with the sheep and pure magic with the dogs but not much else really."

"Is that why you didn't tell him the code word?"

"I've told him that bloody code word a thousand times. He forgets things. That's why he's going to lose the farm after I'm gone. Some bastard will cheat him and he'll have nothing." The old man's chin sank to his chest as he slowly shook his head. "I love that boy but I don't think he can manage when I'm gone."

"How long has he been guarding the site up on the hill?"

"Must be twenty-five years now. He takes it very seriously even though I don't think he understands what it is he's guarding. He's up there checking the area day and night in all weathers."

"Sounds like he has served his country well." Jim turned to Ivan "Well Sergeant Major, what rank would you say the guard commander of this site warranted?"

Ivan looked puzzled and then the penny dropped. He smiled. "If it was up to me I think I would give that job to a Sergeant because of the value of the site being guarded. Is that what you were thinking?"

"I was thinking Corporal, but you have more experience of setting up guard details so I bow to your judgement." Jim looked at the old man who still had his head sunk to his chest. "I think your boy deserves some reward for his years of service. Let me make a call and then if that goes well I may have solved some of your problems."

He walked out of the cottage, pulling his mobile phone from his pocket as he went.

Helen was sitting on the wall outside waiting for him. "How's it going?"

"Not bad. I thought you had gone off to the pub with the others. I would have had you come in if I'd realised."

"No. I didn't want to get in the way so I thought I would just wait here."

He looked at her, admiring her stillness and calm. "You really are a remarkable woman."

She smiled. "So why are you standing there holding the phone? Need to call your bookie?"

"Not quite. I need to clear something with the Prime Minister."

He dialled the number. The conversation was brief. As he finished he saw Helen smiling at him.

"You really are a kind person under all that military bearing, aren't you?"

"I try. Come on inside, it looks like the rain is about to start again."

They walked up the short path and as Jim opened the door he touched her fingers and squeezed just a little. They entered the small sitting room and Geordie stood to let Helen sit down. Jim resumed his seat opposite the old man.

"I have a proposition for you," he said, "if you agree I'm going to swear your son into the Army and back date his service for twenty-five years. He will be discharged back into civilian life as soon as the hide has been emptied and the material handed back to the Bank of England. He will leave with the rank of Sergeant and will get an Army pension for the rest of his life. Army pensions are not over generous but it should allow him to live here without much difficulty."

The old man raised his head. His eyes were brimming with tears. "You'd do that for my boy? Even after he shot at you? Are you allowed to do it?"

"I wouldn't normally be allowed to but I have the Prime Minister's permission and he is contacting the Ministry of Defence right now to set it up."

It was too much for the old man by the fireplace. The tears ran down his wrinkled cheeks. His shoulders shook, until Helen knelt in front of him and hugged him.

Chapter 33

Geordie and Ivan left the cottage and walked back to the pub in the village. The light drizzle had started again and the road between the cottages shone brightly. They turned into the pub through the old front door. The four Special Forces soldiers were sitting around a scarred oak table with their prisoner amongst them. The wreckage of a substantial country lunch lay before them. Ivan stopped and motioned them to follow him. The two engineers waited outside until the other five men had joined them then they all walked back to the cottage where Jim and Helen were standing in the small front garden. The old man was standing in his doorway, his hand on the door jamb for support.

"Peter. I told you that one day someone would come for the things we have been guarding." The younger man nodded. "Well, that day has arrived. Take these people up the hill and show them how to open the room. And Peter, don't forget about the trap. You remember what I told you about that?"

His son nodded again slowly. "I remember."

He started back up the lane out of the village. The team walked with him.

Jim and Helen stayed in the cottage garden for a few moments. Jim said, "This still has to stay a secret. You have done your country a great service but nobody can know, at least not until we have found all of the gold."

"I've kept this secret so long that I think I can manage to keep doing it. Don't you worry about that."

Helen kissed the old man's cheek as they left the garden. They walked up the lane. Jim looked back to see the old man still standing in the doorway watching them. He raised his hand slightly in acknowledgement and went back into the cottage.

Coming out of the village they saw the rest of the group climbing slowly up the track ahead of them with Peter leading the way. As Jim and Helen arrived at the start of the track the others disappeared over the brow of the low ridge. They climbed up the incline and found the rest of them sitting around the depression in the ground near the ruined cottage.

Ivan looked up "We thought we'd better wait for you, boss. Wouldn't want you to miss the great reveal would we?"

"Too true. Right then, Peter, how about you showing us the way in to your big secret? How's the nose by the way?"

"It's fine, Dr Potts straightened it out for me. He says it will be as good as new."

Peter climbed to his feet. He walked around to the side of the ruin and started to pull stones and nettles out of the way. The others watched as he tossed these to one side until a metal ring was revealed in the base of the old wall. Peter leaned in and grabbed the ring. He squatted down and heaved slowly backwards. The ring seemed to be solid but after a moment or two of heaving it gave way and pulled backwards revealing a length of greased cable that led into the wall. He continued pulling until they heard a crack and a groan from behind them. All of them spun round to see a small, low door opening in the hillside away from the depression in the ground.

"Well, damn me," said Geordie, "that's five quid I owe you Ivan."

"What was the bet?" asked Helen.

"I said the entrance would be in the bottom of the depression where the old miners had been digging their tunnel. I reckoned they would have the gold stashed in the tunnels of the caverns below us."

"And I said that was just too obvious for these guys" smiled Ivan. "I reckoned they would have done something a bit cleverer. Never mind, Geordie, you can bet me double or quits for the next one."

"Can you and your hooligans mount a security cordon around us while we see what's going on," said Jim to the leader of the Special Forces team "I'll make sure you get a look inside before we empty it."

The four soldiers moved outwards without a word and in seconds had dropped out of sight.

Helen watched, astonished. "How do they do that? I didn't see anywhere to hide and they've vanished."

Jim smiled down at her "Magicians never reveal their tricks. Come on, I think you may find the next bit more interesting."

He took her hand and led her to where Geordie and Ivan were now standing with their new companion by the slightly open doorway. Ivan seemed to have forgotten about having a private word with his shooter. Peter was pulling away the overgrowth that had built up over the last seventy years.

"Best you let me go in first," he said. "My old Dad told me where the trap is to stop people stealing stuff." He pulled the door slowly open on the stiff hinges. "Mustn't pull it more than half way to start with or we'll be in trouble." As he spoke the rust in the hinges gave way and the door swung fully open. "Oh shit!" Peter said as he stepped forward to pick up the grenade that had been pulled out of the recess in the wall.

As he stooped, Ivan leapt forward and smashed into him with his good shoulder, pushing him violently behind the now open door. Jim grabbed Helen by the arm and swinging her around flung her to the ground away from the doorway, making sure to land on top of her. Geordie saved himself by diving the other way just as the grenade exploded. Jagged, white-hot fragments of metal flew in all directions. But none of them were wounded, although Jim had a large tear sliced across the back of his jacket by a piece of flying shrapnel.

Geordie sat up first. "Looks like all that safety training on the grenade range paid off, eh?"

"Anybody hurt?" said Jim, rolling off Helen onto the wet grass.

"We're fine," said Ivan, "but I think I've opened up that wound again. I'm leaking."

"It's a good job I wasn't wearing my good shoes," Helen said. "All this rough foreplay would have had the heels off them for sure."

Jim helped her to her feet and watched her brush the wet grass from her hair. "Quite remarkable," he said.

They waited until the smoke had cleared from the small entrance before them. The shrapnel sizzled in the wet grass as it cooled but none of them felt the need for a souvenir.

Then Jim said, "OK, Peter any more surprises that you know about?"

"That's the only one that Dad told me about."

"Good. OK, Geordie, I think we need your mining expertise again if you don't mind." Jim gestured to the entrance. "Peter you might want to sit over there away from the doorway."

Geordie moved forward, pulling a small flashlight from his pocket. He started to enter the tunnel.

"Remember what I keep telling you" said Ivan "Check the corners and make sure of your footing before you go forward. Take it easy and don't get complacent, the old man said that Peter forgets things so there could be more nasty things in there."

Geordie smiled over his shoulder at the big Sergeant Major. "Yes, Mum, and I'll be home before dark."

"See that you are you cheeky bugger."

Geordie moved slowly into the narrow tunnel. The smell of the grenade was still strong in his nostrils as he checked carefully for any further unpleasant surprises. After a slow, careful fifteen feet he was confident the first part of the tunnel was safe. He found himself facing another low metal door let into the side of the tunnel to his left. The rusty metal handle was by his shoulder and he reached up to grip it with his right hand. He pressed down gently increasing the pressure until he felt the judder as the handle started to move. Once it reached the vertical position he pulled gently and was surprised how easily the door opened.

With the door barely open he peered inside to check for any trip wires on cables linked to explosive devices to catch the unwary. Satisfied that there was nothing waiting for him he opened the door in slow, careful stages checking repeatedly as he did so. It took him a good four minutes to swing the door fully open. He leaned into the space beyond.

He was about to move forward into the low, dark chamber when he looked down to see the wooden plank across the bottom of the low doorway, that had no business being there. In a world of rock why would there be a need for a wooden door step? He slid back into the passage and lowered his chin to the floor until he could peer under the edge of the plank where it had rotted away. He shone the flashlight in and could just make out the ugly shape of a fragmentation grenade lying in the dust and debris, that had accumulated around it over the last seventy years. After all this time it was perfectly possible that the explosive would be inert, but the one at the doorway had been effective so there was no way he was taking any chances in this enclosed space.

He shuffled backwards away from the grenade and contemplated his options. Making his mind up he rolled onto his shoulder and called down the tunnel to Ivan whose face he could see, watching his progress.

"Ivan! Found another little surprise package in here. Can you get me a length of string or wire or something similar?"

"How long do you need it?"

"Only a few minutes."

"Hell of a time for old jokes, Geordie."

"Sorry couldn't resist it." Geordie looked along the length of the tunnel and worked out how far from the outer door to the booby trap. "I guess about five metres or a bit more should do it."

"Back in a minute."

Ivan's face disappeared from the tunnel entrance and Geordie lay on the cold stone looking around him. No markings were obvious, all he could see were the chisel and pick marks where the tunnel had been expanded. There were faint scrape marks in the floor where he guessed the gold crates had been dragged in. Certainly the tunnel was too low for anything that heavy to have been carried.

Ivan reappeared and crawled into the tunnel dragging a length of wire. He passed it to Geordie's outstretched hand. "Here you go. Part of an electric sheep fence. What's the problem?"

"Grenade lying on the floor just inside the tunnel where it turns into a chamber. Looks like the pin is out and the lever is being held down by what is supposed to look like a doorstep."

"Be nasty in here with all those fragments bouncing off the rock. The old boys obviously wanted the pride of Germany to get shredded, if they ever came in here. Got to admire them. I'll get out of your way."

He shuffled backwards out of the tunnel, leaving Geordie alone.

The big ex-miner slid himself towards the booby trap and stretched out his arms. If this all went wrong he hoped that by being flat on the floor and as far back as possible he might avoid the worst of the blast and most of the fragments. He formed a loop in the end of the wire and gently hooked it over the far corner of the wooden plank. Satisfied it was firmly in place he slowly shuffled backwards out of the tunnel, careful not to touch the wire lying alongside him.

He slithered out through the doorway into the wet grass and stood up. "Best we all move to one side of the door. In fact the rest of you might want to get well clear. I have no idea what the shrapnel is going to do as it bounces around in there."

Helen looked puzzled. "What's shrapnel?"

"Nasty sharp edged bits of hot metal flying at high speeds," Jim said, "it's usually the casing of the shell or grenade that gets sent flying by the explosion. Named after the officer who invented it during the Napoleonic wars. Very effective but not nice, if we are on the receiving end."

Helen quickened her step away from the tunnel mouth and caught up with Jim and Ivan. They saw Geordie slip behind the outer tunnel door and pick up the wire. He pulled and a second or two later they saw a short plank of wood slide out of the entrance. Helen sighed and went to stand up. Both her arms were grabbed by the men either side of her and she was dragged down again.

"Never trust explosives, Miss. Especially not old explosives. The rule is to give it a minute and then another one for the wife and kids."

The fuse in the old grenade finished burning and did its work. The sound of the explosion was muffled but the smoke boiled out of the tunnel and they heard Geordie coughing behind his door. They stood and walked forward.

"OK, Geordie?" Ivan called.

"Yeah, no worries, but that stuff does stink." Geordie appeared from behind the door and peered into the tunnel. "Hell, that was effective. The shrapnel is scattered all along the tunnel. It would have made a hell of a mess of anyone in there. Unkind minds our friends had back in the day."

Peter walked up behind them as they contemplated the tunnel.

"Good job my old Dad never let us go in there for a look round. Not sure why Granddad didn't tell us there were two surprises in there."

Ivan nodded slowly. "Two so far. Geordie, don't assume anything. There could be more booby traps in there. Take it slow and careful."

"I'll crawl around like I'm on egg shells."

Helen smiled up at Jim. "Ivan really is a Mother Hen, isn't he?"

"No. Not really. He is a highly professional and experienced soldier. As a senior NCO his first priority is to look after his people, to try and make sure they all come home."

"Well, that told me," she said.

"I didn't mean it that way. There is no way you could understand without serving in the military. All people on the outside see is the shouting, they don't realise it has a purpose and isn't bullying."

They watched as Geordie's feet disappeared into the low tunnel. Peter turned to Jim. "Do you think they'll have those bombs at the other entrance?"

"Do you know where there is another entrance?"

"Yes. A bit. Dad says there is a way in from the Peak Cavern underneath. But he says it's hidden so none of the Blue John miners or any of the tourists will stumble across it."

"Do you know where it is? Can you show us?"

"No. I know it's there but Dad has never shown it to me. He is the only one left who can find it, but his old legs are not strong enough to climb around in the caverns. It gets pretty rough once you get off the tourist paths."

"We'll forget that one for the time being." Jim walked to the tunnel mouth where Ivan was peering in as Geordie's feet moved out of sight into the side chamber. "Is he still checking as he goes?"

"He is. He knows if he kills himself in there I'll make his life a misery."

They waited and watched, listening to the sounds of Geordie moving around carefully out of sight of the entrance. Then his head and smiling face reappeared, in the tunnel and he crawled towards them. As he emerged from the tunnel into full daylight he looked at the four people now clustered around him.

"Well, it's cramped in the chamber but at least you can turn round. And Helen, this is for you."

He passed over a small rectangular block wrapped in what looked like oilskin paper. Helen took it and was surprised at how heavy such a small package was. She opened it and looked at the three soldiers who were now smiling at her.

"Is this what I think it is? How much of this is in there? It looks like solid gold."

Jim nodded. "It is. That's part of the haul your Granddad helped to load during an air raid in 1940. That's one of the smaller bars. We thought you might like to show it to him when you get home. It might be nice to close the circle for him."

"I think he will be thrilled to see it. I guess I'm not allowed to keep it?"

"Sadly, no. It all has to get back to the Bank of England. But no reason that bar can't travel through Sussex on the way to London." Jim turned back to Geordie. "So what is the situation inside?"

"Not sure yet, boss. There was a stack of five boxes in the chamber off the tunnel and one had been broken open, so I could bring that bar out."

"That's a lot less than we found at the first site. I thought we had been told there were four equal loads."

Ivan nodded his agreement "I wonder if this is another bluff? If they left just a part of the haul here then maybe a German search party would be satisfied and not look any further?"

"It's possible. Did you manage to look any further in there?"

"Not yet. I'm going to need better light and some heavy hand tools to search properly."

Chapter 34

Geordie set about dragging the five boxes of gold bars through the narrow, awkward entrance tunnel. Ivan helped him to stack them a few feet from the entrance, while Jim and Helen completed a large circuit of the site looking for any signs of a further entrance. As they returned Geordie was sitting on the pile of boxes easing his thirst from a plastic bottle of water.

"Been back inside, boss, now that the chamber is empty but I can see damn all that looks like another exit. As far as I can see it's solid rock with no joins anywhere. Don't know what to suggest:"

"Could it be a double bluff of some kind?" Ivan said. "They make a hide like this with all these traps and build another one somewhere completely different to put the real haul in?"

"It's possible of course," said Jim, "but why pass down only the phoney site to the Guardians? Unless Peter's Dad is holding out on us for some reason?"

"Could be. What do you think, Peter?" said Ivan, turning to the shepherd beside them.

"I dunno" he said "this is the only place he ever told me about. He's not a liar."

"He didn't strike me as a liar either. Ivan, you and Geordie take a walk back down to the village and tell him what we have found and see if he has any ideas. You might pick up a sledge hammer while you're down there so we can see about tapping the walls and floor of the chamber. Any void behind the rock should sound hollow."

The two soldiers turned to go. "What will you be doing, boss?" said Geordie.

"I think Helen and I will go and have a look round your chamber to see if we can see anything you missed. See you later." He turned to Helen and held out his hand. "Come on. I have to justify having a fresh pair of eyes on this job."

She smiled and followed him back through the entrance and into the tunnel. They climbed into the chamber where the gold had rested for so many years and slowly, inch by inch, they tracked the flashlight around the walls and the floor. Nothing.

After a moment Helen said, "Shine the light up here in the corner will you? I've just had an idea."

Jim shone the flashlight beam into the top right hand corner of the chamber and watched .as Helen ran her fingers across the rock.

"There's a crack here, very thin, but it runs in a semi-circle right up here in the corner."

"I saw that but it's way too small to be a doorway."

"You are tired, aren't you? Not sure I should keep you up so late tonight."

"What do you mean?"

"In both the hides you have explored there has been a metal ring for you to pull to release a secret door or hatch. What if there was a ring concealed behind that small piece of stone? Maybe that's the answer?"

"Damn me! I must be tired. If you could move into the other corner I'll try and prise it out with my penknife."

Helen shuffled past to give him room to work. As she passed he leaned in and gave her a kiss on the cheek.

"We'll see how tired I am after dinner."

She grinned as she settled into the corner. Jim got to his knees and opened his penknife to the largest blade and proceeded to work it into the crack. It took a few moments to find a place where the blade could slip in, then he levered against the stone. After a few seconds of effort the stone gave way and a piece of rock about five inches across tumbled to the floor of the chamber. Behind it was the metal ring they had been hoping for. As he sat back an object fell from a recess above the ring and rolled out into the chamber. It took a second for the knobbly shape to register.

"Down!" he screamed as he threw himself across the chamber pushing Helen into a ball in the corner with his body wrapped around her as far as he could.

He cringed, waiting for the white hot fragments of the Mills grenade to punch into his exposed back and legs. After twenty seconds, which felt much longer, Helen started to move.

"Stay still!" he hissed. "It's another grenade and the Lord only knows what shape it's in."

He gave it another slow count of thirty before slowly rolling over towards the grenade. The sweat was running down his face and into his eyes. He wiped them quickly and the grenade swam into focus. The pin was missing but the trigger arm was still in place. He reached out slowly and grasped the deadly bomb so that the lever could not fly off and ignite the internal fuse. Clutched in his hand it was now a lot safer, but his whole body felt weak and he trembled from the sheer relief.

"Helen. Would you go out through the tunnel please and send anybody who is there away from the doorway while I get this damn thing out of here."

She crawled out through the tunnel without a word. He waited, to give her time to get clear. Then crawling on his elbows, so his hands could maintain their grip, he followed her. He emerged into the daylight to find Helen and his two men standing with Peter at the edge of the ridge watching his progress anxiously. He sat down on the bullion boxes, then raising his head he called across to his team.

"Ivan, I could use a grenade instructor right about now."

Ivan walked forward and Geordie held Helen's arm to stop her following him. "Not now, Miss, they're busy. Just be a minute or so."

As Ivan reached him Jim held the grenade up for inspection. He turned it over in his hands so the Welshman could see all sides of it.

"A Mills 36 Grenade if I remember my basic training correctly. The trigger lever didn't fly off because it's corroded in place by the look of it. If that was free we could just throw it somewhere safe and let it go off but that isn't going to work and we can't have some kiddie finding it. Don't go away, I'll be right back."

Jim smiled weakly and nodded. Sitting in a damp field holding an unstable grenade was not his idea of fun. If this went off it was going to ruin his whole day. Ivan came back holding a large screwdriver and an equally large pair of pliers.

"I picked these up when I was getting the sledge hammer," he said "Right, what I am going to do is to unscrew the bottom plate that holds the fuse and detonator in place. Once those are out it will be safe enough to leave inside the old hut until we can come back and blow it up. Just keep that lever from springing off, will you?"

Jim waited as his Sergeant Major took a firm grip of the grenade's body with the pliers and inserted the screwdriver in the slot in the base plate. Holding one and turning the other he tried to remove the plate. Nothing moved.

"I think it must be corroded in place. What we need is some honest to goodness foul language to persuade it."

Ivan started to try to unscrew the plate again. He went red in the face from the effort and issued a stream of invective that would make a Drill Sergeant blush. But it worked and the base plate turned. Once it was moving it was the work of seconds to open it and remove the fuse and detonator assembly.

"OK, boss. I'll have that now" Ivan said, removing the grenade from Jim's cramped fingers. "I'll pop it over there in the rocks, just in case." He walked towards the ruined hut.

Helen gave him her sweetest smile as she walked past him towards Jim. "Very instructive Mr Thomas. I'll have to remember some of those, next time I go to church."

For the first time in a very long time Ivan blushed.

Chapter 35

With the grenade safely out of the way the team retired to the pub in the village to consider their next move. Once they were sat around the table cradling comforting mugs of strong tea Geordie was the first to speak.

"The people who built this hide seem to have taken things a bit more seriously than the lot who made the hide near Morecambe Bay. Three booby traps so far and we haven't found the main stash yet."

Ivan turned to Jim. "Whatever we do, I think we need to be damned careful about pulling on that ring you found. Heaven only knows what surprise that's linked up to."

"I agree. I think we need to run a length of rope down the tunnel and into the chamber. We should be able to pull it from outside. If there is something else we should be clear of it when it goes off."

"That hiking shop we got the boots and jackets from had nylon line at the back of the shelves. If I'm quick I should be able to catch them before they close," Geordie said, rising from the table.

"Hang on. I'll come with you," said Ivan, sliding off his chair and standing. He looked down at the other two. "We'll come back here once we have the rope, unless you want to meet us up at the site?"

"Here will be just fine," said Jim. "I think we need to eat before we get into the next part. No telling how long it will take."

Ivan nodded and followed Geordie out of the pub and back into the late afternoon drizzle. Helen reached across the table and took hold of Jim's hand. It was steady now, the shock of the incident with the grenade had passed. He was his old self again.

"I think that's the second time you have saved my life on this adventure," she said.

"And score one for Ivan when Peter opened fire on us. I think it was a mistake to involve you this closely in this search. I can't risk losing you again."

"Jim, if you start treating me like some wimpy girl you will lose me anyway. I don't need to be wrapped in cotton wool. And what happens if I'm not there to find the clues for you? I'm involved and you just lost this argument before it started."

"I think I'm allowed to be concerned about you, aren't I?"

"I'll give you that one. But I am now part of this and don't you try and push me away."

"You really are a remarkable woman, you know."

He was still looking into her eyes when the other two reappeared through the front door of the pub. Geordie had a coil of green line over his shoulder and Ivan was fiddling with a couple of metal snap hooks as he walked.

"We called in on Peter's dad on the way back down," Ivan said, "Peter was in there and had told him what we'd encountered. I think he was a bit shaken by finding his old dad had not told him about all the booby traps."

"Maybe he didn't know either?"

"That's what they think. Apparently one of the original team had two sons serving in 9ᵗʰ Battalion of the Sherwood Foresters. They were both killed in France in 1940. They think he was pretty bitter about that and they guess he went back in and 'improved' the hide to try and get some revenge on the Germans. I'm guessing he wasn't thinking too clearly about 'own goals'."

"Interesting, but that doesn't help much. We still don't know what else this character has installed in there. We need to be even more careful from now on. Let's eat and then go back up to the site. We'd better let the security team get something to eat while we're there."

The food was the usual plain nourishing, comfort food served in pubs across the north of England. But it was well made and certainly filled a hole. They set off back through the rain to the site of the hide. Walking up the quiet streets between the grey stone cottages, Jim realised he needed a new jacket soon. The slices cut across the back by the flying shrapnel were allowing water to enter and run down the back of his legs.

Once back at the site, they called in the security team and arranged for them to go into the village in twos to get something to eat, leaving the second team of two on watch. Ivan had secured one of his snap hooks at the end of the line and handed it to Geordie who had been nominated to climb back into the hide to secure the line to the ring in the chamber wall. As Geordie disappeared in to the tunnel, Ivan paid out the line behind him. It took only a few minutes for the line to be snapped onto the ring and for Geordie to crawl carefully back out. They all moved out of the direct line to the tunnel and Ivan started to pull on the line. He increased the pressure steadily, waiting to feel the 'give' as the ring pulled back towards him. Feeling nothing, he dug his boot heels into the turf, wrapped the line around his back and leaned into the pull. After two minutes of this tug of war. the line went slack and Ivan fell back onto the wet grass. He reeled in the line until the snap hook appeared, still looped through the iron ring. A length of metal cable was trailing that with a stout steel pin at the end.

"Well, it looks like the mechanism was fairly simple and this looks complete" said Jim, indicating the assembly at the end of the line. "Do we have a volunteer to be the first back in to see what we achieved?"

"That'll be me boss," said Geordie, "I'm still the best miner you've got."

He walked back to the tunnel entrance with Ivan, who said, "Remember mate, check everywhere, this group could have left more traps in there."

"I know. Believe me, I'm not going to forget that in a hurry."

He dropped to his knees and started the slow crawl into the tunnel, checking as he went. He reached the entrance to the chamber and looked in. Nothing seemed to have changed. Whatever the ring and pin had been attached to had no effect. He crawled in to the chamber to examine the corner where the ring had been. All he could see was a hole drilled at the back of the stone recess. He sat in the middle of the chamber and shone his flashlight around the walls, looking for any further clues. Nothing.

Geordie sighed heavily and turned to crawl back out of the tunnel. As he did so he heard the sound of rock grinding on rock and felt a tremor through his hands and knees. As he looked round to identify the source of the sound the floor below him swung down and to one side as the hidden trap door opened. He was dropped the four feet down into another chamber. He managed to break his fall and to land without smashing his knees onto the granite below. It was still a painful landing. He checked himself for damage as the rock dust settled around him. The flashlight was still illuminated and showed that in front of him the floor fell away in a roughhewn slope to create a larger chamber with standing headroom. At the end he could see the stack of sturdy wooden boxes that the Bank of England had used to pack their gold bars.

Chapter 36

Geordie struggled to his feet. He was pretty sure no bones were broken but he was also sure he was going to have a fine array of deep bruises after his fall onto the granite floor. He stood in the well that the opening hatch had exposed and yelled for the others to come in.

The first face to appear in the tunnel doorway was Jim's. He stopped and looked around the chamber where the floor had fallen away.

"Are you alright?" he said, tasting the gritty dust that was still circulating, as it ground between his teeth.

"I'll live, boss. The drop into here was a bit much but, bottom line, we've found it. There's a ruddy big pile of those gold crates in here and some interesting boxes over to one side. I haven't checked for booby traps yet but I think it might be a damn good idea."

"You look a bit battered. Might be a better idea if you climbed out and I'll go in and make the safety checks. Once you get out, will you ask Ivan to round up the Lieutenant from the SAS team? I need to speak to him about getting this place emptied."

Geordie climbed slowly and painfully back out of the hole and Jim backed out of the tunnel to let him through. As soon as the big ex-miner was clear of the entrance way Jim climbed back in and went carefully down into the new, larger chamber. Using his flashlight, he very slowly and carefully checked the whole area for booby traps, but found no sign. He lifted one of the top crates and moved it across to the raised area below the trap door. Leaving it there, he moved across to where the larger boxes stood against the left hand wall. He carefully opened the first one, checking for hidden trigger cables. Finding nothing suspicious, he opened the box fully and stared down at the gleaming golden guineas inside. He could not guess how many there were but the box felt damned heavy.

He hauled the coin box to one side. It felt like it would need two men to lift it out of the lower chamber and manhandle it through the tunnel. He could see that this was going to be harder work than emptying the Morecambe hide. He returned to the pile of larger boxes and equally carefully opened the next one. This too was full of gold coins but of a type he had never seen before. He stood up and stretched to ease his back. This was really going to be hard labour and then he had to plan how to get it all away from here. He tore himself away from the treasure chamber and climbed back into the access tunnel, then out into the open air.

It was full dark as he emerged to find his team and the lieutenant waiting for him.

"Well, boss," said Ivan, "what's the verdict?"

"Geordie was right. We've found it and it's going to be bloody hard labour to get it out of there. And then we have another issue. That track up the side of the ridge seems to have eroded over the years and I am pretty sure a conventional vehicle will not get up there anymore. We need a heavy duty four wheel drive truck. Something that can take the rough ground but also carry the load."

"Then what we need is an Army cargo truck," said Geordie. "I've got the driving licence for one of those. Do we go and get one, or have one brought here?"

"Or do we call in the Bank people with their security trucks?" said Ivan.

"I think it's best if we go and pick one up, then less people are involved. The same reason we don't use the Bank people, it would get us too much attention having all those trucks around. Ivan, can you take the hire car and drive Geordie down to the barracks at Sutton Coldfield to pick up a vehicle. Unless there are problems you should be able to get back here before dawn so we can park it up here, hidden from the village by the ridge line."

"Can do, boss. But I think I'll take him down to the pub for a shower and a change of clothes first. Nobody is going to hand over Army equipment to someone who looks like that."

Jim looked at Geordie and was forced to agree. His sergeant did look worse for wear with torn clothes, hair full of dust and a trickle of blood running down from the cut on his forehead.

"Oh, I don't know," said Helen, smiling, "I think he looks rather dashing if a little worn round the edges."

"Thank you, Bonny Lass. At least someone appreciates masculine beauty. Away then, Ivan, we have a ways to go to find this truck." And with that the two men turned and walked away towards the village.

Jim watched them go then turned to the Special Forces Officer who stood quietly by waiting for his instructions.

"Did your lads manage to get something to eat?"

"They did, sir. Thank you. What do you need from us now?"

"Firstly, I need to make sure the site stays secure. Your men can go into the tunnel for shelter if they wish to but don't let them go into the chamber beyond. There is still a very real possibility of further booby traps. They need to get as much sleep as they can since, once the truck gets back, I will have to use them for labour to shift the bullion out of there. They will also need to be awake as a guard detail on the truck as we drive it south."

"That's fine, sir and where will you be?"

"I'm going to get some sleep too. It's going to be a long day for me as well tomorrow."

The young lieutenant looked at Helen and smiled. "Yes sir."

Chapter 37

Jim was walking back up towards the site as the sun peered over the hill tops. He had picked up Peter from his father's cottage as he walked by and they were accompanied by a very excited collie dog who ran back and forth sniffing everything and trying to encourage them to walk faster.

"Nice dog" said Jim.

"Aye, that's Bracken, my best. He hardly needs any commands when he is working the sheep. He took over as lead dog when Sam got too old."

As they came in sight of the trackway up to the site they could see the military truck was off the road and at the bottom of the slope. Geordie and Ivan were checking the slope to make sure it was wide enough for the heavy vehicle to make it up. Satisfied, they walked back to the vehicle and greeted Jim.

"Morning, sir," said Ivan. "Looks like we should be able to get up there as long as we don't slide on this wet grass. I'll take it really slowly."

"I thought Geordie was going to be driving?"

"He was but the bruises he picked up falling into the pit have stiffened up and you know these trucks can take a bit of muscle in low gear and four wheel drive."

Jim turned to Geordie. "Looks like you won't be heaving the boxes around in the tunnels either? Probably best if you take over from one of the SF guys and watch the track for unwelcome guests. Then they can all have a workout with our special weights."

"Thanks, boss. Didn't want to wimp out but I am ruddy stiff this morning and not in a good way."

"No need to be smutty, Helen isn't here to appreciate it. Right, if you are ready Ivan, let's see if you can get this beast up there."

Ivan climbed into the cab of the heavy, camouflage painted vehicle. He started the engine and they could hear the gearbox grinding as he set the controls for all wheel drive and low ratio. The three men stepped clear as he started the truck creeping slowly forwards. At very slow speed, Ivan took the heavy vehicle up the track, careful not to have the wheels start to spin and lose traction. With the engine growling, the truck climbed slowly and without a pause up the track and over the ridge, out of sight of the village.

As Jim walked up behind it he checked the tracks left in the grass. There had been little room to spare and at one point half of the offside wheel had been above the drop.

"We are going to have to be very careful coming back down with tons of extra weight on board."

"You could always go the long way round," said Peter. "That track is wider and flatter."

"There's another, easier way up? You might have mentioned it."

"You never asked me about it. It's up the hill towards where I was watching you from and then it drops down to the road further up the valley."

"Well, if you know anything else that might make things easier don't wait to be asked, eh?"

They reached the top of the ridge and found that Ivan had backed the truck up to the tunnel entrance and dropped the tailgate. The lieutenant was waiting with him as they approached. The dog ran across and greeted him like a long lost friend, jumping up, wriggling around his legs and then rolling over to have his belly tickled.

"I see you've met Bracken. Looks like you have a new friend," said Jim.

"Yes sir, it certainly does. What would you like from us this fine grey morning?"

"First off, my Sergeant is slightly injured so if one of your men can hand him a weapon he will be our security. Then Ivan and I will go in and make a final check for booby traps. After which, with Peter's help, we seven will do the hard work shifting the material out of the hide and into the truck."

"Fine, sir, my last two should have finished their breakfast down in the pub by now so we should be ready for some weight training by the time you've finished your checks."

Jim and Ivan entered the underground hide and carefully checked, once again, that no further traps, for the unwary, had been left in the piles of gold crates. In itself that was hard labour as each box had to be moved slowly to be checked under, to ensure there were no spring triggers or grenades in place. After almost two hours of painstaking work they were satisfied it was safe to begin the harder labour of moving the gold up to and through the tunnel.

The work settled into a dull but taxing routine. The low, narrow tunnel in particular generated skinned knuckles and bruised heads, all accompanied by a deal of heartfelt swearing from the soldiers, as they worked. Helen arrived but rather than embarrass them she quietly withdrew, back to the warmth of the lounge in the pub, leaving them able to vent their anger on the awkward boxes and the unforgiving tunnel walls.

The truck bed slowly filled with evenly spread flat boxes, then the larger crates of coins and other artefacts were manhandled out of the ground and up into the back of the vehicle. With the chambers empty, for the first time in over seventy years, the tired and sweaty men leaned against the truck and contemplated their prize.

"Do we know how much all of that is worth?" said one of the Special Forces soldiers.

"Not really, but at today's price of £749 per ounce you can be sure it's the most expensive Army truck on the motorway today. Now, what I would like is for you, Lieutenant, to ride up front with my Sergeant Major driving and your three men need to be in the back as security. We will stop at the Fish and Chip shop in the village to get you something to eat on the way, then we don't stop again until London. OK?"

The SF men all nodded and started to climb into the vehicle to make themselves as comfortable as possible on the hard wooden crates. Geordie walked back from his position watching the track and handed the MP5 submachine gun he had borrowed back to its owner. With Peter in the cab to show the way, Ivan slowly drove the large vehicle up the slope towards the new track down into the valley. Geordie and Jim closed the entrance hatch into the tunnel and covered it over with grass and debris as they had originally found it.

Jim straightened up and started to move off.

"Just one more job, boss," said Geordie and fishing in the pocket of his jacket, he brought out a small block of explosive and a detonator. "We need to get rid of that last grenade before some daft kid finds it and takes it to school."

"Bloody hell! I had forgotten that in all the heaving and grunting."

"Ah well, that's why you bring a Sergeant along on a job like this, for the small details. I borrowed the charge from the engineer detachment at the barracks when we picked the truck up."

Geordie walked across to the ruined hut and placed the charge on the grenade. He inserted the detonator and started the timer. He walked slowly away watching his footing so that he did not stumble and fall inside the blast radius. Both men walked to the top of the ridge and then ducked down behind it. The sound of the explosion was muffled by the stone walls but was still loud enough to convince them that the explosive in the old grenade had still been viable. They checked that the explosion had destroyed it completely, then set off to walk back down into the village to pick up Helen.

As they passed his cottage, they called in to see Peter's dad. Peter was there by now and confirmed that the truck was in the pub car park waiting for them. Both of the civilians were relieved to hear that their task was now complete with the gold on its way back to a nation that would never know what these two men had done for it. They shook hands with Jim and Geordie as they left. The two soldiers paused just long enough to stroke Bracken's head and then set off down the street.

Chapter 38

The drive though the countryside and then south down the motorway was uneventful. They had reduced the need for heavy security by emptying the second hide by stealth. Jim sat in the back of the hire car and ignored the conversation between Helen and Geordie. They had been incredibly lucky with the first two hiding places and had scored a major success with both of them, but the clues for the next two hides were very thin. A painting of a horse-drawn cart seen on the side of a van seventy years ago, with no indication of where it came from, was going to be tough to find.

The other hide seemed to be somewhere near to Stonehenge on Salisbury Plain. The land around there was open and had been crossed for many years by thousands of troops using the military training area. Not to mention the thousands of tourists who visited the ancient standing stones. Anything hidden around there must have been artfully done and would probably be hell to find.

He finally fell asleep. He woke when the sound of the engine changed as Geordie throttled back to leave the motorway as they reached London. It was late and the streets were much emptier than during the day, which would be a relief to Ivan hauling the big truck through the streets of the capital.

They pulled up at the back of the Bank of England. Jim was pleased to see the four SAS men spread out away from the truck and vanish from view. Ivan was leaning against the cab as they waited for the bank employees to open up to receive the second treasure as Jim walked over to him.

"Hi boss, long, day eh? I'm just about cream crackered after all that driving. Good job its Friday so I can get a lie in tomorrow morning."

"A break would be welcome, but I think I am going to be up worrying about our clues to the rest of the gold wherever it is hidden. The clues we have are not a lot of help."

"Speaking of which, I've got a niggle at the back of my mind."

"Go on."

"Well, we know there were 20 tons of gold given to the Auxiliary Units and it was split into four equal loads, right?"

"That's right. So what's bothering you?"

"I've been driving trucks like these for most of my army career and you know how heavy the steering gets when they are fully loaded? Especially at slow speed."

"I'll take your word for it. But where are you going with this."

"This truck didn't feel difficult enough to be fully loaded. I don't think I was carrying the best part of five tonnes. We might have a fifth problem, or maybe more."

Jim stared, then slowly said, "I really hope you are wrong for a change. We are going to have to check the figures with Sir Richard when we see him."

"What figures would those be, Major?" said the cultured voice from behind him.

Jim turned to see the Bank of England Governor striding towards him across the broad pavement. Tonight he looked very different from the cultured aristocrat he had appeared in Downing Street, with a lumpy blue, woollen jersey over his brown corduroy trousers.

"Ivan here has identified a possible problem. I think we need to go into the bank to talk about it rather than out here."

"Very well, come on inside we can talk while we watch the unloading. The doors are open now if you would care to have this vehicle driven inside."

They watched as Ivan climbed back into the cab and drove the army truck down the slope and into the bank.

"Not the most secure vehicle I have ever seen, Major. Could you not have called for an armoured security van?"

"Don't you worry, Sir Richard, that truck had four heavily armed SAS soldiers on board, it doesn't get much more secure than that."

Sir Richard grunted and led the way into the bank. As they passed the hire car Jim waved for Helen to join them.

"Another member of my team, Sir Richard. This is Helen Jennings, the granddaughter of one of the men who loaded up the gold during an air raid all those years ago."

Sir Richard bowed slightly but said nothing as he took Helen's outstretched hand and held it for just long enough to make her uncomfortable. They moved into the bank unloading area and watched the old gold crates being lifted onto motorised pallet trucks that took them away in batches, through a wide corridor, to some vault they could not see.

"Very well, what is this problem with figures you think you have?"

"Well, Sir Richard. Our understanding was that the bank shipped 20 tonnes of gold bars and other artefacts out to the Auxiliary Units in four equal loads. Is that correct?"

"As far as I know, yes. But what is the significance of that?"

"Based on twenty years of experience handling trucks like that one, my Sergeant Major does not believe we had 5 tonnes on board tonight. The truck felt too light."

"Oh really! You think you can weigh gold bullion by the feel of a truck's steering wheel? Forgive me if I am a little doubtful, Major."

"Nevertheless, I think it would be prudent to check how much we have recovered so far to see if it is half the amount originally sent out during the war."

"I don't think that is necessary but no doubt you will go over my head if I decline?"

"No doubt at all, Sir Richard. I have no wish to leave this job only partly done. That is not the Royal Engineer way."

Chapter 39

The ringing of Jim's mobile phone woke him. It took him a couple of seconds to recall he had not set the alarm for this morning. He rolled to his left and reached across Helen to the phone on the bedside table.

"Sorry," he said, as she grunted at him. He thumbed the button to connect the call and said "Wilson".

"Ah, Major. Richard Wallace here. Sorry to wake you so early but since your request has kept me out of my bed all night I was sure you wouldn't mind. It seems I owe you another apology. It seems that you can actually weigh gold bullion by the feel of a truck's steering wheel."

"I'm sorry, Sir Richard, I'm still a little hazy. What are you talking about?"

"You told me last night that your Sergeant Major didn't think he was carrying a quarter of the gold we gave to the Auxiliary Units in 1940. It seems he was correct. With two loads here we expected there to be some 10 tonnes, but when we checked through the night we came up short by two tonnes."

"So somewhere between the bank and the hiding places each load lost a tonne of gold? That's no coincidence. Somebody planned that. Sir Richard, thank you for the update and I hope you catch up on your sleep shortly."

Jim heard the disgruntled Governor mutter as he hung up the phone and could not help but smile. He was beginning to enjoy irritating this pompous individual. He sat up in bed and started to work out what he knew and whether any of his information might help to find the location of the gold that had been spirited away.

He felt a tap on his arm and looked down at Helen.

"Well, if you are going to wake a girl up this early you might at least provide some entertainment."

He smiled and snuggled down next to her, sliding his hand across her firm, flat stomach and leaning in to kiss her. She reached up and pushed him onto his back before throwing a shapely leg across his.

"I think you should let me drive this morning, before I go off to see my girlfriend for coffee and gossip."

"Always happy to oblige a lovely lady."

Chapter 40

That Sunday morning Jim and Helen strolled along the embankment of the Thames holding hands like a couple of teenagers. They had a quiet lunch on a floating restaurant close to Cleopatra's Needle and watched the traffic ploughing up and down the murky river.

Over the coffee Jim looked into those steady brown eyes and said, "OK, so what have you been waiting to tell me?"

"You're getting better at reading the signs," she said. "My Granddad is coming back from his holiday so I need to go home to Henfield to look after him."

"When do you have to go?"

"Tomorrow morning."

"Not much notice. You could have told me that a while ago."

"I could but that would have put a damper on this weekend and I didn't want that."

"Fair enough. And I have enjoyed the weekend with you. I'd better ring my team and tell them I will be late in tomorrow."

"Why? I can take myself to the station."

"Don't spoil it, I was going for the romantic goodbye on the station platform."

"Good plan. You really are getting back into the swing of this dating thing, aren't you?"

Jim stood and walked to the stern of the boat to phone Ivan and Geordie. Ivan answered immediately, as usual, even though he was jogging across St James's park at the time on his usual Sunday fitness run. Geordie took time to answer.

"I didn't interrupt anything, did I?" asked Jim.

"Sadly, no boss. Sam is at a final rehearsal for the play she's in. It opens tomorrow and there were some minor glitches to iron out. I was just dozing on the sofa and watching an old episode of Friends."

"I never did like Friends. I could never see the point of it."

"Not very PC to say that, boss."

"Not PC? How do you mean?"

"Well not liking Friends could be classed as 'Rachel Prejudice'."

"I'm sure that means something to fans of the show. You'll have to explain it to me tomorrow over lunch."

He returned to Helen.

"There is something you could do for me when you get back to your Granddad."

"Anything," she said.

"He recalled seeing four removal vans at the bank when they loaded the gold. But we now know that the gold was divided into more than four loads somehow. Can you ask him to try and remember if there was another vehicle there that night? Could he have misremembered?"

"Why would you think he might be wrong?"

"It was a long time ago, on a dark night, during an air raid and sadly he is an old man whose memory might be fading. The mind can play tricks and memories deteriorate over time. Maybe jogging his memory a little with that bar of gold will bring it back for him."

"Well, I'll try. But he has been telling me that story since I was a little girl. I think it was the most important event in his life. And the details have never varied, as far as I can recall."

"That's what makes me wonder. He may have told the tale so often that, even if he has forgotten details, the telling and retelling have made it accurate in his mind."

"Alright, I'll give it a whirl. Now, how are you going to entertain me until my train tomorrow?"

He stepped closer. "I'm sure we can think of something."

Chapter 41

Jim took Helen to Victoria Station to catch the Brighton train. He stood like the forlorn star of an old black and white movie, watching her pass through the ticket barrier and on to the train. She looked back as she stepped aboard and gave him a small wave before disappearing inside the carriage. He turned away and wandered through the milling crowd to the underground station to catch the Circle Line train back to Westminster and his team.

He arrived in the office in time for the second coffee of the day and called his two men across to the conference area for a catch up. They sat in the red plastic chairs and sipped at the scalding brew before Jim spoke.

"Our next clue is that there was something up by Stonehenge on Salisbury Plain. But that seems to be all we have. Any ideas?"

"I've got nothing," said Geordie, slowly shaking his head.

"Ivan? How about you?"

"I have a few thoughts. We all know from military training exercises on the plain that it's mostly rolling grassland with virtually no streams and just a few small woodland areas. Very few villages and those are quite small, so everybody would know everyone else's business. There are no caves, or rocky outcrops that could conceal one and any digging to make a bunker would probably get seen and commented on. So how about hiding in plain sight?"

"What are you thinking of?"

"The Barrows."

Geordie looked puzzled "Wheelbarrows?"

"No. The burial mounds scattered across the plain. You must remember them. It was a major offence if any military personnel strayed onto one for any reason. They were all surrounded by barbed wire and had warning notices around them. The proper name for them is a Barrow."

Jim nodded thoughtfully. "Any idea how old they are?"

"Last time I was down there one of the guides at the Stonehenge visitor's centre told me there are a number of different types and they can be between 2000 and 4000 years old. Does that help?"

"It might. The Ordnance Survey has been mapping Britain since some time just after the Jacobite rebellion in the 1700s. By the 1930s they had had detailed maps of the country for years and were keeping them up to date. Now, since the Ordnance Survey belonged to the War Office for most of its life, military areas would be especially well mapped and so the maps for Salisbury Plain should be pretty good."

"Sorry, boss. Being a bit slow today. How does that help and what has it got to do with 4000 year old graves?"

"Aha! Now that's the good bit. As Ivan said, the Army has always been careful not to damage the barrows so it would need to make sure they were properly marked. So if we compare a map from the late thirties with one from, say, the fifties we might be able to spot any barrows that appear on one and not the other."

Geordie blew on his coffee and thought about it for a moment.

"It can't be that easy, surely?"

Ivan smiled. "It's a start and we don't have anything else at the moment. Oh and by the way..."

"What?"

"Don't call me Shirley."

Geordie groaned at the old joke.

Within the hour the two soldiers were back with armfuls of maps which they proceeded to spread on the empty desks and tables.

"That was fast. Where did you get all these?" said Jim.

"We took a chance that they had a map store in the MoD Main Building down by the river and here we are. We have maps of the area around Stonehenge from 1937, 1946 and 1960."

"Right then, grab a coffee and we can make a start. If I take the 1960 maps I can call out the grid reference of each barrow around Stonehenge and you two can tell me if it is on one your maps from the previous years."

Geordie and Ivan looked at each other and both sighed.

"Right you are, boss," said Ivan, "that sounds like a ruddy slow day ahead of us but I can't think of a better way with old maps."

After three hours of this tedium they had found nothing amiss. The field of red crosses on Jim's map was growing outwards from Stonehenge covering every barrow they had tried. So far every one on the 1960 map had been there in 1937 and 1946. Thoroughly fed up they took a break for lunch in the staff restaurant. Conversation was desultory. Their lead was taking them nowhere and they had nothing else to go on.

They walked back to the lift and stood in silence as it carried them up to the fourth floor. They walked past the taxation staff to the narrow staircase up to their overlarge office and stood looking at the field of red crosses on Jim's map.

"How far have we got?"

"We are at least ten miles from Stonehenge in all directions with no anomalies that might be worth following. It can't be further away than that, can it?"

Geordie wandered to the large board they had set up at the end of the office. Stuck to the top left hand corner was a copy of the doggerel they had found in the hide on the shores of Morecambe Bay.

"Can you come and look at this a minute?"

They walked over and stood next to him looking at the board.

"What have you seen, Geordie?"

"Well, if you look at that rhyme it tells us where the hides are, or at least it fits for the two we have found, right?"

"Right, so what's your point?"

"Look again, boss, it doesn't say anything about barrows or ancient burials."

Ivan and Jim looked at the rhyme.

In a Barn by the Bonniest Bay

We hide our treasure away

Near the deepest Hole

We live by the Bowl

By the Standing Stones

Where there are no Bones

Another Cave no?

Where the rich folk go

"That's true but it doesn't say anything about anything else, either."

"Boss, you said something about hiding in plain sight and you also said you could not dig on the open plain without some nosey beggar seeing you, right?"

"Right, but where are you going?"

"Did either of you ever watch the film 'Raise the Titanic'?"

"A long time ago, yes, but what are you talking about?"

"I watched it over the weekend while Sam was rehearsing. She has a hell of a lot of films on disc. Anyway, do you remember the quote 'Thank God for Southby'?"

"Vaguely, but I still don't see it. What about you, Ivan?"

Ivan smiled. "I think he might have something, boss. There was some stuff they wanted to hide and instead of taking it on the Titanic they buried it in a grave in a country churchyard."

"That's it, boss. Where can you dig a hole that will not attract attention? A graveyard. Especially in war time when there might be more customers."

"Back to the maps gents. Find me a graveyard."

Chapter 42.

As they climbed out of the car the rain sliced horizontally across the Plain in a way familiar to generations of British soldiers who had slogged across it time and again. The flat, gently rolling Plain offered no resistance to a cold wind from the north east and the rain reduced visibility as they looked around.

"Oh yes. I remember this place alright. Baking hot in the summer and like this the rest of the year. Except, of course, when it gets really cold and your sleeping bag freezes to the ground."

"Never mind, Geordie, you have all this to look forward to when you get back to the Army properly." Jim said, raising the collar of his Barbour jacket and retrieving the cap from his pocket. "Alright, it's your theory so where do we start to look?"

The three of them looked around the grey stones of the cemetery. Here and there they saw slightly bigger tombs, but the majority were just head markers, many with the inscription faded by the years of harsh weather.

"My vote is to find a nice warm vicarage and to ask the vicar if we can see his parish records," said Ivan. "We might even score a nice cup of tea and a few chocolate biscuits."

"Sounds like a plan to me. Geordie, lead the way. That building behind you looks like a vicarage."

They trudged through the grave markers along neatly trimmed gravel paths. The stones might be sacred to the memory of any number of once loved people, but now they just looked sad, wet and cold. As they approached the vicarage, the door swung open and the round smiling face of a country woman appeared.

"It must be someone very close for you to come on a day like this, my dears?"

"Good morning, ma'am. I'm Major Jim Wilson and I wonder if we could speak to the vicar?"

"You just did, I'm Sarah Mansfield, vicar of this parish. Come you in out of the rain and let me close the door before the dog gets out."

The old Labrador behind her wagged its tail gently but showed no sign of wanting to quit its place by the fire for the joys of running around in the storm. It watched as the three men came in and shrugged out of their coats.

"Come in and warm yourself," said the vicar, "the kettle has just boiled so there's tea if you would like some and I should be able to find some biscuits for you."

Jim introduced the other two. Ivan smiled broadly and lowered himself into the overstuffed armchair to one side of the fireplace. He leaned forward and tickled the old dog behind the ear.

"If you have any chocolate biscuits I may have to consider converting away from the chapel."

"Oh don't do that, they need a big broad chest like yours for those amazing choirs. The choccy biscuits come free, if only to stop me eating them and putting on even more weight."

She bustled away into the kitchen and the three men looked around the neat sitting room with its pictures of local scenes on the wall and family photographs on the sideboard. Over the fireplace hung a larger photograph of a handsome, young man in army dress uniform. Geordie got up to have a closer look and was surprised when the dog growled at him.

"Don't mind Corby," said the vicar as she entered the room carrying her tray of tea and biscuits. "He was my son's dog and he doesn't like people going near that picture. Strange really, you don't expect a dog to understand what a picture is, do you?"

She set the tray down and looked up at the young man above the fireplace.

"He was so proud of that uniform. He had wanted to be a soldier all his life. I thought going away from here to university might change that but it never did."

"Where is he now?" asked Jim.

"Outside with the rest of the family. They brought him home from Afghanistan in a sealed coffin. It was one of those roadside bombs. Some of his troop came to see me after their tour of duty. They tell me he never knew what hit him, so he didn't suffer. I think they thought that might be some comfort. Nice of them to try." She sniffed a little, then turned to Ivan with the plate in her hand. "Your chocolate biscuits, we don't want to let them go to waste."

The vicar sat in the armchair on the opposite side of the fireplace to Ivan and picked up a biscuit.

"Now then, how can I help you gentlemen?"

"Well ma'am we would really like to get a look at some of your old parish records. The ones from 1940, to be specific."

"And why would you want those, Major?"

"This is going to sound churlish, so I apologise up front, but I would rather not tell you."

The vicar sat back in her chair and steepled her fingers in front of her face. "So why would I let you rummage through my parish registers if you won't tell me why?"

Geordie sat forward. "Ma'am, before Corby decided not to like me I was looking at your son's photograph. I noticed from his collar badges he was a Royal Engineer."

"And?"

"And because we are all Royal Engineers too, I thought you might just trust us. The boss here would tell you if he could but it really might be very important and it is a secret that we have to protect."

Jim leaned forward. "Unless of course the word 'Cromwell' means something significant to you?"

"The only significant Cromwell I know is the Lord Protector from the 1600s. I take it that is not who you mean?"

"No ma'am, 'Cromwell' is a sort of password for something we are searching for and if it doesn't mean anything to you, with regret, I really can't say any more."

The vicar contemplated the three of them for a long minute of silence. She looked across at Ivan who was tickling Corby behind the ears again.

"Corby seems to have taken to you, Ivan and he is generally a good judge of character. Finish your tea and follow me to the study. All the parish records are in there, we should be able to find the 1940 volume without much difficulty."

They gulped down the last of their tea and followed the vicar along the wood panelled passage to the study, the old wooden floors creaking beneath their feet. She led them into the room with a desk to one side and packed bookshelves on three walls. The fourth wall had a large bay window looking out onto the cemetery and the church beyond. The vicar stood, in the bay, looking out into the rain as they gazed around them.

"My son and his father, plus all the rest of the family are just here outside the window. I sometimes practice my sermons for them when searching for the right phrase. On a dry day Corby goes and lies out there to be near his old master. It's nice to see them together again."

She turned from the window with watery eyes and walked to one of the bookshelves lined with blue books. She ran her finger along it until she reached the half-way point.

"Here you are. The Register of Births, Marriages and Deaths for this Parish in 1940." She pulled the large heavy book off the shelf and handed it to Ivan. "I hope you find what you're looking for. I'll have our lunch ready at about one o'clock if that suits you? If you need any help with the entries just give me a call."

She left the room and Ivan went to the window. The grey stone of the head markers contrasted with the white stone of the military marker for her son. The badge of the Royal Engineers was clearly marked with his Name, Rank and Serial Number, plus the date and location of his death. He sighed and turned back into the room, there were way too many of those headstones nowadays.

Jim was leafing through the pages that were yellowed with age. The carefully inscribed information was still clear.

"Seems to me, gents, that we need to find any recorded deaths after the gold was picked up, for about three or four months. We then need to see if they exist in the register of births or marriages. If they have a history here they are almost certainly genuine and of no real interest to us."

He turned to the relevant pages and they found that there had been only five burials during the target time. Birthdates were recorded in one of the columns so it was the work of only a few minutes to check the Marriage Register for the relevant years to eliminate each of the five in turn. Having drawn a blank they carefully placed the registers in the right order on the bookshelves.

"Well, it seems we are going out in the rain again. I suppose it was too much to hope that we would stumble across something on the first try. We'd better make a move to our next cemetery."

"Hang on, boss. I don't know what the vicar has planned for lunch but it smells wonderful and it would be rude to leave after we have been invited, eh?"

"Fair enough, Ivan. I suppose you are due a home cooked meal but no hanging about afterwards, even if you get offered more biscuits."

"Would I do a thing like that? I'm hurt you would even think it of me."

Chapter 43

They pulled into the entrance of the next cemetery on their list and were looking at the dreary headstones and sodden grass through the misty car windows when Geordie's phone rang. He stepped out of the car to take the call. He climbed back in again to the back seat moments later and leaned between the two front seats.

"Fancy a break from graveyard's in the rain?"

"I wouldn't mind if you have a better offer. What's up?"

"That was Sam on the phone. Her granddad wants to speak to you but he won't tell her what about. I guess they really bought into the security training back in the day."

"Can we phone him?"

"We could, but he only lives in Salisbury. That's about a twenty minute drive from here and if we time it right, we should be in time for afternoon tea."

"That should suit you, Ivan."

Ivan nodded slightly. "But I think I would prefer my tea next to that big fire in the vicarage if I was to have a choice."

"I think we bothered the vicar quite enough last time. Let's go and see granddad. Do you know where he lives, Geordie?"

"Not far from the hotel we are booked into for tonight. So we could drop the car off and walk round if you wanted."

"Let's see what the weather is like when we get there before we decide."

Ivan put the car in gear and turned out of the graveyard heading for the road to Salisbury. The journey took more than the promised twenty minutes with the rain sluicing down the windscreen faster than the wipers could deal with it. The streets were quiet as they drove into the city, with few cars venturing out and even fewer pedestrians braving the downpour.

"There's a really good curry house just up here on the left," said Geordie, "if anybody fancies it. I make a point of coming here every time I get a break from an exercise on the Plain."

"In this weather I think a curry might go down really well. What do you think Ivan?"

"Maybe, but I've got a call to make before I decide, if that's OK with you?"

"No worries. You can make the call while we're speaking to Geordie's grandfather-in-law. If that term exists."

The rain showed no sign of easing so they drove directly to the house and parked outside the small, neat garden. The door of the house stayed closed as they climbed out of the car and dashed up the pathway. Ivan stayed in the car to make his call and promised to join them in a couple of minutes. Jim and Geordie sheltered in the porch of the house and knocked on the door. They heard the shuffling footsteps approaching and then the door swung wide. The old man stood back to let them enter and they both shook hands with James Lanton as they did so.

"Hello, Mr Lanton," said Jim, "I hear you want to speak to us."

"Hello, Granddad," said Geordie.

"Cheeky bugger, I'm Sam's granddad, but I forgive you. But only because you make her so damned happy."

He led the way into the neat sitting room with yet another blazing fire.

"Geordie, go make the tea, you know where the kitchen is, I want to talk to the Major here."

Geordie did as he was told and Jim sat himself down in the chair that the old man waved him into. The old man sat down opposite him and looked at him for a moment before he began.

"You know I was a messenger boy for the Auxiliary Units up around the Plain during the war. Well at the end of that I was the perfect age to be called up and after training I was sent out to the war in Korea. That was a nasty little war; mostly forgotten about now, of course. Anyway, I got shot there. Chinese machine gunner got me in the shoulder, upper arm and through the lung. I think that boy knew his business, it was damn good shooting."

"I'm sorry but does this have anything to do with the Auxiliary Units?"

"Indulge an old man, Major, I'm getting to it. Everybody is in such a rush these days. Anyway, I was laying there in the mud with blood pumping out of me when one of the regimental medics got to me. He controlled the bleeding and stopped up the hole in my lung so I could breathe. He was still working on me when the next burst of machine gun fire took him. He died in an instant with a bullet through his head. Fell across me and shielded me from the mortars that started about then, though he didn't know it. That was 'Chalky' White and he came from a village out on the Plain. That Chinese lad did me a bit of a favour, really. I met my Elsie in the hospital they took me to. She was a nursing assistant back then. Lovely girl."

"Where is your wife?"

"Oh, Elsie died a while back, but it won't be too long till I see her again."

"I'm sorry for your loss, Mr Lanton."

"Yes, well anyway, after I got back I took my new wife on a cycling holiday for our honeymoon and to show her a bit of Wiltshire. We went out to Stonehenge and then out to the big stone ring at Avebury. On the way we went to see Chalky's old Mum so I could tell her how her boy died and what he had done for me. She lived in a cottage in West Lavington on the way to Devizes when you are coming from Stonehenge."

Geordie reappeared with the tea on a tray and set it down on the small table in front of the fire. "I've even got a plate of biscuits for Ivan."

"Well, you go and get him and let me finish my story!"

Geordie looked at Jim, who nodded very slightly and the Sergeant headed for the front door.

"Where was I?"

"West Lavington."

"Right. But that's not the interesting bit for you. On the way to Lavington you pass through the village of Tilshead. It was hot, so we stopped at the pub there for a drink and a bite to eat. While we were sitting at the table in front of the pub was when I saw him."

"Saw who?"

"One of the men who used to meet me in the woods around Stonehenge. He was walking along the road in Tilshead bold as brass and damn me if he wasn't dressed as a parson with the dog collar and everything. I asked who he was and the barman told me he really was the parson for the village. Now, what do you think about that?"

"That's really very helpful but why didn't you tell me about it at Sam's wedding?"

"Probably because I had forgotten all about it. Talking to you made me start thinking about those days again and it came back to me last night when I was in bed. That cycling holiday was magic for me and Elsie, we never managed to do it again after the kids came along."

"Well thank you for telling me your story, Mr Lanton."

"Is it any use to you?"

"Oh yes. With just a little luck you may have saved us some days of tramping around in the pouring rain." Jim looked up at his two men as they entered the room. "And I'm pretty sure these two will be delighted with that."

"Delighted with what, boss?" said Ivan as he reached for his first chocolate biscuit.

"Mr Lanton here has just given us a very useful clue and by the way don't pinch all the chocolate ones. You need to save room for a curry."

They thanked the old man for his information and made their way back to the car. The rain was finally stopping with just a few drops falling in the wide black puddles. As they got back into the car, Ivan cleared his throat.

"Err, boss. How do you feel about me taking the car tonight and missing out on the curry?"

"No problems for me. Why, have you had a better offer?"

"Something like that. I'll see you for breakfast."

Chapter 44.

The next morning the three met up for a seriously challenging full English breakfast in the pub they had stayed in. Even Ivan was wondering if he could do it justice.

"How was the curry? Everything Geordie promised?"

"One of the best I've had, it even rivals my favourite curry house in Birmingham. You would have enjoyed it."

Geordie smiled slightly. "Boss, Helen was right you know, you really are out of practice at picking up on clues."

"What have I missed this time?"

"I think you will find that the Sergeant Major had prettier company than us last evening. Maybe a certain lady vicar?"

Ivan said nothing and carried on working his way through a very fine Wiltshire sausage. Jim looked at his two companions and shook his head.

"Now how would you know that?"

"Boss, Ivan may well be a fan of the chocolate digestive biscuit but even they don't put an expression on his face like the one he was wearing yesterday at the rectory when he looked at the Reverend Sarah."

"Is he right, Ivan?"

"Pardon me, but that's a bit private, if you don't mind."

"That's a yes, then. We'd better finish up here and get on the road out to Tilshead. The name rings a bell but I can't place it."

"Remember a couple of years ago we were test flying that new drone aircraft out on the Plain and they put us in those wooden huts at Westdown Camp? The village just down the hill from that camp was Tilshead. Only a small place, nestled in a bit of a shallow valley."

"Now that you mention it, I do remember. Shouldn't be difficult to find the church in a place that small. I wonder if they have their own cemetery?"

The team drove slowly into the small village of Tilshead about an hour later. The village was an unusual mix of modern houses, older buildings and thatched cottages, but somehow it all seemed to belong. As they drove along the high street they spotted the church and cemetery on the right, tucked back from the road. A little further on they pulled over and parked outside the Rose and Crown. Geordie checked the menu on the blackboard outside the pub.

"Looks like we have found the place for lunch, unless there is another nice lady vicar here, eh Ivan?"

"Wind your neck in son, I've told you that's private."

"Sorry mate, just pulling your tail a bit."

"If you two have finished, can we now go to look for something important?"

"Sorry, boss," they chorused.

A couple of hundred yards along the street they turned in to the path that was signposted for the church and the school. As they walked along it they saw the church to the right, set among the gravestones. The small village school was at the end of the cemetery up a slight rise. They walked through the graveyard and tried the door of the church. Locked.

"OK, let's not waste any time. Split up and take a wander around to see if anything looks out of place. I'll go and see if I can scout out the local vicar."

Ivan wandered down the slope while Geordie set off upwards and Jim headed for the school to try to find somebody to ask for information. He tried the doors and they too were locked. He set off out to the main road again to try the small shop they had passed on the way into the village. Ivan and Geordie continued to wander along the paths and between the headstones reading about the "dearly departed", "beloved mother" and other traditional messages, to be found on English headstones.

Tucked into a quiet corner under the wide arms of a large tree Ivan spotted a possible anomaly. He made a point of not shouting across to Geordie but continued walking without changing pace. He hoped that would be enough to convince the owner of the face he had seen peering over the wall that he had missed the clue. He worked his way back to the church door to meet up with Geordie.

"Nothing here as far as I can see, Ivan."

"No, I think we are wasting our time. Let's go pick up Jim and see about that pub you fancy."

Geordie noticed the use of Jim's first name. Not like the big Sergeant Major to be disrespectful of an officer. Particularly one of this standard. Then the penny dropped. Somebody was listening. He played along.

"Yes, well, that story about a famous rock star being buried here always did sound a bit far-fetched. But the picture would have sold well. Worth a try eh?"

Ivan nodded and smiled. With a tiny movement of his head he pointed out where they were being observed from. Geordie didn't look until they were walking back down the main path.

"Dark jacket, grey hair, standing behind the wall?"

"That's him. Been there ever since we started looking at the stones. Got your camera? Get a couple of general shots of the cemetery and see if you can zoom in on him without being obvious."

Geordie wandered a little way back up the path pulling the camera out of his pocket. He turned slowly as he took pictures around the church. The man by the tree seemed confident he was out of sight. He didn't move when Geordie pointed the camera in his direction. The high powered zoom brought his face into clear focus as Geordie took the photo.

They met Jim as he was turning into the cemetery on his way back from the shop.

"Just heading back to the pub, Jim. Geordie here has a thirst you couldn't buy for a quid."

If Jim was surprised by the use of his first name he didn't show it much. Just the one eyebrow raised slightly as he turned to walk with them towards the Rose and Crown. As they turned into the car park Ivan glanced quickly over his shoulder. The man from the graveyard was standing by the sign to the church, watching them.

"I think we have a winner, boss. If we can find a quiet table we'll tell you why."

They entered the pub. Jim and Ivan selected a table away from the bar and Geordie went to get them three pints of beer and a menu.

"OK, Ivan, what have you got?"

"Couple of things boss. Firstly we had company while we were looking at the headstones. Somebody trying to keep out of sight watching us. He watched us along the road to here as well. If he was legit I'm thinking he would have spoken to me, you know how protective these villagers can be."

He stopped as Geordie reached the table carrying the beers. He waited until the sergeant had settled himself before continuing.

"Go on Ivan. The barman is well away from us" said Jim, looking over at the bar.

"You remember the young lad's gravestone at the first cemetery we visited? Military pattern with regimental badge and the usual style for a soldier. No matter where a serving soldier dies he always gets issued with the same style of headstone, right? Well, in this graveyard there is a headstone for a soldier that is not like that. It says he was killed in a training accident on the plain, so he was a serving soldier and even if he got a local headstone to start with, he would have got the proper one when things settled down."

"Interesting. And did your watcher see you reading it?"

"I don't think so. I didn't stop, just wandered by trying to look bored."

Geordie handed the digital camera to Jim.

"That's him, boss" he said, pointing at the screen on the back of the camera. "But you can see him close up soon. I can see him through that window behind you. He is coming across the car park and he has somebody with him this time."

Jim peered at the small screen on the back of the camera while studiously ignoring the two men who walked into the pub and stood at the bar. He did notice they were taking surreptitious looks at the three of them while pretending to look around the room.

"Ivan, have a look at the camera screen and tell me if the headstone is in any of the pictures, will you."

Ivan took the camera and flipped through the pictures. "It's in the lower corner of the photo you were looking at boss. Probably too small to see any detail though."

Jim turned to Geordie. "Could you take a walk out to the car and bring the laptop in here. I'd like to see that picture a bit bigger and while you are there can you pick up those pistols you have hidden under the seat. With guns being produced at the last two hides I think we might need to be prepared, if Ivan is right."

Geordie took a gulp of his beer before standing and making his way out to the car. Jim noticed that the men at the bar turned round, ever so casually, to watch him go and one moved a pace to the side to keep him in view as he crossed the car park. He was back in a couple of minutes with the laptop in his hand.

"There you go" he said handing it over "I've got everything you wanted."

Jim fired up the computer and connected the camera to it. It was the work of seconds to access the camera's memory and to call up the picture he needed. He smiled as he looked at the larger image and then zoomed in on the headstone.

He turned the computer screen towards Ivan slightly. "Is that the stone you think is out of place?"

"That's the one. It just doesn't seem right for a military headstone, does it?"

"No, but I think someone has been having a little joke as well. Remember when we were being briefed at Number 10 I told them how I used to go to Richard Holmes' lectures at Sandhurst?"

"He's the history lecturer, right'"

"He was and a brilliant one at that. He was an expert on the Peninsular War and one of the books he quoted from was "The Recollections of Rifleman Harris", one of Wellington's soldiers who went right through that war. His first name was Benjamin, if I remember correctly. Now look at the headstone again."

Ivan moved the computer and peered at the enlarged image. His smile broadened as he read the inscription again.

"Rfn Benjamin Harris, The Rifle Brigade. Died in a training accident on this plain 18th September 1940"

"It does seem a bit strange. If he was killed in training why would he be buried here? Surely they would have taken him to the military cemetery in Larkhill Camp? Says nothing about him being from this village."

Geordie looked at the screen as Ivan turned the computer around for him. He smiled too.

"I think we have a candidate. Ivan wins the big prize this time. So what's our next move?"

"Well the best bet is to check the parish register again. But it seems that this village is too small these days to support its own vicar and so one is shared between a group of small villages around here. The lady in the shop has given me his phone number. So I guess we call and see if we can get a look at the records."

"Then what?"

"Then if the evidence stacks up we go and find a coroner to issue permission open up the grave to exhume the body and see if there is anybody actually in there."

Chapter 45

The vicar turned out to be a chubby young man with a face that was far too red for the exercise he had taken walking up the gentle slope of the graveyard. He seemed flustered and unsure. Jim walked forward to meet him with his hand outstretched.

"Good afternoon, vicar, good of you to come over here so promptly."

"Hello, Joseph Wesley. Wonderful name for a Church of England vicar, eh? Always happy to help and to be truthful I was glad of an excuse to leave the group I was talking to. They had got to the part where they back-bite everyone in the village who isn't in the church support group. I don't enjoy that part much, I must confess. Now, how can I help you?"

As he spoke he pulled a large iron key from his jacket pocket and was unlocking the heavy, wooden church door.

"We would like to have a look at your parish records for 1940. We need to get a little more information about Rifleman Harris who rests in your graveyard."

The vicar's hand froze half way through turning the key. He let go of it as though it was red hot and stood straight, staring at the door in front of him. Jim looked down at the hands hanging beside the cleric. They were trembling and the man's face had paled noticeably.

"Here, let me help you with that" Jim said leaning forward and turning the key "These old locks can be a bit tricky at times, can't they?" He pushed the door open gently and waited for the vicar to move.

"I don't think we have any records from as far back as that. They must have been lost, I think."

Jim noted the distinct quaver in the man's voice, that hadn't been there before. This young man was scared, really scared.

"Well, you won't mind if we check on that, will you?" said Jim as he placed a hand on the young man's shoulder and gently pressed him into the church.

It was cool and calm inside the church with the usual plaques on the walls commemorating village worthies from years gone by. The altar was a simple affair, suitable for a country church and the carpet up the aisle was worn and threadbare. The vicar walked along the carpet almost in a daze, with Jim closely behind him.

Jim indicated that Geordie should close the door and keep watch for uninvited guests. The door swung quietly closed making hardly a sound and locked with a heavy clunk as Geordie turned the key that was now on the inside. Ivan followed Jim and the vicar up the aisle to the polished wooden door on the right of the altar. As they passed through they found themselves in a small plain room with vestments hanging on wall hooks, wrapped in plastic garment bags. There was a wooden chair, a mirror and a large oak wall cupboard with a heavy duty padlock securing its doors.

Jim contemplated the nervous young man in the clerical collar. Ivan shrugged his shoulders. They could see no reason why he would suddenly have become so frightened.

"The records are in there," said the Vicar, indicating the cupboard.

"Would you like to give me the key to this padlock, vicar?"

"Not really," said the young man as he pulled the key ring from his trouser pocket with trembling fingers. He held the ring out to Jim who took it carefully from him.

"What's the matter, reverend? What is so worrying about a soldier in your graveyard who has been dead for seventy years or more?"

"Oh, Lord I have to tell somebody. It's not him. There are some people in the village here that came to my home one night just after I took over the parish. They made some threats about what they would do if I ever took any notice of that grave. They didn't say why, but they were very clear about what they would do to my family and then to me."

Ivan took out the camera and turned the screen towards the vicar.

"Is that one of them?"

The frightened young man did not speak, he swallowed hard and nodded briefly. Ivan looked at Jim who put his head to one side to indicate that Ivan should go back to the main door to support Geordie. The big Welshman left the room, without a word and Jim turned back to the vicar.

"Sit down, vicar," he said, indicating the upright wooden chair by the wall. "I don't think this will take long."

He turned to the oak cupboard and unlocked the padlock. The doors creaked as he opened them to reveal the bound copies of the parish records. With a small village like this a few years of births, marriages and deaths would fit comfortably into each volume. It took him a few moments to find the volume that covered 1940. He looked through until he came to September of that year. Of Rifleman Harris, there was no mention. He had been buried in the churchyard with no record having been made, it seemed.

Jim put the volume back on the shelf and closed the cupboard doors. He locked it. Turning back to the vicar, he handed him the ring of keys.

"Did you find what you were looking for?"

"Yes. Well, more accurately, no."

He was about to explain further when Geordie appeared through the doorway.

"Company, boss. Our friends are coming up the path."

Jim turned to see an expression of abject terror on the face of the man sitting on the high backed chair. He seemed incapable of movement or rational thought.

"You stay there please, Reverend. We have some business to attend to with some of your less friendly parishioners."

Chapter 46

Jim left the vestry room and stepped out into the church. As he walked towards the main door he saw that Ivan and Geordie had moved into the shadows on either side of the entrance. Both were close to the wall with their pistols drawn. As he approached the door it shook as a heavy knock came from the outside. He looked to left and right and both his men nodded.

He reached for the iron key in the solid oak door and turned it. Pulling the door open he found himself facing two angry looking men.

"Come on in, gents," he said, stepping back from the door. "I have been wanting a word with you."

The men pushed through the door and moved towards him. The one to the left pulled a knife from under his coat and held it low ready to strike at Jim's stomach.

Jim looked down at the weapon and turning to the second man said "And have you got the fork to go with that?"

"Don't you be a smartarse with me," began the first man. He stopped as the two soldiers stepped silently forward and rested the barrels of their weapons at the base of each man's skull.

"I don't think you want to be insulting people in a church now, do you?" said Ivan with a more pronounced Welsh accent than usual.

The knife clattered to the stone floor. Jim smiled at the two men whose eyes were darting from side to side, to try and find a way out of the situation.

"I think you two might be more comfortable if you sat down in the back pew here," he said, indicating the highly polished wooden seat. "Then we can have a little chat and get to know each other. Won't that be nice?"

The two men shuffled into the pew and sat down, staring at Jim.

"Now, what I would like you to do is to put your hands under your legs, palms up wards and move really close together so your shoulders are touching. That should slow you down just enough so that if you try anything silly my two friends back there can blow your heads off. Understand? Good."

Jim moved around and sat on the front rail of the pew in front of them with his back to the altar. He looked at them for a long moment before he spoke.

"Right then, we came in here to find some information about a grave outside this church. As soon as we asked the vicar about it he clammed up and got very scared. We found the information on our own without his help though. With a little persuasion we also found out that you two had threatened him and his family."

The first man opened his mouth to speak, but Jim shook his head.

"I don't really want to hear what you have to say about that just yet. I'm giving you some information at the moment. Now, if you come near the vicar or any of his family ever again, or if he or any of his family have an accident of any kind, those two heavy calibre pistols behind you will be back and your brains, such as they are, will be scattered to the four winds. Is that absolutely clear to you?"

Both men nodded quickly.

"No, this time I want to hear you say it. I want to hear you say that you understand that actions have consequences. And I want you to assure me that you know I am just the right kind of bastard to deal with scum like you."

"Yes, I understand. He won't be harmed."

"Me too. I won't touch him or his people."

"Good, now tell me. What's really in that grave?"

Neither man spoke. They looked at Jim in stony silence. Jim looked up from the two on the bench to Ivan, who stood behind them. The Welshman tapped the barrel of his heavy pistol just behind the first man's ear.

"Don't you start being rude again. Answer when you're asked a civil question."

"That bloody hurt!"

"It was supposed to. I don't like bully boys like you."

The second man was taken by surprise when Ivan swung the pistol to the left and clipped his behind the ear as well. He lunged forward and made as if to stand up but reconsidered when he felt Geordie's strong hand on his shoulder and the barrel of the gun returned to the back of his skull.

"Now," said Jim, "shall we try that again? What is in that grave?"

"We don't know. We were just told to make sure it was never disturbed."

"Told by whom?"

"If we told you that we would be dead before the week was out and then our families would get it too."

"Fair enough. We'll do it the hard way then. Geordie would you go and find the tool shed for this place. Somebody must be maintaining the grounds. We need a couple of spades and probably a pick, if you can find one."

Geordie pocketed his pistol and headed for the door. The two men turned their heads to watch him go. When they turned back they found that Jim was now holding another large, black, army issue automatic pistol.

"Just in case you thought that changed the odds, gentlemen. Tell me something. Does the word Cromwell mean anything to you? No? Oh well, that clears up one thing for me."

They waited silently until they heard the clatter of tools being dropped outside the church door. Geordie re-entered and looked across at the silent tableau.

"And there's me thinking you would all be best pals by now. Ah, well. Anyhow, I've got the tools you asked for. Where would you like them?"

"Right, you two. Stand up slowly and move to the door."

"Might be an idea to search them first. Don't want anybody trying anything silly now, do we?" said Ivan

Ivan pushed the two men to the stone wall of the church. He kicked their legs apart in turn, none too gently and then handed his weapon to Jim.

"Hands apart and high up on the wall, both of you. Now move your feet backwards so you are leaning. That'll do. Stay like that."

The big Welshman stepped forward and placed his foot across in front of the first man's ankle. "I'm going to be kind to you now and tell you that if you move I will whip my foot back and you will hit the floor face first. It usually breaks the nose. If you want to try it just have a go. I'd love to demonstrate. No?"

He set to work sliding his hands down the arms, back, chest and legs of the first man. Jim moved to ensure he had a clear shot should there be any trouble. Satisfied, Ivan moved to the second man. A second later, he found the small calibre pistol stuck in the waistband of the man's grubby trousers.

"Naughty. That's illegal in this country."

The man said nothing, just waited for the body search to be over. Ivan stepped back and retrieved his automatic pistol from Jim. He slipped the small pistol he had found into his jacket pocket and nodded to Jim.

"Right, gents. Outside and pick up your tools. You are going to do some digging."

Reluctantly the men walked out of the church and picked up the tools, that were lying there. Geordie had stepped back to ensure he was out of reach should they decide to swing a spade at him.

"You know where the grave is. Off you go."

The party of five walked around the corner of the church and across to where Rifleman Harris was alleged to be waiting under the spreading branches of the tree. The two thugs started to dig with ill-concealed malice. Making little effort, they were looking around for a chance to make a run for it. Geordie leaned against the wall nearby and spoke to Ivan who waited on the path on the other side of the grave.

"I reckon our two grave diggers here are eyeing up their chances of avoiding work, don't you Ivan? How far do you reckon they would get?"

"With the accuracy and stopping power of a 9mm Browning Hi Power Automatic and the speed of a bullet, less your reaction time of course I think they might make four to five yards. Oh sorry, I should call them metres nowadays."

"Do you think they are doubting our will to fire, then?"

"Do you know, I think they just might be. Would that be right, gents? You are doubting the will to open fire, on scumbags like you, from men who have completed multiple tours of duty in Iraq and Afghanistan? Bad bet there lads; now stop dicking about, start swinging that pick and dig properly before I get angry."

Jim grinned to himself as the spades started to work appreciably faster. The two men were staring to sweat. He noticed the vicar coming around the corner of the church. He seemed agitated.

"You must stop digging. You can't disturb a grave without a court order. It's illegal."

"Don't worry vicar. I am pretty sure there is no body in there. It's a hiding place for something important we have been looking for."

"Oh, what's that?"

"Sorry vicar, I'm afraid I can't tell you that. But at least your two friends here are getting the exercise they deserve."

The vicar looked uncertain as he watched the digging. He stood next to Jim, then said, "Should your two friends have guns? It's illegal and dangerous."

"It certainly would be, Padre, if they weren't highly trained soldiers carrying Army issued weapons on government business. We are quite legal, I can assure you."

As he spoke, they clearly heard the sound of a spade striking something solid down in the grave. He stepped nearer to watch the two thugs clearing the soil away from the top of a metal box, buried only two feet below the surface. They stood up and straightened their stiff backs.

"Not time to rest yet. Get that box out of there and opened before you try and take a break," said Ivan, in a tone that brooked no argument.

They carried on shovelling and cleared the top of the box which, it was now clear, was two separate, painted, metal cases. They heaved the first one out onto the graveside, then the other. As they went to climb out of the hole, Geordie pushed the first one back with the sole of his boot.

"Now you toss those tools over there beyond the boxes and sit you down in the bottom of that hole. I reckon you must need the rest by now."

The two men threw the tools as instructed and sat down with their backs resting against the ends of the excavation. Geordie moved around to the end of the hole, where he could see them both clearly and held his pistol ready to correct any unfortunate behaviour on their part.

With Geordie watching the two men in the hole, Jim and Ivan picked up a spade and a pickaxe and walked to the two dirty metal boxes. The pickaxe made short work of the four padlocks securing the two lids and the spade levered the first box open. As the lid rose they saw sheets of waxed brown paper. Ivan pulled the paper away, to reveal a row of M16 automatic rifles. He lifted one out and beneath it he found a row of Sterling submachine guns with automatic pistols between them. Around the side of the box were spare magazines for all three types of weapon. Ivan examined the rifle in his hands.

"Heavily greased to stop rusting and with that waxed paper over and around them they should still be fully functional."

He turned to the second box and raised the lid. Row upon row of plastic explosive blocks with detonators and timers in plastic boxes. Jim and Ivan were still staring into the two boxes when the vicar stepped between them. His indrawn breath hissed between his teeth, as he saw what had been revealed.

"Sacrilege. To bury such things in hallowed ground. That's just awful."

"True enough, Padre. But now we need to know who owns them," said Ivan, stepping to the edge of the grave and looking down. "Now then, you two, I have my own idea about who these things belong to but you are just about to confirm my suspicions, aren't you?"

The two men looked at each other and one then looked up at Ivan. Whatever he saw in the Welshman's eyes seemed to convince him.

"We don't know. We really don't, we were contacted and told we would be paid to bury these things here and we would be well paid each month if we made sure nobody interfered with them. Well, the pay keeps coming through and with the Unemployment Benefits as well, we do alright so we didn't ask any questions."

"So who handed the boxes to you and when?"

"That would be about five years ago now. Two Irish fellahs in a truck met us out by the road down to Imber village. They handed them over and just left. A surly pair they were as well. We had an arrangement with the old vicar and put them here one night. He didn't mind the phony headstone."

Ivan turned and looked at Jim over his shoulder "My guess would be IRA," he said.

"Mine too, but that's up to the police to sort out. You keep our two friends here and I'll see if the Wiltshire Constabulary would like to claim a nice big arms bust, complete with two terrorists."

"Oy! We ain't terrorists!"

Geordie looked down at the two agitated men in the hole. "You are now, mates. You are now."

Chapter 47

The Wiltshire police vans drove away down Tilshead High Street carrying the two very unhappy thugs. The Special Branch Inspector had agreed with Jim that the three soldiers had never been there. It had been the painstaking work of his team that had uncovered the terrorist arms cache and so of course they would take all the credit. It had been made very clear to the two prisoners that it would be extremely unwise to contradict the police version of events. The recently updated anti-terrorist laws allowed the police to hold the two men for seven days without giving them access to a lawyer, so Jim was confident he and his team would be long gone by the time they started making a fuss.

The three soldiers and the vicar watched the vans until they were out of sight around the corner of the road.

"Anybody fancy a nice cup of tea? I've got a kettle and some mugs in the back of the robing alcove in the vestry."

"That's good of you, Padre. I think that would go down really well after all that digging. Ivan, Geordie; how about you?"

Both men agreed though Geordie looked wistfully towards the pub. They followed the priest back into the church and waited while he genuflected briefly towards the altar.

"I was quite surprised when they didn't react to the 'Cromwell' code word," said Ivan. "I was convinced we were on a winner with that grave and the odd headstone."

Jim was looking at Ivan as he spoke and so walked into the back of the vicar, who had come to a sudden stop. He turned to look at the three soldiers, his eyes wide.

"Did you say Cromwell?"

"Yes. Why does it mean something to you?"

"It certainly does. Tell me what you are doing here while, I make the tea."

He made the tea and brought the four steaming mugs out into the church where the three men were sitting on the front pew.

"Well? What does Cromwell mean to you three?"

While the other two sipped their tea, Jim explained that they had a mission from the government to recover something that had been hidden in 1940. He couldn't tell the vicar what it was due to the classification of their task but, with the coincidence of the date, the vicar could see why they were investigating the strange grave.

"I see, tell me the code word again."

"Cromwell."

"Right then, if you have finished your tea I need your help with something. Bring the mugs with you and follow me."

They followed the vicar into the vestry again. He took the mugs from them and placed them carefully in a small sink, they had not noticed before, behind a curtain. He pointed at the large and beautifully carved oak wall cupboard that housed the parish records.

"If you could pull that a couple of feet from the wall I'll show you something interesting about this church."

The three engineers heaved the heavy cupboard away from the wall. Behind it there was a wall of blank stones that had obviously been there since the church was built. The vicar squeezed into the gap between the wall and the cupboard.

"Now, let me see if I can remember this," he said, as he placed his hands on two stones, that were separated by about half a metre of other unremarkable stones.

He pressed and nothing happened. He adjusted his position and pressed again, the strain showing in his flushed face. The stones sank into the wall with a scraping sound, followed by a heavy clunk and a louder scraping noise, as the wall moved back a couple of inches on one side and a crack opened at the other.

"There you are, gentlemen, the door to Cromwell. It hinges to the left, if you push on the right hand side."

He moved out of the way, to let the others move in.

"Ivan, I think this one is yours," said Jim. "Same rules as before, move slowly and check everywhere. We don't want any of the surprises we've found before."

Ivan moved forward and pressed on the right hand side, of the newly revealed door. It swung grudgingly open with a grating of stone on stone. Ivan continued pushing until the door had swung back as far as it was able to go. He peered inside, to find a narrow opening with stone stairs leading down under the main church.

"It looks bloody tight in here, but at least it looks properly built."

The vicar leaned around the oak cupboard and offered Ivan a flashlight he had retrieved from one of the drawers. Ivan took it and peered once again into the opening.

He sat back on his heels. "Thanks Padre, that's going to help. It really is dark in there. Right then, if I yell come after me, otherwise stay out of the way in case I have to get out in a hurry."

He squeezed his wide shoulders around the turn and started down the narrow stone staircase. He took one step at a time, checking carefully for trip wires or anything else that might trigger a trap. Fourteen steps down, he found himself at the bottom, of the steps in a small foyer, facing a heavy wooden door with a black, iron latch. The latch was stiff with age but gave in to the force of Ivan's hand and clunked upwards. He pressed gently against the door and with a protest of rusty hinges, it swung slowly inwards. There were no cables or wires, attached to the door to set off any devices. As far as he could tell the floor was solid. He stepped through.

As Ivan made his slow way down the narrow passage Jim turned to the vicar.

"So how did you become a Guardian?"

"Guardian? What's that?"

"You don't know what's down there, do you?"

"No idea. When I took over this parish the retiring priest sat me down and made me promise that if anyone ever came here with the password Cromwell I was to open that door for them. He made me promise that I would never set foot on those stairs and then he showed me which stones to press. That's the first time that cupboard has moved away from the wall in all my time here."

Jim wondered what had happened to the group over the years, that had left this cache with no Guardians. They would probably never know who to thank for their faithful service.

Sighing, he stood and returned to the head of the hidden staircase. He peered around the corner and looked down to where Ivan had disappeared, into the gloom. He could just see a glow from the flashlight moving slowly.

"Ivan! Are you OK down there?"

"Fine boss! Just checking for any surprise packages from the old boys!"

Jim looked around the vestry of the small church. It was not ancient and would probably have raised little interest from an invading army. He shook his head. He had to admire the men of the Auxiliary Units. They had proven to be highly adept at hiding their precious charge.

Ivan reappeared, covered in dust and sweating.

"It's bloody stuffy down there. I don't think that door has been opened in a very long time. Just came up for a breather and to let some air get down there."

"What have you found so far?"

"Not much yet. At the bottom of the stairs is a small room with a door in the left hand wall. I got that open without much trouble and it leads into another passage. This one is a bit longer though still narrow and the floor slopes down gently. At the far end there is another old wooden door and opening that is my next step."

"Obviously there have been no booby traps, up to now, but don't get complacent, eh?"

"And, Ivan," said Geordie, with a big grin, "check the corners."

"I wouldn't forget that one. But as you say, boss, so far nothing. I wonder if this group relied on concealment more than the others? And maybe they didn't want to damage this church with explosives?"

"Maybe, but don't rely on that. These guys have proven to be pretty ruthless in guarding the material so far."

Ivan nodded and went across to the small sink behind the curtain. He drank a mug of cold water and swilled his face to clear the dust.

"Time I got back to work," he said, stepping back to the oak cupboard and vanishing behind it. They could hear him grunting slightly as he eased his large frame through the entry door and onto the staircase.

Chapter 48

Down in the crypt, Ivan made his way carefully back to the second wooden door, still checking to make sure he had not missed any hidden surprises. His break up the stairs had allowed the air to freshen, but not much. It still smelled musty and old. He stood in front of the door and ran his flashlight beam around the edges. He checked the heavy metal latch and then got down on his knees to look under the door. Seeing nothing worrying he stood again and operated the latch mechanism. Once again, the heavy metal was reluctant to move after so many years, but eventually gave in to the force that the Welshman applied.

Gently, very gently, he swung the door inwards, checking for any sign of a trap. With the door now fully open, he checked again before stepping through into yet another passageway. With his nerves tingling, he moved forward. If he had not been on edge and anticipating trouble, he might not have felt the slight movement as the stone slab beneath his boot dropped a little as he stepped on to it.

Seeing that the passageway before him had a bend in it, he flung himself forward and dodged around the corner, expecting the blast of a grenade followed by the flying metal fragments at any second. Turning the corner, he flattened himself against the wall and waited for the explosion. There was nothing. He slowly straightened up and dared to breathe again before muttering some choice swear words, under his breath.

As he turned to look at the part of the passage he was now in, he heard the unmistakeable sound of a moving stone grinding against another. He nervously looked back in time to see a large block of stone crash down from the ceiling of the passage. Had he still been there he would have been crushed, if the mechanism of the stone trap had not deteriorated over time. He did not know what had slowed the stone's fall, but he was mightily relieved that it had.

As the stone dust cleared he could see that the passage was comprehensively blocked by the thick blade of stone that had dropped. There was a gap at the top, to be sure, but nowhere near wide enough for him to wriggle through. He had never been claustrophobic but trapped in this small space he was beginning to reconsider that stance.

Rather than stand around bemoaning his fate, Ivan decided to do something useful. He turned back to consider the dog leg passage he had sheltered in. Once again he was facing a heavy wooden door with rusty iron fittings, that had once been painted black. He pressed the latch mechanism down and forced the old door open with his shoulder. It moved reluctantly until it was wide enough for him to slip past. As he stepped into the gap he heard Geordie's voice behind him.

"Ivan! Are you OK?"

"Yes, I'm fine. The block missed me. All I have is a mouthful of granite dust."

"Can you get back out? It looks pretty tight from this side."

"No chance. You'll need to break it down. In the interim I'm going to carry on and see what else we have down here."

"OK, I'll see if I can scare up a sledgehammer or something. Don't go away, will you?"

"Smartarse!"

Ivan heard Geordie move back towards the vestry, then carried on through the doorway. He stopped inside and used his flashlight to check for any other nasty surprises. Seeing nothing, he moved gingerly forward, paying close attention to the feel of the floor beneath his feet. Nothing moved as he reached yet another turn in the narrow, stone lined passage.

He peered around the corner and in the beam from his flashlight he could see a pile of wooden boxes of the type used to transport the gold. He could see that a couple of them had deteriorated over the years and fragments of wood lay on the floor. The larger boxes that might contain the artworks were nowhere in sight. They would have been difficult to manoeuvre through the passage he had travelled, if they were of any significant weight. He stepped forwards.

The boxes were stacked to the low ceiling. He shone his light and looked inside one that the end had fallen off. He could see the dull yellow glow of the gold reflected back at him. He looked around the storage room. It was a dead end. He was stuck in here until the other two smashed the granite blockage out of the way behind him. With nothing else to do he slid down the rough wall to sit on the floor to wait. He shone the flashlight around the small crates, considering how best to move them through the awkward passageway. Clearly the box handles could not be relied on.

He was still considering options when he spotted the slight anomaly in the dressed stone at the edge of his flashlight beam. He stood up stared at the ceiling in the blind end of the passage. Reaching up, he caught his fingers in the slight inconsistency and pulled out a piece of stone. Beneath it he could see a rusty metal ring dangling from a short length of cable that vanished into a crevice in the stonework. He pulled it and was rewarded by a square slab of stone popping upwards by about a finger width. He put the flashlight down on the gold stack, then pushed up on the slab with both hands.

As the stone slab rose slowly he could see the roof beams of the church above him and a wooden pew, to the side. Placing one foot on a gold box, he pushed himself up. Luckily he had chosen a sound one and his head and shoulders emerged in to the church between two pews. He scrambled out and looked around. He was alone but could hear voices from the vestry.

Walking quietly along the threadbare carpet of the main aisle, he approached the vestry door and peeped in.

Geordie and Jim sat with their backs against the wall while the vicar sat on the straight backed wooden chair. They were planning how to get him out of the tomb that had appeared and trapped him.

"I suppose explosives would do the job but the damage to the church would be a worry" said the vicar.

Geordie coughed. "A more immediate worry would be the damage done to Ivan in that enclosed space. The pressure wave would certainly rupture his eardrums and might even rupture his lungs. Either way, he would not be a happy camper."

"A pneumatic power tool might do the job but it would take a lot of time to get the equipment here and to set it up," said Jim, "plus the noise and dust in that enclosed space would be fairly grim for Ivan."

"So we are back to muscle and a fourteen pound sledge hammer to break up the granite. We can probably get one through the gap to Ivan so we could be working from two sides, but it's still a bloody long job and not easy to get a swing in that enclosed space."

Ivan said quietly, "Or we could rub a magic lantern and create another exit for him to climb out of."

The three men spun towards the door. Ivan was gratified to see all three jaws drop open. Jim was the first to recover and he scrambled to his feet. He gripped Ivan's shoulders. "I should have known you'd pull some kind of stunt. How the hell did you get out?"

"Nice to see you too, boss. Glad to see you were worried about me, any chance of another mug of that tea, vicar. My throat's coated in granite dust from the surprise our pals left behind."

Geordie gripped Ivan's arm as the vicar put the kettle on. The relief on his face obvious. "Looks like they'd been watching some old movie about the Pharaoh's tomb when they came up with falling stone doors."

"Luckily for me it didn't drop instantly or I would have been up a certain smelly creek without a paddle, down there."

Jim, still smiling broadly, said, "So is there anything of interest down there? And how the hell did you get yourself out?"

"Let me get this tea down to clear my throat and I'll show you the other entrance." He looked at the vicar's back, then whispered. "And yes, the gold is down there. The new door should also make it a lot easier to retrieve too."

Chapter 49

With the pews moved out of the way for access, the clever counterweight system under the slab became obvious. Getting in and out of the gold chamber was far simpler than struggling through the narrow passage would have been. Now they were faced with the problem of retrieving the gold and keeping it secure while they did so. Geordie sat by the main door of the church with a loaded pistol in his pocket while Ivan walked up the hill, behind the village, to see if there was an Army unit in residence at Westdown Camp that could provide a truck.

Jim heaved the stone slab back into place so that the floor of the church showed no sign of being disturbed, except for the screwdriver he left in place to allow it to be opened from above. He walked outside to the churchyard to make a call on his mobile phone. As he settled down on a gravestone and opened the phone, it rang. It was Helen.

"Jim, is this a good time? I have an interesting idea for you."

"Always a good time for you. What's your idea?"

"You remember you told me that there might have been another vehicle at the bank that granddad has forgotten? I have been trying to get him to recall but with no luck. I think you might be right, he has been telling that tale so long it has become fixed in his mind and he can't go back and think about it another way."

"Sounds possible but how does that help?"

"I was watching a TV show this morning in the kitchen while I made lunch and they had a hypnotherapist on who was talking about getting people to revisit old memories."

"I don't think having your granddad bark like a dog or remember he was Cleopatra in a previous life is going to help much."

"I'm not talking about some stage hypnotist. This is a recognised method of helping people to recall things they have suppressed. Apparently it can help in the case of major trauma. Is it worth a try?"

"Anything is worth a try if it gives me an excuse to come down and see you. How do we get hold of one of these people?"

"I'll sort that out, you just tell me when you can get down here. Anyway, you need to collect that gold bar from me. Granddad was quite excited by it."

"I'm in Tilshead, in the middle of something interesting right now. I'll come back to you as soon as I have sorted some things out."

"I'll look forward to it."

Jim closed the phone down and sat thoughtfully, on the cold stone grave marker for a few moments. Could it work? With no other clues it had to be worth a try. He pulled himself together and opened his phone again. With the team leader's number on speed dial he was soon in touch with the SAS section that had been so much help at their last two sites. He knew these men were effective and trustworthy plus, by using them again, he kept the secret to the minimum number of people.

Within two hours the yellow and white Augusta 109 helicopter from Hereford was landing outside Westdown Camp on the hill overlooking the village. In the middle of a military training area, army uniform would not excite any comment, so the four men in camouflage strolled down into the village then to the church. They wore nondescript berets rather than the distinctive ones used by the SAS, so the only sign that they were unusual was the non-standard weapons they carried.

They strolled up to the door of the church and wandered in. Geordie had been watching them approach and so swung the door wide for them to enter. Jim walked down the aisle to meet them.

The team leader spoke first. "Hello, sir. Got your labourers here again. Anything interesting for us this time? A nice nuclear booby trap perhaps?"

"Sorry, nothing so dramatic. This group relied on gravity rather than explosives for their booby traps. I'll show you what I mean in a minute. The good news is that we will be mostly working inside the church so no cold drizzle to contend with. Plus, the vicar makes a very good mug of tea if you ask him nicely."

"Right then, where do we start?"

"If one of your team can relieve Geordie on over watch he can give us a hand with hauling the material out of its hiding place. Ivan has arranged a truck from the camp and he will bring that in to the graveyard as soon as we are ready to start loading it. So our first job is to get the stuff out and stacked by the door. Then the truck is here for the minimum time to avoid getting the village people curious."

Jim led the way to the slab in the church floor and helped Geordie to raise it. As he did so the vicar walked out of the vestry and along the aisle towards them. Jim straightened and looked at the slightly florid face approaching him.

"Sorry, reverend, I'm going to have to ask you to stay in the vestry for a bit while we deal with this."

"Deal with what? I think my parishioners and I have a right to know what you are taking from under our church."

"In a fair world that would be true, but I am very afraid that I can't allow that."

Jim turned to the young SAS lieutenant and indicated the vicar with a movement of his head. The young man with the cold eyes and the camouflage uniform stepped towards the country vicar and taking him by the arm, steered him towards the vestry. The vicar tried to break free of the grip on his upper arm, but to no avail.

"Never you mind, sir, there's nothing there that will hurt the village and I hear you make a fine mug of tea. Perhaps you would like to show me?"

Jim turned back to the hole in the floor in time to see Geordie drop down through it. A second or two later there was a grunt as Geordie passed up the first box. The men formed an impromptu chain and started passing the boxes to the doorway. The pile slowly grew. As Geordie worked his way down the pile in the cellar, he came to the boxes that had rotted and started to pass up individual bars.

There was a pause. Jim looked down onto his sweating sergeant.

"What's up, Geordie?"

"Just looking at these broken boxes. They are made differently and marked in a language I don't recognise."

He handed up one of the box lids from those that had broken apart. Jim did not recognise the writing either.

One of the SAS men looked over his shoulder and grunted. "Norwegian," he said, "I recognise it from my time doing mountain survival training in the Norwegian winter. Bloody freezing, that was."

"Thanks," said Jim. "I wonder how that got into a hole in the ground in Wiltshire? No matter. You've had your break, Geordie, let's get this finished."

The work continued for another hour and even with their level of physical fitness, they were feeling the strain in their shoulders and backs. Geordie climbed slowly out of the hole in the church floor and stretched to ease his muscles.

"Nice job, Geordie. No doubt your reward will be in heaven."

"If it's OK with you, boss, I'd like to go and get a pint of reward at the Rose and Crown. With all the dust, in the cellar I've got a mouth like the bottom of a parrot's cage."

"I think you've earned that. Ivan brought the truck round while you were caving, so the rest of us can load that while you get a wet."

"Cheers boss, much appreciated" said Geordie, as he slipped quickly out of the church before anybody could object.

Chapter 50

With the borrowed truck loaded and the Special Forces soldiers positioned in the back on guard, they set off for London. As they pulled out of the churchyard Jim saw the vicar, standing in the doorway of his church and gave him a cheery wave before opening up his mobile phone to let Sir Richard know they were coming and to get the Bank of England work party ready to receive them.

The weather was miserable as they drove along the trunk road, then on to the Motorway towards London. Despite the heavy canvas cover, the rain and the blustery wind made the conditions in the rear of the truck deeply unpleasant for the four men in there. Jim and Ivan were reasonably comfortable in the cab of the vehicle, but Jim was very conscious of the men behind him. He checked the map in his lap and looked out through yet another burst of pouring rain.

"Ivan, there is a service area on the motorway just before we get to Farnborough. Pull in there and we will let these drowned rats get a hot coffee, before the final run into London."

"I think they would appreciate that, boss. Plus, the roads might be a bit quieter if we arrive a little later."

The blue and white signs for the service area appeared on their left and Ivan started to slow down. As they came alongside the slip road he changed down a gear and allowed the heavy truck to drift left towards the welcoming signs of the service area. He drove past the car park and around the circuit to the truck parking area. Seeing a gap between two large cargo vehicles, he slipped the Army truck into a place where it would be less obvious to the casual observer. Jim opened the door, jumped down and walked around to the tailgate.

"Alright, gents, a fifteen minute break for you. Get inside, get a coffee, get a bit warm and then we are back on the road again."

The young team leader was the first out of the back of the vehicle. He walked across to where Jim stood watching the remaining Special Forces men climb down and stretch. Geordie joined them, having parked the hire car nearby.

"What about you and Ivan, boss? Are you going to get something?"

"No, we'll stay here with the cargo. If you could bring a couple of takeout coffees back with you, that would be appreciated."

"Will do," said Geordie, setting off after the other four soldiers towards the buildings where they could get a coffee and a break from the damp, cold truck.

Jim took a look round the heavy green truck before climbing up into the back to get out of the rain. With large cargo vehicles either side of them and with Ivan looking forwards he felt they were sufficiently secure. He heard the air brakes of another vehicle pulling into the parking area but thought nothing of it until a hand appeared on the tailgate of the truck he was sitting in, rapidly followed by a face and the other hand holding a Sterling submachine gun.

"I guess you must be the Major?" said the newcomer. "You sit very still and you might just get out of this with a whole skin."

Jim said nothing. The empty feeling in his stomach said it all for him. How the hell could he have been so stupid? The ease of the first two recoveries had lulled him into a false sense of security and now he was paying for it.

A second man climbed over the tailgate and sat on the side board of the truck. He too carried a Sterling and Jim noted uneasily that the cocking handle was pulled back. The weapon was ready to fire. At a range of less than eight feet an automatic weapon firing 9mm bullets could make an awful mess of him.

He felt the vehicle rock slightly as a third man climbed into the cab alongside Ivan. The first man stepped down from the tailgate, pulled out the locking pins and allowed it to fall open. Jim could now see five men behind the truck. With another in the cab there were at least six of them. A medium sized cargo truck backed up, guided by yet another man. That made at least eight of them. The back doors of the smaller truck were swung open from inside. Nine.

Jim's mind raced but he could see no way out of this. He watched as two of the armed men took up position to watch for the return of his people. They would be walking across a wide open tarmac parking lot and would have no chance no matter how well trained they were.

The first man spoke again, "Now, Major, I guess you are trying desperately to work out how to leap from the truck and overpower us all, or something equally heroic. Not a good idea, I promise you. Any of us would be delighted to have an excuse to blow you into the middle of next week, so you stay quiet and do as you're told like good little soldiers should."

Jim said nothing. It would be at least ten minutes before his men came back and he needed to find a way to warn them before that.

Chapter 51

Geordie stood in the small queue at the coffee bar and contemplated the menu options. Three of the SAS men were sitting close to the radiator in the corner of the café while the fourth picked up the order for all of them. The truck driver waiting in the queue behind him cleared his throat.

"I know you guys are trying to avoid the cross loading but I'm in a bit of a rush here, mate."

Geordie turned and looked at him. "What cross loading?"

"The cross loading from your truck into that smaller one."

Geordie blinked. "Best you take my place in the queue, mate. I need a leak anyway."

Geordie turned away from the coffee bar and walked into the corner of the café, careful not to rush and draw attention. He reached the table and sat down.

"I think we've got trouble, guys."

"How so?" said the team leader.

"The truckie at the bar thinks we are spinning out our time in here until the cross loading from our vehicle has finished. I think we might want to go now, eh?"

The four other men at the table looked at each other and then stood. The team leader gestured for them all to leave the café and they followed him into the large open entry hall where they would not be overheard.

"Right, gents, nice open truck park between us and the problem would make a wonderful killing ground. We need to go out the other side of the building and circle around out of sight but quickly. We should carry out a recon, but I think we need to get out before they expect us. Agreed?"

They all nodded and looked around for another exit. "We'll use that fire door over there on the motorway side of the building. John and Paul go left, use the embankment alongside the motorway for cover. Mike, you are with me going right. We circle around into firing positions and if necessary open fire together. A cross fire should ruin their day rather nicely, I expect. But if possible get in close; we don't want any civilians getting involved"

"What about me?" said Geordie.

"That pistol of yours is pretty useless for this job, so stay inside the building and don't let any civilians come out towards the trucks. The last thing we need is for these bastards to take hostages."

"But ....."

"No buts. We don't have time. Digging big holes is your thing, this is ours. Guard the door."

Geordie moved to the main exit doors and took a position to ensure nobody could get past him. He watched the four Special Forces soldiers disappear through the fire exit and move rapidly left and right.

Geordie turned to look through the sliding glass doors to the vehicles standing in the truck park. He could see the radiator grill of the smaller vehicle that had backed up to their army vehicle, in between the two large articulated trucks. Even knowing they were there he could see no sign of the attackers. He could see no sign of the four soldiers either. The temptation to pull his pistol and run to the aid of his friends was strong, but military discipline held him in place.

Out of the truck now, Jim watched the hijackers moving the boxes of gold across into their own vehicle. They were working hard and fast, paying him no attention. The man guarding him, with an automatic weapon, from less than ten feet away gave him no chance to act. His frustration with himself was intense, but he tried to calm down and gain as much information as possible, to pass on to the police, to try and catch this group once they moved off.

"So, how had you planned this robbery if I hadn't been stupid enough to stop here?"

The man guarding him grinned. "Oh, don't worry, we had it all set up. You had about three more miles to run before we pushed you off the road with our other truck. She's a thirty eight tonne Volvo, you wouldn't have stood a chance. At least this way, you lot get to live. Provided you don't do anything stupid, of course."

"You can't hope to get away with this. Every copper in the country will be looking for you."

"Don't you worry about that, Major. We have a really nice plan all sorted out and it's going to work a treat."

"Not sure you're right about that son" said Jim as the SAS Trooper, known as John, rose silently behind the guard from under the truck they were next to. The soldier grabbed the robber's neck in a nerve pinch and reached around to grab his submachine gun as he passed out. He eased the inert body of the guard to the ground and handed the Sterling to Jim.

"There you go, sir, something for you to play with. Follow me under the truck."

He slipped quietly under the Army vehicle and waited until Jim joined him. He held his finger to his lips and then showed Jim five fingers, then four, then three in a silent countdown. As he reached zero the three remaining Special Forces men stepped out of their hiding places in front and behind the two screening trucks and moved swiftly to cover the sweating robbers labouring to move the gold. They had all put down their weapons to allow them to work except for the two men who had been watching the buildings and waiting for the soldiers to return from their coffee break. These two spun round with their weapons raised as soon as they realised what was going on behind them.

It was a foolish mistake. The two troopers on that side of the work detail fired two shots each, in a classic double tap and the two guards dropped to the ground. By now Jim and his rescuer had emerged from under the truck and the remaining members of the gang had no option but to surrender. Jim walked to the passenger door of his own vehicle and tapped gently on the side window. The attacker guarding Ivan turned and looked down into the barrel of the submachine gun that Jim held steadily pointing between his eyes. Without a word, he handed his own weapon to Ivan and then turned away from the window to be met by a very effective Welsh fist, powered by hard muscle and anger. Jim reached up and opened the door, to allow the limp body of the unconscious man to slither to the ground.

Ivan looked at Jim "Our turn for coffee then, is it?"

Chapter 52

With submachine guns all around them, the would be robbers transferred the gold, they had already moved, back into the Army vehicle. Once that was finished, the two dead men were picked up and loaded into the smaller truck along with the two unconscious ones. The remaining robbers had their hands secured behind them and they too were loaded into the same truck and the doors closed behind them.

Ivan walked across to the buildings to allow Geordie to stop blocking the doorway to the increasingly irate group of truck drivers who wanted to complete their journeys. His story about a military exercise happening in the truck park had worn thin and he was seriously contemplating drawing his pistol to keep the truckers inside and safe. He thanked them all profusely for their cooperation and walked back with Ivan to find Jim on his mobile phone.

Jim closed the phone as they approached. "Hampshire Constabulary are on their way and I have asked that they bring their Special Branch people with them. If they treat these people as terrorists we will have more control over them. Plus, they can be interrogated for longer."

"So how did they know to attack us? They must have been tipped off by somebody. Do you reckon it could have been the vicar?"

Jim shook his head. "Not likely. They would not have had time to organise this between us leaving Tilshead and now. No, it took time to set this up and to get the people and arms together. The vicar never had chance to call anyone while we were shifting the gold."

"Well," said Ivan, "if not him then who the hell was it tipped these buggers off?"

"Good question and well phrased. I don't know, but we need to find out quickly. Hopefully out friends in blue can persuade them to tell. And speaking of which, here they are."

The three of them turned to watch four police cars swing into the truck park at high speed with the blue lights flashing, but no sirens. They skidded to a halt and police officers boiled out.

The senior officer looked around, then said "Is one of you Major Wilson?"

"That's me," said Jim, stepping forward "I'm afraid I am dumping you with a pile of paperwork as we have to get going."

"You can't leave the scene of a crime without making statements and satisfying me about what went on here. You said, on the phone, there had been some fatalities so you are certainly not leaving."

"We certainly are," said Jim, pulling the Prime Minister's authority letter from his pocket. "Read this and get your Chief Constable to phone that number if you need to."

The Police Inspector looked up from the letter and then towards the panel truck that held the prisoners. He turned and followed the two trails of blood from where the guards had been shot and noticed the blood dripping from the bottom of the truck's doors.

"Bloody hell. What's been happening here?"

"As far as you are concerned it's a terrorist attack on an Army vehicle. There are other things going on that will not appear in your report or in the press, at least not yet. You need to make sure those prisoners do not get any messages out to anyone.

Their mobile phones and their weapons are in the cab of their truck for you."

"OK, Major, let me check with my Chief Constable before you rush away. While I'm doing that you can explain to my Sergeant just what the hell went on here."

"Will do. Sergeant, would you like to come over to the van and we can start dealing with your prisoners?"

Jim and the police sergeant walked to the rear doors of the attackers' truck. The soldiers moved to cover them with their weapons at the ready. The police officer looked around a little uncomfortably.

"Do we really need all the artillery, sir? We are quite used to handling criminals."

"Ah, Sergeant, these are terrorists rather than ordinary criminals and my people are taking no chances with them."

Jim swung open the back door of the truck. As he had expected, the men inside were on their feet and ready to make a concerted break for freedom even though their hands were bound. As they tensed to jump they saw five loaded and cocked submachine guns pointed at them and decided against an escape.

"See my point yet, Sergeant? said Jim, smiling slightly.

"I do, sir. OK, all of you people already on your feet, get out one at a time and form a line over there. Sir, if your men could keep them covered while my officers get them out of your bondage gear and into proper handcuffs, then into our vehicles, that would really help."

The prisoners stepped down obediently and walked to the area the sergeant had indicated. The police officers waiting there quickly handcuffed them and stood them facing the large truck next to them. One of the prisoners dropped to the ground and rolled under the truck. As he stood up on the other side, ready to run he found himself facing Geordie, who was now armed with one of the Sterlings.

"Now, bonny lad, did you really think we were that stupid? Get back under there and join your mates before I get cross with you."

On the other side of the vehicle, the sergeant was now staring into the back of the robbers' truck at the four bodies lying there.

"Four dead? That's going to be a lot of paper work."

"Shouldn't be four," said Jim looking over the Sergeant's shoulder, "only two of them were shot as they tried to open fire on us. One irritated my Sergeant Major and I think he has a broken jaw. The other one was knocked out by some kind of Vulcan Death Grip, I have no idea how. You'll have to ask Spock here," he said, indicating a grinning SAS Trooper.

"Now sir" he replied "you must know there is no such thing as a Vulcan Death Grip, all the Trekkers know that. I got him with a nerve pinch to the neck. That stops them yelling or moving. Then push on a pressure point to switch the lights out. He should come round within the hour with just a stinking headache and a stiff neck."

"Where the devil did you learn that?" asked the Police Sergeant.

"Hereford"

"Ahh, that explains a lot. Never mind."

The police inspector came around the side of the truck, putting his mobile phone back in his pocket as he walked. He looked at Jim with more respect than before.

"Seems you were right sir. You will be leaving here without making statements and it seems these men are indeed terrorists. My Chief Constable has despatched two unmarked cars to escort you onwards. Our armed response team will be in them just in case there are any more of these beggars around. They should be here in about fifteen minutes."

"I was rather hoping to be gone by then, Inspector."

"Sir, if I am cleaning up this mess and breaking Lord knows how many regulations and laws, you could wait for fifteen minutes to make my Chief Constable happy, couldn't you?"

"I could and would you thank the Chief when you report to him about our little adventure? I'm sure he'll be calling for you to give him a personal debrief."

"He already has, so maybe you could give me a few details. Like what you have in that truck for instance and why some of your men are carrying non-standard weapons."

"I wish I could but I'm afraid you already have all the information I am able to give you. However, I do need something from you. I need to know who set these people on to us. We have been keeping a low profile so it's quite worrying. I don't suppose you would let one of my specialists here have a word with one of the prisoners?"

"No, sir. That is one line I'm not crossing. They will be interrogated hard but without any crude coercion."

The one Jim had nicknamed Spock looked aggrieved at that "My coercion is anything but crude I'll have you know. Painful it may be, but far from crude."

Chapter 53

The rush hour in London was running down as they left the motorway and headed through the city to the Bank of England. The escorting police cars made the journey easier, but even they could not clear the crush of cars out of the way all the time, so it was fully dark by the time they reached the bank. As the heavy Army truck pulled around to the vehicle entrance the armed police placed their cars both sides of the doorway and took up positions watching the street. The five soldiers from the back of the truck dropped the tailgate and climbed down stiffly.

Jim opened the passenger door and dropped to the floor of the unloading bay. Sir Richard was there to greet him with an outstretched hand and a surprisingly warm smile.

"Well, you did it again. Tilshead this time, eh? Never heard of it myself and I hear you had some excitement on the way back with your spoils? Maybe you should think again about taking my security people along as back up?"

Jim looked at the Governor for a second before replying. "Maybe we should, but the problem was handled rather well by my people."

"How will you keep this event out of the press? It could attract far too much of the wrong kind of attention."

"I'm aware of that, Sir Richard. I've got the Hampshire Police to agree to hold the attackers on terrorism charges. With an armed attack on a British Army truck in broad daylight it seems quite plausible to me. And that way they can be held without seeing a lawyer for seven days. By which time we will have disappeared back into the woodwork."

"Good enough. Would you like to watch my people unload your truck?"

"I would, but I think my lot would like to go and stand by a hot air duct somewhere, its bloody cold in the back of one of these vehicles on a day like this."

Sir Richard called one of the bank employees over and instructed her to take the five soldiers off to a coffee room to get warmed up. He then re-joined Jim, plus Ivan, who had also come over to watch the unloading. With the gold safely stored in the massive vault, Jim and Ivan took their leave having first collected the others. They drove back up the ramp to the street where Jim asked Ivan to stop the truck. He jumped down and went across to the police officers to thank them for their help and to release them back to their normal duties.

Jim climbed back into the cab of the truck and sat looking through the windscreen as the two police cars drove away. He leaned back in his seat and tossed his beret on to the narrow dashboard. Ivan paused before he restarted the engine.

"I know that look, boss. What's biting you?"

"Ivan, how the hell did Sir Richard know we were in Tilshead and how did he know we had been attacked? And another thing, the first one of the thieves over the tailgate knew I was a Major before he had chance to see my rank badges. He had been briefed."

"Are you sure you didn't mention where we were to Sir Richard when you told him we were coming in?"

"I'm sure."

"Then we seem to have a little mystery to solve. Where to?"

"Let's drop the truck at Chelsea Barracks. The Guards can take it back to Westdown Camp tomorrow and I think we could all do with a night's sleep in their transit accommodation."

Ivan started the engine and pulled the heavy vehicle out onto the street. Rush hour was long over and the streets of the capital were quiet. Ivan drove in silence for a while until he turned into Birdcage Walk, to reach the barracks.

"Boss, you don't really think the Governor of the Bank of England could be the one who set us up for those scumbags do you?"

"I don't know. Four tons of gold is an awful lot of money even for Sir Richard. So I don't know, I just don't know."

Chapter 54

The next morning the three team members took a brisk walk back up Birdcage Walk to Parliament Square and into 100 Parliament Street where they had their office. The first order of business was to get themselves a rather good English breakfast in the staff restaurant. They filled their trays and sat at a table remote enough to allow them to speak freely.

Jim swallowed the last of his Lincolnshire sausage and said, "Ivan, I need you to follow up on the last part of that daft verse we picked up in Morecambe. Some nonsense about a cave. Trawl the Internet and anything else you need to find us any possible locations."

"Will do. What are you going to be doing?"

"Geordie and I are going to West Sussex to watch a demonstration of hypnosis on Helen's granddad."

"What the devil for?"

"Apparently it can help him remember things he has forgotten or repressed. We're going to see if he can recall where the rest of the gold went that night."

"Good luck with that. I'm betting I'll have more luck finding a cave."

They parted at the lifts. Ivan headed up to the fifth floor to start his research and the other two set off to catch the train to Horsham. From there they grabbed a taxi to take them into Henfield where they hoped Helen would be waiting with the hypnosis expert as she had promised. They paid off the taxi outside the neat bungalow and walked towards the gate to the garden path.

"We're being watched, boss."

"I'd be surprised if we weren't, a Geordie down here is rarer than a singing rocking horse. They are probably trying to identify what species you are."

The door opened. Helen stood there waiting for them, looking as lovely as ever. She kissed Jim lightly on the cheek and smiled at Geordie as they walked into the hallway.

"Come on through," she said, showing them into the lounge. "This is Katie; she's a friend from the psychology department and a qualified hypnotherapist. Granddad will be through in a minute."

The stocky woman with kind eyes stood up and shook their hands. "Do we have to do the whole barking dogs and clucking chicken routine or do you know the difference between hypnotherapy and stage hypnotism?"

"Helen put me straight on that when she suggested getting your help and I briefed Geordie on the way down here, so we are just here to see if you can help Mr Greenly to remember a special night in 1940."

"What happened back then?"

"I'm really sorry but I can't tell you that and you really must not ask him. All we need to know is, was there a fifth truck there being loaded, or was the cargo they were loading taken away somehow?"

"It sounds important?"

"It is. But it would be damaging if too much was known about it. I promise you it's nothing illegal."

Katie looked over Jim's shoulder as Mr Greenly shuffled in. He seemed unsteady on his feet and looked tired. Jim looked at Helen who smiled and nodded. "He'll be fine. In fact, Katie tells me he will sleep like a baby afterwards and wake up feeling a lot better."

The old man moved slowly to his chair next to the fireplace and sat down with a groan. He did not seem to have noticed there was anyone else in the room.

Katie nodded to Helen who stood up, closed the curtains and the door. Katie waited until Helen had resumed her seat and there were no more distractions. The two men had been warned to sit still and keep quiet during the session. She moved the dining chair she was sitting on alongside Harold's armchair and started to speak to him. Her voice was low and comforting. She did not use any equipment but just allowed her words to wash over him.

Jim watched, fascinated. This bore no relation to the stage hypnosis he had once seen. The warm voice continued, always soft and always reassuring. He could see the old man sink into the chair as he relaxed and his head fell slowly backwards. Jim thought he must be asleep. Now the voice changed slightly as Katie steered Harold's mind back in time to the night when he had loaded trucks during an air raid. The old man's body did not move but his head swung slowly left and right as he visualised.

Katie spoke again "So tell me Harold, how many trucks are you loading?"

"Four. All removal vans from all over the country. Strange they are being driven by men in uniform."

"Harold, have another look. Are you sure there are only four?"

"Yes, I'm sure just the four. No wait. There's another one. It's not a removal van. it's a cargo lorry with a canvas back on it."

"Tell me about the lorry. What colour is it? Does it have an owner's name on it?"

"It's difficult to tell the colour in the dark. It might be black; no its dark green, I just saw it when the searchlight swung by overhead. There are letters on the side, quite big ones."

"What are the letters Harold?"

"It's a G then a V then an R. No, the second letter is W. There was a rope hanging over it. GWR, that's it."

"Is there anything else you can tell me about that lorry, Harold."

"The soldier driving it has an accent. It's difficult to understand him, he slurs his words together and when he says an R it sort of rolls."

"Can you read the number plate or any other writing on the lorry?"

"No, that's all there is. It's too dark to see the plate."

Jim leaned forward and whispered to Katie. She nodded and turned back to the old man.

"Harold, one of the vans has a painting on it. A horse and cart, I think. Is there anything else you could tell me about that one?"

"Horse and cart on the van side, yes. The cart has a flower on its side. It's white, a white rose."

Katie turned and looked at Jim, who nodded. She turned back to the old man in the chair and still in her soft mellifluous voice brought his mind back to the present. She assured him he had done well and suggested he might like to go for a lie down, to sleep for a while. His eyes opened and he looked dazedly around the room before pushing himself out of his chair with a groan and shuffling to the door. He left the room and they all waited until they heard his bedroom door close before they spoke.

"That was remarkable, Katie" said Jim, "thank you so much for that. Now we just need to work out what GWR means."

"God's Wonderful Railway," said Geordie.

"What?"

"It's the old Nickname for the Great Western Railway. All the old steam train drivers used to call it that. It used to run from London down to the West Country."

"How on earth did you know that?" said Helen.

"I'm a Geordie and steam trains are in the DNA. The first commercial passenger railway in the world was the Stockton to Darlington line up in Geordie Land. My old granddad drove locomotives for the LNER right up to the day he died. Had a heart attack on the footplate right in the station. He was dead before they could lift him down."

"Well, you learn something every day. I thought the first real railways were in London."

"No, George Stephenson was a Geordie boy like me. In fact, it's down to him that people from the North East are called Geordie's in the first place."

Helen smiled. "Go on then tell us the tale."

"It came from the coal mines. George Stephenson developed a safety lamp for miners and then Davey developed what he said was a better one. All the mines changed over to the Davey Lamp except up in the North East where they stayed with the lamp they called the Geordie Lamp and so the Geordies got their name."

"Is that true or just one of your tall tales?"

"As true as the fact that me and Katie here are going to the pub for a pie and a pint while you two talk about how wonderful I am. Come on Katie, you can tell me how you got into this black magic skill of yours."

As they stood Helen said, "Thanks, Geordie, we'll join you shortly."

"No problem, Helen, but don't call me shorty."

Geordie and Katie were still giggling about the childish joke as they closed the front door. Jim and Helen watched them go and sat down on the sofa holding hands like a couple of besotted teenagers.

"Can you stay at all?" she said

"Sorry, I can't. But this session with your Granddad gives us a new lead and if that pays off I'd like to take you away somewhere without anybody we know around."

"That sounds good. Do you have anywhere in mind?"

"Not yet, I'll work on it. Oh and by the way, you'd better let me have that gold bar now unless the beer in the pub has become very, very expensive?"

They kissed and he held her close. She sighed and said, "We'd better get over to the pub or they'll think we're up to something."

Chapter 55

Back in London, Jim and Geordie met up with Ivan to compare notes about the progress they had made. Jim described the hypnotherapy and the way the old man had gone back in time, to visualise the scene in the street outside the bank.

"All good, but where does it take us? The GWR must have used a lot of trucks, how do we trace that one? They were operating the railways throughout Devon, Dorset, Cornwall and heaven knows how many other counties. Their trucks could have been going all over the place."

"I've been thinking about that. This was wartime with strict rationing in place. Fuel was very limited for non-military use. Trucks of that time could not have made it up from the West Country to London and back again on one tank of fuel. They must have authorised it to collect fuel in London or issued spare cans. Either way, somebody might have signed off on it. If there are records from that time we might drop lucky."

"Worth a go."

"Plus we have Geordie here who is something of a steam train fan. He could be our wild card when going through the records. He can probably chat up the record keeper by talking about ancient trains."

"No need to take the mickey, boss."

"I'm not. I'm deadly serious. These records have probably been archived and the sort of people who look after ancient records are commonly interested in whatever was going on at the time. You make friends with them and it could be damned useful."

"I'd better read up a bit more about the GWR so I can convince them, eh, boss?"

"Go ahead, buy a couple of books if you think that will help. Now, Ivan, what did your search reveal?"

"Well it was going nowhere very fast until you called about the white rose on the side of the van. That narrowed it down to Yorkshire, the white rose county. Still it's the biggest county of them all so there was plenty to look for."

"And what did you find?"

"There are a number of caves in the Dales but nothing in them suggests the rich people that get mentioned in that crap verse, so I kept on looking. Then I found that there are two villages near Hull that are called North Cave and South Cave."

"Sounds promising. Did it lead anywhere?"

"I think it may have. In South Cave there is a manor house called Cave Castle, built back in 1780 something, that has now been converted into a Hotel, Spa and Golf Complex. Looks quite a nice place, judging by the website."

"That would fit. So did you book us in there?"

"I did indeed. And I took the liberty of booking you a double room in case Helen wants to join us again. She was quite useful in Castleton. She could help with chatting up the staff if we need to."

"Nice thought. I'll give her a call and see if she's free.

As he stood and walked down the room to use his mobile phone he did not see the smiles his two men exchanged.

Chapter 56

Having met up with Helen at Kings Cross Railway Station in London, the four companions travelled north together and left the train at Brough. As they carried their bags across the lattice metal footbridge to the station exit they could see the waters of the wide, muddy Humber River reflecting the late afternoon sunlight between the village houses. A short taxi ride brought them to the village of South Cave and, in the centre of the village, to the gothic gate house of Cave Castle. The driveway sloped up from the gatehouse, past manicured lawns and an attractive duck pond, before swinging round to the car park in front of the impressive main building.

Jim paid off the taxi as the other three retrieved their bags and walked into the hotel reception area. They were looking around as Jim joined them.

"Nice place for a government funded holiday," said Helen. "Are you sure we are in the right place?"

"Not really, no. This is the place Ivan came up with based on the clues we had, including your granddad coming up with the white rose of Yorkshire painted on one of the vans. We'll just have to have a sniff around and see what we come up with."

With that, they wandered to the reception desk and checked in. Having dropped their meagre luggage in their rooms they met up in the bar area for a coffee. They made their way to a table set in a bay window overlooking the grounds.

"Ivan, did your research indicate anywhere we should start looking?"

"I've got nothing, boss. All I came up with was this place as a likely location. After that we just have to start looking, as you said?"

"That's what my understanding was, I just wanted to make sure we were all on the same page. My thinking is we might all split up tomorrow and follow various trails."

"Works for me, boss," said Geordie. "Do you want to divide up the jobs now? I don't mind searching the wine cellar, if they have one."

"That's really big of you but I have a slightly different idea. Helen, will you take the hotel? Chat up the staff and the management, see if they have heard any rumours or old stories. Try and get a guided tour of the non-public areas. Ivan and Geordie, I've got you down for some prowling around the grounds. This is quite a big property and there are various bits of woodland on it. It's seventy years or more since the hides were built, the ground could have shifted or eroded and something might be visible if you're alert for it. And before you ask, no I'm not going to lounge in the bar. I'm going to try and find out about the Home Guard they had around here, where they based themselves, et cetera. and see if there are any records. Now, how about dinner? We could also investigate to see if their wine cellar has anything nice in it."

Ivan and Geordie headed straight for the dining room, leaving Jim and Helen to follow in their own time.

Helen looked at Jim. "So do you want me to start chatting up the staff tonight?"

"No, I thought we might have an early night."

"I was hoping you might say that. Shall we skip dinner entirely or eat later?"

Without another word she stood up from the table and headed towards the wide staircase. Jim gulped the last of his wine and set off in pursuit. As they climbed the stairs he admired the shapely legs climbing in front of him and the way she held herself as she walked.

She stopped at the door of their room and as she fumbled the key into the lock he reached up and slowly started to unzip her dress. She turned the key, pushed the door open and turned to him with a secret smile.

"My, we are eager, aren't we?"

He stepped into the room, gripped her shoulders and kissed her while kicking the door shut behind them.

Chapter 57

Breakfast the next morning was well up to the standard of the dinner the night before and they sat looking out across the golf course as the mist slowly cleared, sipping on the excellent coffee. Jim put down his empty cup and sighed.

"Well, I suppose I had better get you all started or we'll be sitting here in the warm all day. You all happy with your assignments?"

"We'll be fine as long as the rain holds off and Helen here can get us some recommendations about the wine for lunch during her chatting up," Geordie said.

"I'll see if I can find the local vicar and the local library, if they have one in a village this size."

"It might be worth skimming through the Internet as well to see if there are any mentions of this village during the war," said Helen. "Though I imagine it was a bit of a sleepy hollow back then."

"Not as much as you might think, there is an aircraft factory in Brough, the village where we got off the train and it was here during the war. Hull got quite a pasting from the Luftwaffe, so I think they might have been waiting for the Germans to land around here."

"That makes this sound a bit more promising," said Helen, as they stood up to go their separate ways.

Four hours later they met up in the reception area, ready to go in for lunch. Geordie and Ivan had muddy boots and wet trousers, so went up to their rooms to change while Jim and Helen went into the bar to wait for them. There were two pints of cold beer on the bar waiting for the two men as they returned.

Both of them reached for the glasses and downed half of them before drawing a breath.

"Thanks for that, boss" said Ivan, "I was spitting feathers after all that blundering about in the woods."

"Did you find anything?"

"Brambles, lots of bloody brambles and rabbit holes. I think I have stumbled on just about every rabbit hole in Yorkshire today. I may even have used a bad word or two."

Geordie smiled. "I could hear him across the greens. Good job there weren't any golfers about this morning, you'd have quite put them off their stroke."

"What about you Geordie, anything?"

"Sorry, boss, no. But there's a lot more to look at yet. This place has about 150 acres or more, plus the farm land around it. Going slowly, it could take a couple of days just to walk it thoroughly:"

"Helen, any joy?"

"Some, but I'm not sure it takes us anywhere. The house was built in 1787 and has had a number of owners. It was pretty run down during the war and just after but, as you can see, it has been improved. It was built on the site of the original castle which dates back to Norman times, though there are very few traces left. One piece that might be interesting, in 1866 they found an underground passage that led from the site of the old buildings direct to the Parish Church which you can just see behind the trees at the back of here."

"Nothing else? No rumours, ghost stories, anything like that?"

"Not that I have been able to find so far. How about you?"

"Not bad, as it happens. It turns out there was activity around here from the Auxiliary Units. The local group had three of what they called patrols. One here in South Cave, one in North Cave and another in Brough. Not long ago a cache of improvised explosives was found in a wood, on the far side of this village, called the Little Wold Plantation and there is a statement in the records that the Auxiliary Units had their Operational Base there, although the OB itself has yet to be found. The one in North Cave has been found and there are photographs of it on the internet."

"So, are we looking in the wrong place?"

"I don't think so. We know that the gold was entrusted to special groups who would have been separate to the operational patrols. This still seems like a good location to search."

"What's the plan after lunch?"

"More of the same, I'm afraid. Although I'm going to spend some time tramping the woods with you two. Looks like Helen is going to be the only one staying dry."

Chapter 58

Jim was slogging through a dripping wood looking for any signs of a base that had been exposed by weather, erosion or land slip and finding nothing. With no leads, finding a small base that had gone undetected for over seventy years was starting to look like a wild goose chase. The clues were thin and the weather miserable. He was ready to give up on this thankless search when he felt the vibration of his mobile phone in the damp pocket of his trousers. He took it out and flipped it open, checking the caller ID, as he did so.

"Yes, Helen? I really hope you have found something."

"Sorry, I just thought I would call to see how you are doing? I've spoken to all the staff now and I have had the grand tour of all the non-public rooms and there is nothing obvious here. Unless you have any better clues we could be searching here for a year and still find nothing."

"I know. I'll talk to you when we get back in."

He wiped a rain drop from the end of his nose and felt a cold trickle of rain that had found its way inside the back of his jacket. This was a waste of time and effort. He lifted his phone to call Ivan and Geordie to stand them down when it vibrated in his hand and that annoying tune played again. He really must get round to changing that ring tone. He pressed the green button and took the call.

"Yes, Ivan. Are you as fed up as me?"

"Maybe not, boss. Do you remember that book you showed us, on the train, about the Auxiliary Units? There was a picture in there of an outside latrine that was used to cover the entrance to one of the hides. Well, I've found a disused latrine covered in vegetation deep in one of the woods. Fancy a look round? Geordie is already on his way."

"Where are you?"

Ivan described his location and Jim set off across the empty fairway towards the piece of woodland that Ivan was searching. He blundered through the brambles to find Geordie and Ivan standing next to a small, dilapidated, three-sided hut with a roof that was long gone and a rotten wooden door that lay in front of it.

"Having fun, boss? I think this just might brighten your day."

Ivan turned and reached down to lift the remains of a wooden seat that had once served the earth closet toilet. He looked at Jim and Geordie like a magician about to produce a startled rabbit.

"If you look down in here with the flashlight you can just see a metal ring set into the wall of the shaft. Don't worry, all the dung has long rotted away. At least, I hope so."

Jim and Geordie looked into the dank, dark and dismal hole. Just peeping out of the forward wall was a small, rusty metal ring.

"Have you tried it, Ivan?"

"Not yet. I thought you might like to have first go at shoving your hand into the toilet?"

"Thanks. Very thoughtful of you. Well, I suppose it must be my turn."

Jim leaned in to the damp hole and reached down to the ring. It was rusty and slimy in his hand. He took a grip and pulled it outwards towards the centre of the shaft. There was definitely something attached to it. He pulled harder and felt something give way with a small clunk. He pulled again and the edge of a horizontal door became visible. He forced his thumbs into the small opening that had appeared and pushed out and down. The door gave way and fell across the latrine shaft. The three men stood and looked down at the slimy, muddy and heavily rusted metal plate below them.

"Well, I don't fancy trusting my weight to that. Not with what is probably down at the bottom of the hole. Even if it is seventy years old."

"Ivan, how could fossilised poo hurt you? You must have been in worse holes over the years?"

"I probably have, but not voluntarily."

Jim knelt down and leaned into the hole. Where the metal plate had been he could now see an opening that led down into the earth. Without the metal plate to stand on first, it would be impossible to scramble down without a serious risk of falling to the bottom of the shaft, however far that might be. He stood and looked around.

"With ropes slung from that tree," he said, "we should be able to belay down and into the entrance shaft fairly safely. That should also make it safer and easier getting back out if we can't find the secondary access."

Ivan and Geordie contemplated the tree Jim had pointed at and nodded slowly.

"It's going to take a while to set that up and we don't have any rope with us this time. I doubt we could be ready to try it until well after dark."

"You're right, Geordie. Let's get this closed up again and make sure there is no sign we have been here. Then let's head back to the hotel. I'm ready to get out of these wet clothes and into a cold beer about now anyway."

Chapter 59

The next morning found the three soldiers back at their latrine, with climbing ropes borrowed from the South Cave Scout Troop. Geordie scrambled up the overhanging tree and fixed the ropes in place, then dropped them down to Ivan who fed them into the latrine opening through the space where the roof had once been. Geordie slid down the rope hand over hand and landed next to Jim.

"Alright, so who gets the joy of climbing down into a disused toilet?"

"Since you two don't seem too enthusiastic I guess it's my turn. Unless you object, Ivan?"

"No, I think I'm with Geordie on this one. I would hate you to feel you hadn't been a full part of the search."

"Thanks, that's really big of you both."

Jim stepped up onto the lip of the latrine pit and slowly lowered himself down to the access opening. Had he been able to stand on the lowered door it would have been far easier but, with that rotted away by metal corrosion, he had no choice but to use the rope to swing in. His feet struck the far side of the access passage and he slowly walked himself down the damp wall. Once fully inside he could lower himself down to the floor below. He stood and looked back into the latrine pit. The lip of the access opening was level with the middle of his chest. With the drop down door useable it would have been a simple climb back out.

Crouching down and turning on the lamp on his caving helmet, he found a narrow horizontal passage, leading away from the pit. He checked carefully for booby traps and then moved slowly into the low passage. After three steps he came to a right angled turn to the left, then he could see another turn, to the right this time. He recalled that when he was shown the hide at Coleshill a blast wall had been built to protect the base from grenades that might be tossed in. The turns in the passage would have served the same purpose.

He shuffled forward and reached the right turn. As his head lamp swept the area he saw a boot lying on the concrete floor. He moved his head to sweep the beam of his light and found the other boot, then the trouser legs of the body that was lying there with its grinning skull up against the wall of the room he was about to enter. He swept the headlight beam backwards and forwards picking up the shapes of the grenade fragments that lay around.

He shone the light back onto the crumpled remains. The skull had a few remnants of skin and hair still attached, but most of the bone shone a dull white. The finger bones jutted out from the remains of the jacket sleeves and he could see ribs where the shirt had rotted away. Very clearly, this had happened quite some time ago.

He moved back to the entrance and was about to shout when he heard Helen talking to his two men. He would have to keep her out of here. He did not want her to see the grisly remains in this dark, mournful place.

"Ivan! Geordie!"

The entry way darkened as the big Welshman leaned in. "Yes, boss? Have you made it round the 'U Bend' yet?"

"Ivan, you need to keep Helen from coming down here. I've found a body and it's in pretty poor state. Once we have completed the search we are going to have to notify the police about this. Somebody is missing a relative."

"Can you tell what happened?"

"Pretty sure it was a grenade and in that enclosed space, with all the ricochets, I think it was damned effective."

"Do you need me to come down?"

"Not yet. I'll complete the search and then we can decide what to do next."

Jim moved back along the passage and stepped carefully over the remains. He moved further into the bunker until he reached the remains of a wooden door at the other end of the room. The wood was rotten and crumbled into a soggy brown pile of fragments, as he pushed it. He leaned through the doorway and swept his headlight around the chamber beyond. It was empty. Only a few paper and wood fragments were scattered on the concrete floor.

He checked again for further booby traps and entered the chamber. Examining the paper he found that anything written on it had long gone in the damp conditions. The wood was different though. He could still read the markings. He picked a piece up to examine it and like the door, it crumbled to nothing recognisable. Moving to the next piece he shone his light on it without touching it. With a sinking feeling in the pit of his stomach he moved to the next piece and the next. These were the remains of the boxes the gold had been stored in. Somebody had beaten them to it and nearly four tonnes of Treasury owned gold was gone.

He carried on exploring the underground base and found a wider and taller tunnel leading away from the room where the gold had been stored. He followed it carefully, checking all the time for traps, that might yet be lethal. Eventually he reached the end, to find a stout looking wooden door standing open, leading to a cross tunnel. Judging by the distance he had come he guessed this was the old tunnel that led to the church, which had been found way back in the 1860s. The Auxiliary Unit people must have known about it and exploited it when constructing their base. This would have made removing the gold a lot easier for the thieves, with the parish church nestled up a quiet back lane, away from the village main street.

Jim sat in the tunnel and contemplated his options. If he reported the body normally there would be a fuss and would draw attention to his team. An anonymous call to the police would excite even more interest and publicity. Yet he could not leave the body where it lay. Somewhere a family was wondering what had happened to a loved one. He would have to involve the Police Special Branch again and they would need to work up some cover story to explain the grisly discovery. He sighed and stood up. He could not appear in the church unannounced so would have to go back through the secret base and struggle back out of the latrine pit. Not an inviting prospect.

Climbing back up the sloping passageway from the old tunnel Jim came back into the chamber where it looked like the gold had been stored. He made another check to see if there were any other useful traces, but found nothing. He then made his way past the disintegrated door to the chamber where the body lay. He paused as he passed and looked down at the twisted remains. He could hardly imagine what a grenade exploding in here would have been like. He hoped the end had come quickly.

As he went to step over the body he noticed there was something beneath the bony remains of the left hand. He stooped and moved the finger bones gently to one side, to expose a Webley .38 revolver. It must have been well oiled, as the rust on it looked only superficial. Checking the pockets of the tattered jacket, he found a mildewed wallet with the remains of a few old style pound notes. In the other side of the jacket he found the soggy remains of a police warrant card. So much for Inspector Spelling. He slipped the weapon and the warrant card into his jacket pockets and moved on to the exit into the latrine shaft.

As he struggled around the awkward turn, Geordie and Ivan leaned down, grabbed him by the upper arms and lifted him up out of the hole.

"Wouldn't want you falling through the hatch and into whatever is still down there, boss."

"I would have to agree with you on that one. Though it would make the perfect end to a lousy day."

Helen turned to look at him "Lousy? Why what's wrong?"

"The gold is gone and there is a body down there and I think it's the Police Inspector we were told about who was following up a clue. No trace of the people who stole the gold though."

"The gold is gone? All of it? Are you sure this is the right place?"

"I'm sure. There are some fragments of the gold boxes still down there and they have the Bank of England markings on them."

Helen seemed to be even more disappointed than the rest of them. With a crestfallen look she turned away and stared into the trees. At that moment her mobile phone rang and she flipped it open to read the caller ID. She glanced at them then walked away, saying she had to check up on her grandfather. She walked into the woods before speaking into the mobile phone. Geordie climbed the tree to retrieve the climbing rope, while Ivan and Jim waited.

"I did get one souvenir, though," said Jim and handed the revolver to Ivan. "A bit rusty but it might clean up for a museum or something."

Helen returned from her call. "He's fine," she said, seeming a little more cheerful now "and it's just about time for a rather nice dinner with some of that good wine."

Chapter 60

Sitting in the large office in 100 Parliament Street they started their research into how to find a single GWR truck in 1940 among the records of a company that no longer exists. Geordie tried the Internet and almost immediately brightened up.

"It seems we could be in luck. The archives of the Great Western Railway still exist and they're stored in the Steam Museum in Swindon. Looks like we need to book to go down there for a visit but, after that, all we have to do is trawl through mounds of dusty paperwork for days on end."

Jim looked over his computer monitor. "Sounds promising. At least we have a place to start. Can you book us in with whoever runs the place while I go and break the bad news to Sir Richard that he is light about four tons of gold. I think that sort of news needs to be given face to face."

Jim was gone for a little over an hour. By the time he returned they had an appointment booked with the chief archivist to see the GWR records and hotel bookings were done.

Ivan handed Jim a coffee as he came through the door. "How did it go, boss?"

"Surprisingly well. Sir Richard had no faith that we would find anything, if you recall, so he seems to regard anything we do find as a huge bonus. We have agreed not to tell the police about the theft, or the body, until we have found the fifth load and then they can make their enquiries. But he holds out little hope of recovering anything from the South Cave cache."

"That's good. Well, Geordie has arranged for us to visit the archives tomorrow and we have a car booked and ready to go down to Swindon as soon as you say the word."

"No reason to hang about here. Let's get some lunch and go. Geordie are you ready?"

"Sure am, boss. I have all the address details and the phone number for the museum. They'll be expecting us first thing in the morning."

The archives turned out to be housed in a modern, well run facility and were nothing like the dusty stacks of paper of their imaginings. Geordie, with his knowledge of the age of steam railways, took the lead and soon the archive personnel were putting themselves to considerable trouble to help narrow the search. Even with their help, trawling through considerable amounts of paper looking for a single authorisation that might not even have been filed was no trivial task.

The first day passed in just trying to work out where to look and the second was not much more productive. By the end of the third day, hopes of finding anything of use were fading. Only discipline and a lack of alternative ideas brought them back on the fourth day, to start grinding their collective way through the paper once again. Four hours into the day Jim was ready to give up and called a break.

"Come on you two, time for a walk round the museum to straighten out your backs and get some fresh air."

"Just finish this box boss and be right with you" said Ivan as Geordie stood up from behind his latest pile of box files.

"Are you sure you're not building a fort over there, Geordie?"

"It's beginning to feel a bit that way, boss. The temptation is to settle down for a little kip behind the piles."

"Well I'll be damned!"

"It's OK Ivan I didn't really mean it."

"Not that. I think I've found it. Look at this."

Ivan held out the large ledger he had been reading through. His finger pointed to a line of neat writing in what was obviously the work of a fountain pen, like most of the entries. The clerks of the time had prided themselves on the neatness of their ledgers, which had been a considerable help to the search.

Jim took the ledger and read the entry that concerned a vehicle being authorised to travel away from its depot and the issue of fuel ration cards to allow the journey to London and back. The dates fitted. Ivan had found the clue that might identify the truck involved.

"Where was the vehicle from? Does the driver get named? Anything?"

"Not much detail. But the ledger itself might be the clue. According to the front cover this book was from the maintenance yard that serviced the Box Tunnel, whatever that is."

"Never heard of it. How about you, Geordie?"

"Never heard of it? Really? It's a tunnel under Box Hill, just under two miles long, another of Brunel's engineering triumphs. The stone they carved out of there was used in a lot of the fine houses in Bath, I think. There's even a story that on one day a year the sun shines right through the tunnel and that it's on Brunel's birthday."

Jim smiled at his two grinning soldiers. "I think we can delay that break a little. Ivan and I will do some Internet searching about Box Tunnel. Geordie, can you see what the experts here know about it? We'll meet up in the café in the museum to compare notes in an hour."

Ivan and Jim moved to the computer terminals while Geordie went away to talk railways with the enthusiasts who knew so much about God's Wonderful Railway.

An hour later they re-joined in the café and found a table away from other museum visitors.

Jim was the last to put down his tray and sit down. "Right then, what have we got?"

"Quite a lot really. The tunnel is fully operational with the main London to Bristol line running through it. It's wider than other tunnels in the country because The GWR initially used a wider gauge track and that left more space between the tracks when they standardised. Because of the traffic through the tunnel we are not allowed in there for a look round, at least not officially."

"Ivan and I found a lot of stuff on the Internet. Some of it pretty weird and a lot of it quite surprising. Ivan, do you want to do the weird stuff?"

"Love to. Well, it seems that the UFO believers think that there are captured flying saucers hidden in tunnels under the hill. A sort of British Area 51. And then there are others who think there are steam trains hidden under there ready for when the oil runs out. It seems that they think a lot of locomotives were sent for scrapping, as the diesels came in, but there is no record of that scrapping actually taking place. From that, they have worked out the engines are hidden and that Box Hill is the only place that is big enough to hide so many."

Geordie smiled. "The archive folk were telling me that one. They think it's really funny."

Jim sat forward. "On the other side of the coin there is some surprising stuff that really is under there. We know that large ammunition dumps were built there during the war to protect them from bombing and an aero engine factory was also set up there as a back-up in case the one in Bristol was destroyed. In the end they never brought it into use but the caverns they dug are still there. There was also at least one communication facility. In all, there are supposed to be about 80 miles of galleries and tunnels under there. Could be an ideal place for the Auxiliary Units to hide a small room."

"Could be but where do we start?"

"Sitting on top of it all is Rudloe Manor. It used to be RAF Rudloe Manor and it is still run by the Ministry of Defence, though it is not quite clear what they do there nowadays. I think it is a pretty fair guess that if there is an easy access point to this complex it is going to be through there. With the PM's letter as authority we should be able to get some cooperation and if not, we'll find another way in."

"It's probably going to be pretty mucky down there so maybe we need combat uniforms and caving helmets again?"

"I suspect you are right, Ivan, we can get changed before we go and see the base commander in Rudloe Manor. It might make him or her more inclined to help us anyway."

Chapter 61

Geordie pulled the car to a stop outside the security post of Rudloe Manor and wound the window down to speak to the guard. All three men showed their military identity cards and were surprised to be refused entry. Jim climbed out of the car and put his beret on before walking into the guardroom. A uniformed RAF policeman looked up from the newspaper on his desk.

"Yes sir. How can I help?"

"I am Major Wilson and I am here to speak to your base commanding officer."

"Do you have an appointment, sir?

"No, this has been rather a last minute decision to come here."

"That could be a problem then, sir. The CO doesn't see anybody without an appointment and we are under strict instructions not to let anyone in who just turns up. Sorry, sir."

"Could you phone his office for me then and see if he will make an exception for me?"

"I can, sir, but I wouldn't get your hopes up. He is very particular about this."

The sergeant picked up the phone and dialled. Jim waited as the sergeant explained what was needed. He shook his head and handed the phone to Jim.

"Major Wilson, who am I speaking to?"

A very officious female voice replied, "I am the station commander's personal assistant and as I have explained to the security man, the commander is very busy. You will have to make an appointment and come back another day."

"That's not really an option I am carrying out a classified task and I need the assistance of this base. Could you ask the ....."

"I am really not interested in your problems. Write in and make an appointment."

Jim found himself listening to a dialling tone. The phone had been put down on him. He took the direct dialling number for the commandant's phone from the sergeant, passed the hand set back and without another word left the guardroom. As he walked back towards the car he pulled his mobile phone from his pocket. This could be quite amusing.

Having made his call he checked his watch and then opened the passenger door of the car and sat down. He watched the road into the camp quietly and within minutes was rewarded by the sight of a car accelerating towards the guard room. He continued watching as a very flustered officer jumped out, hatless and almost ran into the guardroom. Seconds later the police sergeant emerged from the door and pointed Jim's car out to the officer who walked swiftly across to it.

Jim watched him approach but made no move to get out. He waited until the officer arrived at the car before winding down his window and looking at him.

"Can I help you?"

"Major Wilson? I have just had a call from the Chief of the General Staff. I am to give you whatever assistance you need."

"I thought you might change your mind. Very good of you to offer to help" Jim said, trying hard to avoid sounding sarcastic and just failing.

"Perhaps you would like to follow me back to the Manor and we can discuss your needs?"

"Certainly. Geordie, I've always wanted to say this. 'Follow that car'."

They drove into the base and followed the car in front up to a very impressive old manor house. There were few signs of military activity, just a couple of drab Army vehicles parked to one side of the building. They walked up the steps at the front of the building and into the wide foyer.

"Sir," said Ivan, "do you have an armoury? We'd just like to drop in there while you are talking to the Major."

"Of course. My PA will show you the way" said the commandant, indicating the young woman who sat behind a desk.

The lady in question stood up without a word and walked around the desk. She was careful not to make eye contact with Jim as she passed him and he noticed her ears were bright red with embarrassment. Geordie and Ivan followed her out of the building and to the small flat roofed building she showed them. She left them there and hurried back to her office without a word.

Back in the commandant's office Jim sat across the desk from a man who was still clearly stunned at being phoned by the senior military officer of the British Armed Forces.

"Well then, Major. How can I help?"

"I need to get into the tunnel system below this hill. I assume you have an entry point? I would also like copies of all the tunnel maps you have and a guide, to start with, if you have one."

"We don't allow anybody down into the tunnels, there are still sections that are classified and some of the tunnels have not been maintained for years."

"Don't worry about that, we will accept the risk. If a tunnel falls on us it's our own damn silly fault."

"We still don't allow people down there, I'm afraid."

"Do you mind if I use your phone?"

"What for?"

"I tell you what," said Jim, removing the Prime Minister's authority letter from his pocket "you read that while I phone the Ministry of Defence and arrange for you to be posted to the Outer Hebrides. OK?"

The startled officer read the letter while Jim waited patiently. He watched as the man's face turned red and sweat stood out on his forehead. It was clear he did not want to leave this very pleasant station for one where the icy cold winds blew almost constantly.

"I'll have the maps brought here immediately and one of the guides will be at your disposal as long as you need him. Is there anything else I can do?"

"Yes, we would like an office to work from while we are here."

"I will arrange that straight away. Anything else you need, please let me know."

Chapter 62

A young Army corporal wearing a Royal Signals cap badge in his beret was allocated to them as a guide. He spent an hour briefing them on the complicated series of maps they had been given, showing the extensive tunnel system beneath their feet. Danger areas where tunnels were becoming unsafe were marked, as were areas that were still in use for classified activity.

"So then, Corporal," said Ivan, "just how much of this tunnel system do you know?"

"Only a part of it and most of that is in the upper levels. We have been warned off the lower levels as they are supposed to be getting dangerous."

Geordie smiled. "So are you saying you haven't been down to where the UFOs are stored or the park for the Steam Engines?"

"I've never seen either of those, although there is a narrow gauge railway line that served the old Central Ammunition Depot. You can see on the map there where that runs. I've been told that there is still a small locomotive and a couple of flat cars on the old tracks somewhere."

Jim picked up his caver's helmet from the desk and tossed the remaining two to his men. "I think we'd better put a couple of spare battery packs in our pockets. No telling how long this might take. Geordie, have you got the water bottles?"

"Yes and a pocketful of energy bars in case we are not back in time for dinner."

The corporal led them out of the Manor House and across the compound to what looked like a truncated pyramid covered in grass. The concrete pathway led to a pair of steel doors with a large brass padlock. He opened the lock and heaved the first door open, to reveal an elevator.

"Now, I wasn't expecting that" said Jim.

"All mod cons here, sir. Wait till you get underground, people are usually surprised by their first look at the tunnels too."

The elevator doors closed and the machinery hummed, as they dropped. No lights indicated the floor numbers. There were just up and down buttons. The doors slid open as they stopped and the three of them stepped out while their guide hung back.

"Hell's teeth! Would you look at the size of this? These aren't tunnels, this is an underground roadway. I've worked in smaller coal mines than this!"

The corporal joined them. "They could make them this big because the rock is relatively easy to work but still quite stable. At these upper levels we get very little movement or cracking in the rock."

"Well, with electric lighting strung through the tunnels we won't be needing these damned helmets, will we?" said Ivan.

"Oh, you will, sir, if you are going out of the areas that are still being used. The working areas and their connecting tunnels are lit but where they are disused it's disconnected."

"Thanks, Corporal. Now, what about those phones I can see on the walls?"

"Oh yes, sir. If you look closely at your maps you will see them marked. At each major tunnel junction there is a phone. If it has a red tag on it then it's out of service, the ones with the blue tag still work. If you pick up the handset and dial '0' you will get an operator. If you find you need help ever, just find a phone and read the numbers off the tunnel wall. Someone will come and get you."

"With all those maps, we are carrying, I can't see us getting lost, if that's what you are trying to say tactfully?"

"I'm sure you would be right, sir, if the maps were complete. We have found that even in the upper levels there are side tunnels and caverns that are not marked. We think that was done deliberately in case the enemy ever got in here during the war."

"Right then, if we are all ready, our guide here can start the tour. Geordie? Ivan?"

"We're ready, boss. Just admiring the roadway, it looks like you could drive a Land Rover down here easily. I just can't see why the tunnels need to be so big."

"That's any easy one, Sarge. Most of the tunnels were dug in a hurry during war time. They needed to get the stone out PDQ, so they brought heavy digging equipment and trucks down here to get the job done fast. Later on this was going to be an alternative main bunker for the government in case of nuclear war, so they made it more comfortable. The ramps where they brought the vehicles in are still there but the entrances have been blocked."

They walked along the upper level tunnels, their guide pointing out items of interest, with Geordie and Ivan following their progress on the maps they carried. After a time they came to a set of stairs carved into the rock and headed down to the next level. At the bottom they found that the light levels were less than in the upper tunnels. Here they also found disused offices carved into the sides of the tunnels with pieces of old, damaged furniture lying about.

"This was the admin area for one of the ammunition depots. It was abandoned some time ago and just left as it was. The souvenir hunters have been through here but I don't think they found anything exciting," explained the young corporal.

After another hour of walking and looking into side tunnels and bays carved into the walls Jim called a halt. "I think we have the idea now, Corporal. Ivan, if you are happy with those maps, can you lead us back to the entrance. Then we'll call it a day and be back tomorrow morning for our next look."

"What time would you like me to be here, sir?"

"I don't think we need you any longer, Corporal. If you just give me the key to the outer door we can look after ourselves. Unless of course we get lost."

They walked back along the tunnel with Ivan scanning the maps and pointing the way. Geordie walked alongside Jim and waited until the corporal was out of earshot.

"Are we staying on the base overnight, boss?"

No, I don't think so. Too many people asking questions and getting interested in us. We'll find a nice quiet country Inn somewhere nearby and come in daily."

"Sounds good to me. The food will probably be more interesting anyway. Any idea how long this is going to take? It's just that Sam is due back from her play in New York this weekend and I'd kind of like to be there for her:"

"With 80 miles of tunnels and galleries, this is not going to be a quick job. I think we can afford to work a five day week with weekends off. I think that might suit all of us."

Chapter 63

They were back the next morning and the next. For two full days they marched the corridors and tunnels, looking into galleries and alcoves for any clue that might indicate a hiding place. By late Friday afternoon they were tired and not a little fed up. This wasn't going to be a simple search. Jim called a halt and they returned to the surface.

Jim had arranged to meet Helen in London to finally buy her the expensive dinner he had promised her. Geordie was heading up to his home in the North East of England to spend the weekend with his wife and Ivan was heading to a country parish in Wiltshire.

On Monday morning they met up again at the security post of Rudloe Manor. The security sergeant was there to meet them with a beaming smile to hand over the key to the elevator doors.

Jim looked at the sergeant and said "You look cheery this morning, Sergeant. Did you win the lottery over the weekend?"

"No, sir, but nearly as good. I don't know what you did to the commandant but he has been like a bear with a sore head ever since. It's been a joy to watch. And he has stopped being arrogant with visitors too."

"Nice to hear, but you might want to be careful who you say that to."

"Oh I am, sir. I don't need any trouble, but I thought you would like to know that just about everyone on the base would like to buy you a beer."

"We might take them up on that after a few more days in the tunnels," said Jim as the car pulled through the barrier and into the base.

Unlocking the heavy steel doors and taking the elevator down to the tunnel level, they set off hiking along the roadways to where they had stopped the search on Friday afternoon. They considered splitting up but, with so many tunnels and caverns to get lost in, decided against it. Half way through the day they came upon a narrow gauge railway track running next to a large conveyor belt system.

Ivan studied the map. "Well according to this we are on the edge of the Central Ammunition Depot. This seems to have been where ammunition was brought in by a train, then cross loaded onto the conveyor belt to be taken into the depot. The way in is that way." he said pointing to the left.

They followed the track and came to a chamber where the conveyor belt vanished through a hatchway in the wall. The rail track continued into the darkness of a curving tunnel. Geordie followed the track and came back with a happy grin on his face.

"The locomotive and a couple of flat cars are just around the bend. They have a large tarpaulin thrown over them, so they seem to be in decent condition."

"What were you thinking of doing with them?"

"Well, if the track is OK out to the entrance, I wondered if we could get the engine going and take it out to give to the railway museum. It may not be steam but it was linked to the GWR. Nice piece of history for them, eh?"

"Maybe. We'll have to work out who owns it though. Knowing the Ministry of Defence it will be on somebody's books even if they have forgotten it. In the meantime, we need to catch up with Ivan. He was following the conveyor belt."

Following the wide conveyor belt brought them into a large echoing chamber through what had once been fireproof doors.

The ammunition and explosives had been cleared out but the warning signs were all over the walls with fire extinguisher points scattered liberally around. Ivan picked up an old stirrup pump lying next to a metal water bucket.

"Not sure how much use this would have been if a fire had really started in here. Even with all these blast walls, if this depot had gone off when it was full it would have taken most of the hill above with it."

"That's true. So I guess it's a fair bet that the gold would not have been stored in or close to here. I think we can skip through here rapidly and move on into the lower levels."

"Probably right. How do you feel about taking a lunch break here? We can sit on the fire points instead of the cold stone and Geordie can slip back for another look at his toy train."

They settled down to take the sandwiches out of Ivan's backpack. Geordie took his and went for another look at the narrow gauge engine while Jim settled down next to Ivan and leaned back against the cavern wall.

"So then, boss," said Ivan around a mouthful of chicken sandwich, "how did this weekend go with Mrs Jennings?"

"Pretty well. We did all the usual London tourist things including going to the shops in Oxford Street. She certainly has a talent for shopping, that one."

"Sounds like it might be getting serious, then?"

"Do you know, I think you might be right. It's a long time since I have felt like this about any woman. But how about you? I guess you went off to see the lovely Reverend Mansfield. How's that going?"

"It feels comfortable. First time I have been able to say that since my Mary died. Might be something to do with all the people who have died in her family. She seems to understand more than anyone I have ever met. And her cooking is out of this world, which doesn't hurt."

"Good for you. I hope it works out for you both."

"And you too, boss. You and Helen make a bonny couple."

"Well, enough of that. We're gassing like two old ladies here. Can you round up Geordie and we'll push on? Only another four days down here this week."

Back together they set off again, following the maps they had been given. Generally they were accurate but, as the corporal had said, there were side tunnels and rooms that had not been marked up on them. Whether that was deliberate or the maps had just not kept pace with the expansion of tunnels, they could not tell.

They trudged on, noticing now that the side passages had been given street names, carefully painted on smoothed patches of stone at the tunnel junctions; Regent Street, Anson Terrace, Whitehall, King Charles Street, all went past with no indication of anything that might lead them to an Auxiliary Unit base.

Chapter 64

The days dragged by in an unending trudge through the tunnels and passageways. They occasionally found interesting remains, in the notices left on walls and defunct pieces of equipment left lying about. The stone dust coated their mouths and dried their throats. By the time Jim called a halt on the Friday afternoon they were all heartily sick of the vast underground complex.

The same routine dragged on for three more tedious weeks and Jim was glad he had set up the routine of taking weekends off. The two days with Helen each week, in either London or Brighton, allowed him to recover, ready for another five thankless days of searching. His two men obviously felt the same but never uttered a word of complaint. He had chosen absolutely the best people for a task like this.

As the fifth week started he had to square his shoulders and motivate himself for the long hike back to the spot their search had left off the week before. He found himself rerunning his time with Helen in his head as he trudged through the seemingly endless, boring tunnels and corridors of rock. The swell of her breast under his hand and the taste of her lips before and after their love making, the gentle sound of her breathing in the night and the way she kept her eyes open looking into his as they made love. He pulled himself together and refocused on the job in hand.

If nothing else they were getting a surprising amount of healthy exercise. Walking along beside Ivan with Geordie taking a turn reading the maps, Jim noticed that the big Welshman seemed more cheerful than last week.

"Come on then, Ivan, what's up? What has polished your apple? You've been struggling to hide that smile since we got down here."

"Nothing specific. It's just that being with Sarah has lifted a weight off my back. I know we haven't been together long but it just feels right and for the first time someone understands about Mary."

"I know how you feel. She is a lovely person. You deserve each other."

Geordie turned back and waited for them to catch up to him. "Can you feel that?"

Jim and Ivan stood quietly. Jim placed his hand on the stone wall. "Vibration?"

"Why aye. Unless I miss my guess that's the vibration from the main London to Bath rail line. I think we are getting pretty near to the Box Tunnel itself."

"I wonder why they didn't mark that on the maps?"

"Maybe because it's outside the complex. I guess it must have been on the detailed engineering plans so they didn't tunnel into it when they were expanding the galleries."

"OK. Interesting, but it doesn't add anything to the search. Plod on."

They moved forward until Geordie called another halt. "According to this we are just about at the end of this tunnel." He shone his headlight the way they were facing. "In fact, I think the end of the tunnel is just there, it's a dead end, no way out."

"So, according to the map, where do we have to go next?"

"Honestly not sure, boss. We've been marking off the tunnels and caverns we have been through and the bits and pieces we have passed over don't look too promising, since we agree the base would not be anywhere that a lot of people would go."

"Looks like we should take a break here before we head back to the surface and think again. We might as well do lunch here as well."

They settled down with their backs against the tunnel walls while Geordie passed out the sandwiches. Ivan looked inside one suspiciously.

"Ham, eh? That'll do. So, boss, we seem to have run out of tunnels. Any idea where we go next?"

"Not really. The clues were thin anyway, but we seem to have run them to earth and I think we may have to tell Sir Richard he's got all the gold back that he is getting."

"Well, I won't be sad to see the last of these ruddy tunnels."

"Nor me. OK, shall we head out of here? Geordie, you've got the map, so lead on."

"Um, sir, I have a confession to make before we go."

"Go on."

"Well, not all the gold made it back to the Bank from Castleton. I didn't think they'd miss a couple of those small bars and what with the cost of the wedding and everything. Well, long story short, I liberated three bars but when I showed them to Sam she went ballistic and I was feeling bad about it anyway. I thought I could just slip them into the next lot we found. Sorry, sir. Here they are."

Jim took the bars from Geordie and put them in his backpack. He looked long and hard at the big Sergeant but said nothing. Geordie sat, looking like a whipped puppy.

Jim sighed. "No major harm done. We'll just pass them on to the bank."

Ivan stood with a flushed face and looked down at Geordie "And once we get out of here you and I will have a conversation about this."

Geordie climbed to his feet with his head down "Yes, Sergeant Major."

They had started the trudge back the way they had come. Jim was feeling fairly depressed about wasting five weeks in this underground search when he noticed Ivan was no longer with them. He turned to see the big Welshman staring at the alcove they had just passed.

"Problem, Ivan?"

"Maybe not. We passed this alcove on the way down here, if you recall. It looks like a dozen other passing places in the tunnels where trucks could go past each other."

"And?"

"And so why has this one got a name? We didn't see it on the way down as it's on the right side of the wall but now we are going the other way I spotted it."

Jim walked back. "Not sure I see any significance in that."

"Wait till you get here, guys and then see what you think."

Geordie and Jim walked back to the alcove and looked up at the right hand wall. It took a second or two for the penny to drop and then they saw what had grabbed Ivan's attention. Cromwell Place. An unassuming alcove with a name was odd but one using the Special Units' code word had to be worth a second look.

"Bloody hell, we walked straight past it."

"We did indeed. Nice spot, Ivan. Let's take a look."

The three men dropped their packs in the main tunnel and Geordie put down his folder of maps. They moved into the alcove. It was the full height of the main tunnel, carved in a curve back into the rock. It was about six feet deep, at its deepest point. They stared at the stone and ran their fingers across its surface. There was nothing there.

The train vibration came again, more pronounced this time, as the express from London to Bath drove through the Box tunnel.

"There!" cried Geordie. "There is a piece of the wall that moves differently to the rest when the train goes by."

He pointed to a piece of the wall that looked exactly like the rest. With the train gone there was nothing to indicate any difference but Geordie had his eyes fixed on the spot he had noticed. He moved and put his hand on the place.

"Stay there, Geordie," said Ivan as he walked to his pack. He came back carrying a heavy hammer. "Mind your fingers."

The big man swung the hammer at the piece of wall. Then again. At the third try a piece of stone flaked off to expose a metal bar embedded in the wall.

"Well, I'm damned," said Jim. "Not sure which of you takes the credit for this one but that was a remarkable find. Shall we see what happens when we move the bar?"

"After you, boss," said Ivan, tossing the hammer back towards his pack.

Jim reached up to the bar. He pulled down but it did not move. He tried pulling it towards him and although it swung outwards nothing happened. He stepped back and contemplated the bar now jutting from the wall. He reached up and pulled down again. Within the wall they heard a metallic clunk. And then Jim noticed a crack had appeared in the wall five feet to his right.

Jim pointed. Geordie who stood next to it, tried to grab the edge of the stone and pull but was unable to get a grip.

"Can I borrow your hammer, Ivan? If I shove the back edge into here I should be able to lever it open enough to get a grip and pull it the rest of the way."

Without speaking, the Welshman stepped forward, put his shoulder against the wall and pushed. With a grinding noise and a shower of rock dust the wall swung away from him. They stood staring into the square opening that had been revealed.

Their helmet lamps showed what looked like boxes covered in tarpaulins. There were bunk beds against the wall and a table with an ancient radio set on it. Jim went to move forward but was restrained by Ivan's arm.

"Need to do the booby trap check first, boss."

"Surely not here inside a major base? Not with all that ammunition not far away?"

"It's a Sergeant Major's job to be careful, boss. Just let me check for my own peace of mind."

"Fair enough." Jim stepped back.

Ivan made a very careful check around the doorway and inside the room they had found before he agreed that it was safe to enter. They went inside and shone their headlights around. Geordie was the first to remove a tarpaulin.

"Looks like a weapons box to me"

"According the markings this end," said Ivan, "what we have in here is a Lewis Gun. Some museum is going to love that."

Geordie looked puzzled. "Lewis Gun? What's that when it's at home?"

"Probably the first successful Light Machine Gun," Jim said. "Used in the First World War in the trenches and a version was even mounted on the early fighter planes. It could be used by just one man where the earlier machine guns needed a crew because they were so big and awkward."

Geordie used the claw hammer to prise open the lid. He looked inside to find the machine gun was wrapped in waxed paper and the bottom of the box stained by the oil that had been liberally applied to the weapon. He reached in and pulled out one of the drum magazines that were also in the box. He turned it over.

"Mags are filled and ready to go. These guys were ready for trouble."

"And that's not all they had," said Ivan from behind them. "This case has four Lee Enfield rifles with loaded magazines and stripper clips of spare ammunition."

"I fired one of those when I did my basic training at Sandhurst," said Jim. "Bolt action but still very quick to use. The Army of the time was trained to get twenty aimed shots away in a minute during an attack. They were remarkably accurate, too."

"Oh, wow, look at this," said Geordie.

From yet another crate he had withdrawn one of the most famous sub machine guns in the world. He stood there, cradling the gleaming Thompson gun in his arms. He reached back into the box and pulled out a handful of magazines.

"These are filled and ready for use as well. It's a shame they are the straight magazines and not the drum one Al Capone used. Now, that would be cool."

Jim looked around the room and checked his watch. "We could stay here all night looking through this lot but it's going to take us a while to get back to the surface and we need to be fresh for this. Let's pack up and head out, after seventy years or so down here another day won't matter."

Chapter 65

There was a definite spring in their step as they approached the steel entrance door the next morning. Ivan had peeled off to visit someone and caught up again as Geordie swung the door open. They entered the elevator and rode down to the lower level. As the lift doors opened Ivan handed Jim a package.

"Here you go, boss. We thought you would like a souvenir of your climb down into a toilet in the woods."

Jim looked at his two grinning men and opened the package. Inside was a gleaming Webley .38 revolver. It looked brand new.

"Where did you get this?"

"It's the one you took off the corpse at Cave Castle. I've had the armourer here working on it for the last four weeks and he even managed to get you a box of .38 ammunition to go with it" said Ivan, handing the small cardboard box over.

"Well that's really thoughtful of you but I don't see how I can keep it with the gun laws in this country."

"As long as you have the Prime Minister's authority letter in your pocket that shouldn't be a problem, boss. Any police force in the country will give you a firearms licence based on that."

"True. Well thanks, I really appreciate this." Jim slipped the revolver into one jacket pocket and the ammunition into another. "But now, let's get down to the worksite. I think we have a lot to do today."

They shouldered their packs and set off down the tunnels. With a goal in sight the distance to the Auxiliary Unit base did not seem as long today and they made it in good time. Ivan removed the piece of stone covering the door mechanism, took hold of the handle, pulled it out and then down. Once again the door clicked open for Geordie to push it wide.

Jim paused in the outer tunnel. Something was not right. After years of soldiering in many places around the world he had learned to trust his instincts. He stepped slowly back until his shoulder blades touched the wall behind him. He waited, with his head cocked to one side listening and watching the tunnel they had come down. He glanced at the doorway to see his two men standing stock still and silent. After working together for so long they recognised that Jim knew something was happening.

There it was. He heard a footstep from further up the tunnel in the dark. Somebody had kicked one of the small stones, that had been dislodged from the tunnel roof by years of train vibration. There was no sound now.

Jim swallowed and made a small hand gesture to his men to tell them to stay where they were.

"Who's there?" There was silence. "I know you're there, answer me!"

The answer came in the sound of a weapon being cocked, followed by a burst of automatic fire. With his nerves stretched tight, Jim had reacted instinctively to the first sound by diving to the floor and rolling, the way he had been taught in basic training all those years ago. The burst of fire chipped stone from the wall right where he had been standing. If he had not moved he would be dead or severely injured by now. He came up from his roll and dived through the doorway into the hidden base.

As he landed Geordie heaved the door shut behind him and Ivan stepped forward to wedge it shut with a piece of packing case lid. Jim sat up to find his two men watching him.

"It seems we have company and they aren't friendly at all."

"Whoever fired that burst seems to be a pretty good shot, boss and not scared to use his weapon. I think we might have a 'bijou problemette'. Any idea who they might be?"

"You know, Ivan, I think you might be right. If they get that door open we could be up that special creek without a paddle. As to who they are or who sent them; I have an idea but I'm not sure yet."

"Not necessarily a problem, boss." Geordie moved across to the crates. "If these are still working we have enough firepower to start a small war. Particularly if we can find some grenades."

"Even if we find them, I would be very wary of chucking grenades about inside a seventy year old tunnel. We could end up sealed in here if we bring the ceiling down."

"Damn! And that was such a good plan up to then."

Jim stood up and dusted himself down. The dive through the door had put a scape across his forehead but the bleeding was only slight. He looked around the chamber.

"Right, time for some action. If this base is built like all the others we've found there should be another exit. Ivan, our job is to find that other door. Geordie you find us some weapons that are in working order with ammunition that looks like it has stood the test of time."

Without another word, the three of them set to their tasks. Ivan dragged crates away from the left hand wall and Jim examined the wall behind the radio table. Jim looked over his shoulder to see Geordie heaving the Lewis Gun out of its crate and working the mechanism. From here he could see no rust on the gun, the Auxiliary Unit soldiers had been careful it seemed.

The men worked in silence, each intent on his own task until Ivan crossed the chamber to Jim. "Nothing obvious my side, boss. Any joy over here?"

"No. Nothing as far as I can see. Take the other end of this table, will you? I'll have a look behind it."

They each grabbed an end and lifted, but the table did not move.

"That's odd. It doesn't look that heavy."

They each pulled out the two drawers beneath the table top and looked under. At the back of the table they could now see the two bolt heads that secured it to the wall. Jim reached in and tried to turn the bolt head at his end by hand. It would not move. Ivan tried his with the same result.

"Ivan, can you see if there are any tools that might help, while I check the third wall?"

"Not sure that wall is going to be any use though. My guess is that the railway is just the other side of there."

To prove him right the room thundered and shook as a train rushed by. A lot closer than it had been in the passage outside. Jim nodded but carried on as Ivan dived into the smaller boxes scattered around the weapon crates. Jim found nothing, but Ivan found a box of tools and he and Jim went back to the table.

Ivan knelt down and reached under the table with a large adjustable wrench in his hand. He fitted it to the first bolt head and started to turn. It took a deal of strength but the bolt eventually moved, only for half a turn and then locked solid again.

"Stop, Ivan, you've done it!"

Ivan pulled himself out from under the table and looked where Jim was pointing. There was a crack running down the wall behind the bunks. Turning the bolt had released another lock and revealed the carefully concealed doorway. Ivan stood up and walked across to the bunk. He pushed on the wall and watched as it swung back. They lifted the bunk out of the way and looked into the chamber beyond. There were the boxes they had been looking for, stacked from floor to ceiling.

"You know something, boss? I reckon they must have recruited a master stonemason to build these doors. The joins were so tight it had to have been done by somebody with an incredible level of skill."

"I think you're right. A lot of these Auxiliary soldiers were specialists in their own field and they were dedicated people. A very special group."

As usual, Ivan insisted on checking the room for booby traps before letting them enter. While he was doing that, Jim went to check on Geordie's progress with the weapons.

"What have we got?"

"Some bonny weapons in here and they looked after them carefully before they left. The guns were dripping in oil but the ammunition was bone dry so we have a good chance that they will work."

"So what does that give us to work with?"

"One Lewis Gun with ten drum magazines, all full. A Thompson sub-machine gun with another ten magazines, again all full and four Lee Enfield rifles with about a hundred rounds each, all in stripper clips for rapid loading."

"As you said, we can start a small war with that lot."

"That's not all. We have thirty hand grenades with the fuses removed and stored. As you said we don't want to use them in here but we also have four phosphorus grenades which might be quite useful if we need smoke. But my personal favourite is over here."

He turned to a long, thin, polished box that sat on top of another crate. Geordie lifted it up gently and placed it in front of Jim. He slipped the two brass catches sideways and opened the lid. Jim looked in to see a rifle with a highly polished wooden butt and stock. Mounted on top was a long telescopic sight. Geordie carefully lifted the weapon out.

"You remember that book you had on the Auxiliary Units? Well, this is one of the .22 sniper rifles they mention in there. Designed to take out enemy officers or collaborators with minimal noise. Beautiful piece of work isn't she?"

"I thought you'd be more excited by the machine guns?"

"Oh yes, they'll be fun. But this little beauty is a precision weapon. A craftsman's tool."

Ivan joined them. "The gold store is safe to enter and they have a couple of interesting features in there you might want to look at."

"Good. But I think our first order of business is to tell our friends outside in the corridor we are back in the game. Geordie grab that Thompson."

Geordie stepped to the crates, lifted the Thompson and loaded one of the magazines.

"Might as well test it then, eh?" said Jim. "As I open the outside door a crack you put a full magazine down range. With all that rock out there the rounds should ricochet all over the place and even if we don't hit anybody it should frighten the crap out of them. Ready?"

"Ready." Geordie cocked the old weapon.

Jim removed the wedge and pulled the door open a crack. Geordie put the barrel of the weapon in the opening and let rip with the full magazine of twenty rounds. The noise in the enclosed space was deafening but they were rewarded with a scream from the passage outside as they slammed the door shut again.

"That's opened the batting with one for the good guys. Should make them think twice about trying anything. Now let's see about getting out of here."

Chapter 66

With the chamber door wedged firmly shut again, they turned to enter the second room they had opened. Geordie reloaded the Thompson and laid it on the radio table ready for use. The three of them stood and looked at the pile of wooden boxes in front of them.

"Am I dreaming or does that pile look a lot bigger than the other ones we have found?"

"I think you might be right, Ivan" Jim said, "and look at the boxes at the top of the pile. The wood looks newer than lower down. I wonder why?"

Geordie tested the weight of one of the upper boxes. "It's certainly heavy enough to be gold. I wonder if this is the stuff from South Cave?"

"What makes you say that?"

"Well, you said that there was a lot of rotten wood from packing cases in the chamber by the toilet so maybe they re-boxed it when they moved it here?"

"That would fit. Maybe they moved it after that poor soul found it? A bit of a shame they just left him down there, though," said Ivan.

"True, but you have to remember these guys were trying to keep a seriously big secret. They probably didn't know he was a copper."

Jim looked around the room. On the wall that butted up against the railway tunnel he saw a large painted sign on the stone 'Check Before Exit'. Below it he could see a rusty metal handle in the wall. It seemed they had found the other exit.

"So, Ivan, you mentioned some interesting features."

"Didn't think you had heard me, boss. Well, you'll have seen the sign up there about checking and down here is the way to do that." Ivan pointed at two rectangular boxes mounted against the wall. "They seem to be two driver's periscopes from an armoured vehicle of some kind. If you push them out a couple of inches and have a look you might be surprised."

Jim did as Ivan suggested. He pushed the first periscope out a little and then bent down to look through. He found he was looking along the side wall of the Box Railway Tunnel. He pushed the other one and craned round to look through that. Sure enough he could see the Box Tunnel again, but in the opposite direction.

"Presumably that's to guard against stepping out in front of the 8:20 from Paddington? Somebody really thought this through."

"They did indeed. The level of sophistication down here is surprising since they were working in secret and could not let anyone else down in the tunnels know about them."

"Despite having our friend waiting outside the door, is anybody hungry?" said Geordie.

Jim checked his watch; it was some time beyond their normal lunch break. With all the excitement he had completely forgotten about it. Trust Geordie to be practical and remember the need for food.

"Since the opposition can't get at us in here why not? What did the pub pack for us today?"

"Ham and cheese with pickle. At least, that's what I asked for, but I thought you might like to live dangerously."

"More dangerously than being in a seventy year old tunnel, right next to the railway main line with armed unfriendlies on the other side of the door?"

"Yep! I've found a big box of rations left over from the war. Does tinned food last seventy years do you think?"

"I think we'll stay with the ham and cheese. The last thing I need is for you two to be bringing up your stomach linings all over the place."

"You could be right there boss. Sandwiches it is then."

They sat on the crates in the main chamber working their way through the very generous pub sandwiches. Geordie had also thought to bring a can of beer each for them to wash it down.

"I thought it would be more of a celebration about now when I packed the beer. I wasn't expecting to get shot at."

"With any luck Geordie there was just the one of them and we know you have at least winged him. I think once we're finished eating we need to take a look outside and see how your friend is doing."

They packed the empty tins and the sandwich wrappings away in Geordie's pack. Then Jim motioned Geordie to pick up the Thompson again and stand ready.

"Headlights out and pass me one of those empty cans."

Jim removed the wedge from the door and slowly swung it open a fraction. Outside was as dark as a witch's heart with not a sound. Jim tossed the can into the passage and as it clattered to the floor he was rewarded with a burst of automatic gunfire.

He swung the door closed again and wedged it firmly. "Looks like we aren't going out that way anytime soon. It will have to be through the door onto the track. Let's go."

Chapter 67

They returned to the gold chamber and Ivan went over to the two periscopes. He pushed the first one out and recoiled. At that second a train roared down the track.

"Bloody hell! I could read the washing instructions on the driver's shirt. That took me by surprise."

He leaned down again and checked the track once more. He then turned and checked the second periscope.

"All clear both ways but the trains are moving fast so I suggest you get to the space between the tracks a bit quick before one sneaks up on you."

Jim nodded and pressed down on the handle in the wall. It did not budge so he tried heaving it upwards. This time it moved and revealed an irregularly shaped door that had been built to match the brickwork in the tunnel. Despite Ivan's assurance, he looked both ways before stepping out onto the track and then across to the unusually wide space between the tracks.

He found he could see both ends of the tunnel at about the same distance each. That meant he had almost a mile to go to reach the open air. He took the mobile phone from his pocket and found that he had no signal this deep into the hill. He turned to call his men to follow him when the first shot cracked past his head.

He flung himself onto the stones of the roadbed and tried to find a dip to hide in. He lifted his head to see three figures entering the tunnel ahead of him, all carrying weapons. He looked back, over his shoulder, to see another four entering from the other end. Scrabbling into his pockets he retrieved the old Webley revolver and box of ammunition. Breaking the weapon open, he loaded six bullets into the chambers of the pistol and snapped it shut. He lifted his head, to see where his attackers might be and was greeted by another shot that hit the stones close to him and howled off into the darkness of the tunnel roof.

He was fully aware that the attackers were way out of range of the pistol he carried, but he had nothing else. He raised it and fired three rapid shots towards the people in front of him then rolled over and fired between his feet at the other four behind him. Luckily none of them were experienced in combat and all of them dived for the ground despite being perfectly safe at that range.

Jim spotted the recess in the tunnel wall. A workman's refuge, used by rail workers maintaining the tunnel. He jumped up and dived across the track into it, slamming his back against the brick back wall. He took a deep breath, then reloaded his revolver. He did not shout back to his men. They were experienced enough to know what had happened and certainly intelligent enough to know what to do without him yelling and possibly revealing their position.

He looked across the tunnel. He could see Geordie moving quickly assembling equipment without showing himself in the tunnel. Ivan came into the chamber behind him and tapped him on the shoulder. They were ready. Geordie stood and waved to Jim. Jim waved back. The ex-miner swung a canvas bag round once and lofted it across the tunnel to Jim who grabbed it out of the air. It was a bag of Thompson magazines. Next the weapon itself came flying across the tunnel and Jim snatched it to himself gratefully. This was still not a long range weapon but it was an improvement on the Webley and the large .45 calibre rounds would make a very satisfying noise in the tunnel.

The attackers had recovered from their first fright and were now firing at Jim's alcove, to cover their movements as they approached him. He looked at the bent and twisted bullets that dropped to the ground before him. They were small, probably only 9mm, so they were probably using submachine guns. Not very accurate at this range, but a lucky shot could still ruin his day.

He looked back to the doorway across the tracks. Ivan gave him a thumbs up signal and Jim replied with the same. He then leaned quickly out of his alcove and fired a long burst of nine rounds along the tunnel, then spun round and emptied the rest of the magazine in the other direction. As expected, the roar of the Thompson was very impressive with the echoes in the tunnel amplifying it mightily. The attackers in both directions flung themselves into whatever cover they could find.

Geordie took his chance and while the attackers' heads were down he dived across the first track and hit the ground in a shoulder roll, making sure to protect the Lewis Gun he cradled in his arms. It was the work of a second to cock the old weapon and raise himself to fire it. This was a far more effective weapon. The .303 rounds were lethal to over 1000 yards in the old days and the range here was much less. The first burst of fire hit one of the attackers as he rose to fire and sent him cartwheeling backwards with blood soaking his black clothing. The other two at that end of the tunnel vanished from sight.

Jim was firing short bursts from the Thompson at the larger group of attackers. They were fast learners it seemed and they had realised that they were outside the effective range of the old sub machine gun. They kept up a wary fire and continued to move forward carefully, making use of the sparse cover in the tunnel.

Geordie raised the Lewis to fire at the second group when one of them got lucky. A round struck the sergeant in the left shoulder. He fell back to the ground in agony. That was Ivan's cue to leap from cover holding one of the very accurate Lee Enfield rifles. He took a kneeling position and spotted the man who had shot Geordie. He was punching the air in a victory celebration as the .303 round from Ivan's rifle struck him full in the chest and stopped his joy permanently.

Ivan leapt across the track and went down beside his friend. He checked the wound and thrust a handkerchief into it to stem the bleeding. He looked across Geordie's back to Jim.

"Through and through, boss. Painful but it looks like it missed the serious bits."

Jim was relieved and gave Ivan a thumbs up just as another of the attackers got lucky. A burst of fire sent blindly down the tunnel ripped into the back of Ivan's calf muscle, carving a long gouge that spouted blood across the stones. The pain was intense. Ivan was not going to be firing carefully aimed shots anytime soon.

Chapter 68

Jim lay as low as he could to peep around the stonework to assess the situation. Two of the enemy were down and appeared to be dead. That still left him with five attackers to deal with. The question was, how effective would they be? Would their confidence have been shaken by losing two men? He could see no movement in either direction but doubted they had withdrawn yet.

His men lay in a gulley of stones between the rail tracks. The change of track gauge all those years ago had given them a fairly safe place to be, provided they kept their heads down. He could see that Geordie was attempting to stem the bleeding from Ivan's calf despite his own wound. Jim checked the tunnel again and ducked back quickly as another train came flying through on the track nearest to him. As it passed he rolled over and looked behind it, in time to see three attackers rise up and move forward.

A long burst from the Thompson sent them to ground again. But his question was answered; they had not given up yet. Geordie looked across at him from where he had finished helping Ivan and nodded. The two men had exchanged weapons as the Lewis was easier for Ivan to use without moving his leg. He moved the machine gun into place and fired a burst along the tunnel that emptied the drum magazine and sent the empty brass shell casings pinging off the rail tracks. While he was changing the magazine, Geordie brought the Lee Enfield to his shoulder and fired at a movement in one of the safety alcoves.

Jim heard the sharp intake of breath. The powerful recoil from the rifle had jarred the wound in the Sergeant's other shoulder. He saw Geordie's head go down as he dealt with the pain.

Geordie looked over his shoulder to Ivan "You ready?" Ivan nodded.

"You OK, boss?"

"I am. How's the shoulder?"

"Stings a bit. Can you two lay down some fire? I need to move in three, two, one. Now!"

The Lewis Gun roared in the confines of the tunnel and the Thompson sang its own song. The two old weapons spraying bullets in both directions. With the attackers diving for cover Geordie leapt across the track and back into the hidden base. He disappeared from view.

After the burst of fire Jim and Ivan lay quietly waiting for their next chance. There was a sudden burst of indiscriminate fire from the London end of the tunnel and Jim saw two figures leap up and start to run forward. He waited until they were a few yards closer then fired a carefully aim burst of three rounds at the nearest man. The attacker was slammed against the brick wall of the tunnel by the heavy bullets from the Thompson and slowly slid down to the rail bed. He was out of the fight and it looked like he was probably out of luck.

Jim carried on watching and waiting for his next opportunity. He saw a movement and fired again but with no result. He then realised that the remaining two men were squirming their way back out towards the tunnel entrance. They had had enough and were giving up. Over his shoulder Jim could see no movement from the second group that were being covered by Ivan.

Geordie reappeared in the doorway of the base on the opposite side of the tunnel. He was now carrying the .22 sniper rifle. The small calibre weapon would have far less recoil than the other weapons so he could use it accurately with minimum pain. He stayed inside the cover of the doorway and waited for his targets to appear.

Ivan spotted movement from the two attackers left in front of him and fired the Lewis Gun. The scream from the left of the tunnel indicated he had not wasted his ammunition. Jim could see the attackers, in their black fatigues, making a hasty exit, one of them limping badly and clutching his thigh.

"Hold your fire, gents. They've given up," said Jim stepping out of his alcove and crossing to Ivan. His leg had been badly chewed by the round that had ploughed along his calf. Geordie's emergency dressing needed to be replaced quickly to stem the blood. He helped the Sergeant Major to his feet. With Ivan leaning on him he helped the injured man to hop back into the base.

Geordie helped Jim to lay Ivan face down on the stone floor and went to find something to dress the wound. Jim went back to the door and checked the train tunnel both ways. The light from the ends of the tunnel showed it was clear except for the three black clad bodies that still lay there. Geordie returned with a handful of military field dressing pads and set to work on Ivan's leg.

"You two stay in here. I'm going to walk out of the tunnel and see if I can get a signal on this phone. Now that our playmates have buggered off. I'll have an ambulance here in no time."

Ivan looked up "Take the Thompson, sir, just in case."

"Good idea. No point taking any chances. Be back shortly."

The two injured men forced grins and both said, "But don't call me shorty."

Jim stepped out and across the track to where the Thompson lay. He was always amazed at the resilience of British soldiers in adversity. He checked the weapon, loaded a full magazine and put a spare in his jacket pocket. The distance to the outside was marginally shorter towards the city of Bath so he set off that way. He stopped as he came to the black clad body lying crumpled by the track. There was no sign of life but he picked up the Sterling submachine gun from beside the body and tossed it across the tunnel.

He made his way to the tunnel entrance and stepped out. He checked, but could see no sign of the people who had tried to kill him and his team. He leaned the Thompson against the banking and took the phone from his pocket. He opened it up and was glad to see there was a good signal.

The sound of a weapon being cocked was unmistakable and he froze. He raised his head to see one of the attackers rising from behind a bush on the culvert bank. The heavy duty pistol he held easily compensated for the slight build of the man. Jim stood very still as the man approached. All he could see were the two shining eyes behind the black ski mask.

The black clad figure stopped about eight feet away from him. Too far for him to dive and try to disarm him. They stood and looked at each other. The barrel of the pistol looked like the top of a beer keg to Jim at that moment. The man raised his left hand and pulled the mask over his head, releasing a cascade of auburn hair over her shoulders.

"Helen?"

"Hello, Jim."

"Helen?"

"Yes, Jim, Helen."

He shook his head. "But what? I don't understand."

"Oh dear, you really are a romantic fool aren't you? I've been planning this for weeks. With the help of my ex-husband, of course."

"Your ex-husband?"

"That's right, Terry Jennings. He runs one of the most professional criminal groups in South London. That's where the guns and the foot soldiers came from"

"So it was you set up the robbery on the motorway? I was convinced it was Sir Richard."

"That slimy fool? No, that was me. We were just about to jump you at Cave Castle as well but then you popped out of the toilet and said the place was empty. My team were just about to burst into the woods to take you down. A good job they did their final check beforehand."

It dawned on him. "That's when you had to take a sudden call about your granddad. And that trip to see your girlfriend for coffee and gossip was..."

"Was to show Terry that gold bar you so kindly loaned me. He got quite excited by that."

"But, how did you know we were here? I never told you, or anybody else, that we were in these tunnels."

"I took your phone during one of our romantic weekends in London. You were snoring. After scoring 'A' for effort by the way. And I put it back after we had fitted a GPS locator chip in it. Plus of course we followed you back here each weekend."

"But why?"

"Are you serious? There's tons of gold bullion to be had. I could live in luxury on a Caribbean Island for the rest of my life. Did you think living with you on an Army base would compare to that? How sweet."

The small blue box for the engagement ring, in his trouser pocket, pressed into his leg. Mocking him, as his carefully constructed future world collapsed.

"So what now?"

Helen raised the heavy automatic pistol and pointed it at his face. "Sorry Jim. Nothing personal, it's just business."

He watched horribly fascinated as her finger tightened on the trigger. The world seemed to have slowed around him while all his hopes and dreams crumbled.

He felt a pluck at his sleeve as she screamed and her arm flew up. The pistol fired as she spun away from him and fell to the ground.

She lay panting with blood pouring through her fingers from the wound that had appeared in her right upper arm. Jim dazedly stepped over her and picked up the pistol from where it had fallen. He stared down at her.

"Jesus! You were really going to do it. Did I mean so little to you? I had even picked out an engagement ring for you. I thought we had something special together."

She looked up. "So what happens now? Are you going to shoot me?"

"You know I couldn't do that, even after this."

He stood in silence for a moment trying to come to terms with the changed situation. He glanced down the tunnel and saw Geordie walking towards him. He was still carrying the sniper rifle that had saved Jim's life. He looked back at Helen lying on the ground.

"I take it you had an escape plan in place?"

"Of course."

"Then you'd better use it before I call the police. Get out of here before my lads arrive."

"Help me up."

"Help yourself. You're wasting time and by the way, you now owe me one."

"You learn to hate quickly don't you?" she said, as she struggled upright and turned to climb the embankment behind her. She paused and looked back at him "I'm sorry about this you know? Maybe I'll make it up to you one day."

Jim watched as she climbed out of sight behind bushes. A moment later he heard a powerful car engine start and accelerate away.

He looked at Geordie who was still at least two hundred metres away. Then returned to the phone he still had in his hand. He called the emergency services and then waited for his Sergeant to join him.

"Sorry about the crap shot, boss. You were standing between me and that guy. I could only see his arm after he raised the pistol."

"Pretty damn good shot at that distance, even if you did put a hole in my sleeve. At least you put the bastard off shooting me. A shame he managed to get away. But that's a problem for the police later. Speaking of which, I'd better get them up here with the ambulance. The explanations are going to take a while."

He made the second phone call then turned to Geordie. He looked him in the eye and smiled.

"I reckon you just saved my life there so all sins forgotten eh?"

Chapter 69

Jim pushed open the door of the private ward where his two men were sharing a room. As he got inside he saw that Sam was sitting by Geordie's bedside holding her husband's hand. Across the room a smiling Reverend Sarah was looking down at Ivan as he sat in a chair by the window.

"Hi, boss," said Geordie. "So what did the Prime Minister have to say?"

"Funny thing. I tried to arrange an appointment to brief him but he refused to see me. The gratitude of politicians, eh?"

"That's a bit off isn't it? After all we have recovered for him."

"It is. But Sir Richard was very grateful. Very relieved to have all his property back after seventy years missing."

"Well then, sir," said Ivan, "where does that leave us going forward?"

"As far as I am concerned if the PM doesn't even want to talk to me then he obviously has no more use for us as his special team. I have been on the phone to the Commander Royal Engineers and he has agreed to let us go back to the Army. He has given me an engineer field squadron and you two are coming with me. If that suits you?"

"Do we get to choose which regiment?"

"The Army hasn't changed that much. We go where we are told, but at least it will be a proper unit and not some headquarters desk job."

Sam stood up. "Is Helen not with you? I was looking forward to meeting her."

Jim shook his head. "No, I'm afraid Helen won't be joining us, ever."

Chapter 70.

Golden Eights – Factual Context

This story relies on a number of apparently unconnected events in order to work. Do they make a realistic story? I think so and let me lay out the facts so that you can be the judge.

The Spanish Empire was huge and rich. Galleons sailed across the Atlantic carrying gold and silver to Spain for many years and some were attacked by English ships captained by privateers such as Drake and Hawkins. The Spanish naturally regarded these people as Pirates. It seems doubtful that the papers signed by Queen Elizabeth I giving them authority to attack enemy shipping would have prevented a rapid and unpleasant execution for any of them captured by the Spanish. One ship that Drake took, in the Pacific, was named *Nuestra Señora de la Concepción* and the cargo she carried made a rich haul. There was a considerable quantity of gold and silver registered with the Spanish Authorities. In addition, there was an appreciable amount of privately owned gold and silver that had not been declared to Spanish authorities. There were at least 1,300 silver bars plus 14 large chests stuffed with gold and silver coins. The amount of treasure was so significant that it allowed Queen Elizabeth to pay off the whole of her foreign debt with her share and to have money left over to invest in the Levant Company, a forerunner of the hugely successful East India Company. See Stephen Coote's excellent book 'Drake' for more information.

The coins known as 'Pieces of Eight' were the first truly world currency, since the fall of the Roman Empire, due to the purity of the silver used. They gained the name because of the practice of cutting them into eight pieces for smaller transactions. They were minted in various places in the Empire, including Lima in Peru and Mexico City.

Phillip II of Spain was a dedicated ruler and a very religious man. As the head of government he could expect gifts from successful captains of his fleet and the governors of his dominions. These would probably have taken the form of religious artefacts or artistic items made by the indigenous peoples of the Empire for the most part, but a solid gold version of the currency that formed the basis of his Empire does not seem unrealistic. The British seem to think that Drake and others were a huge problem for Spain. The Spanish today think they were far less significant. While the attacks brought a lot of treasure to Britain the sheer scale and wealth of the Spanish Empire of that time is often not really appreciated and the relative proportion of treasure taken was actually small.

In 1940 the British Army had been virtually destroyed as an effective fighting force. Much of its equipment, ammunition and heavy weapons were abandoned in France to allow the Army to escape through Dunkirk. Many troops arrived back in England without even a pair of boots. The German Army was a highly capable force and the invasion of Britain was a very real possibility. Had the Germans managed to land it seems likely that they would have taken control of the whole country, not easily but almost inevitably. The Government made what preparations it could while rearming the Army as quickly as possible. Luckily the vastly outnumbered Royal Air Force was able to prevent the Luftwaffe from gaining control of the skies, without which the invasion, known as 'Operation Sea Lion', could not proceed. This was by no means certain and a huge debt is owed to the young men of Fighter Command, including those from the British Commonwealth and those few airmen who had escaped from countries that had been overrun, such as the Poles and the Czechs.

Operation Fish actually existed and the gold reserves of Britain were shipped to Canada for safe keeping. Had those ships been sunk in the Atlantic the effect would have been fairly disastrous for the war effort. Is it realistic to assume that all the gold reserves would have been put on ships in wartime, travelling through an area known to be infested with enemy submarines, without a back up plan? It seems unlikely that the authorities of the day would not have 'hedged their bets'. Interestingly one of the ships that carried the gold across the Atlantic was HMS Emerald, which was also the ship that took a large proportion of the Norwegian treasury out of Norway to keep it out of German hands.

Churchill's Secret Army did exist and was officially known, in what few documents remain, as the 'Auxiliary Units'. The recruitment of these remarkable people and the bases they created are much as I have described them. Most of their small bases remain to be found, so well hidden were they. Churchill seems to have had a fondness for unconventional forces possibly because of his experiences during the Boer War in South Africa. The Boers created fast moving Commandoes that led the more ponderous British Army a merry dance until they in turn adopted tactics suitable for the South African terrain. Churchill was captured by one of these Commandoes that ambushed a military train on which he was travelling. The most famous of the Second World War unconventional military groups was probably the Special Air Service [SAS] who still exist as part of the British and other Commonwealth armies and were the original model for many Special Forces units around the world. But there were others such as the Long Range Desert Group [LRDG] and even one called Popski's Private Army. The role of the Secret Army was to remain hidden until the Germans had taken over that part of the country and then to cause as much disruption as possible through sabotage and assassination of key Germans and any British collaborators. Captain Duncan Sandys, in a memo to his father-in-law, Winston Churchill, described the role rather well when he said *"They are intended to provide, within the framework of the Home Guard organization, small bodies of men especially selected and trained, whose role it will be to act offensively on the flanks and in the rear of any enemy troops who may obtain a foothold in this country. Their action will particularly be directed against tanks and lorries in laager, ammunition dumps, small enemy posts and stragglers. Their activities will also include sniping."*

The people recruited to this organisation were sworn to secrecy and their role was so secret they did not even receive the Defence Medal which was given to virtually everyone who served in any capacity during the war. During the 1990s when their activities were partially declassified a number of them applied for this medal but, due to the lack of records, many were unable to prove they had served and were refused.

The Auxiliary Units did build highly effective hides across the country and many have yet to be found. It is also true that they used hidden triggers to operate entry doors. One of these was famously demonstrated to General Bernard Montgomery along with the rabbit holes being used for observation and he became a major supporter of the Secret Army. The headquarters and training base for this shadowy force was in Coleshill House and at the time of writing a small museum is being created by a group of dedicated volunteers. You can find their website at www.coleshillhouse.com. Classified information, being released slowly from British Government archives, has also allowed the production of a very informative book by John Warwicker titled "Churchill's Underground Army". One thing that has emerged since I started to write this book is that within the Auxiliary Units there actually was an even more clandestine group called the Special Duties Section. I doubt if they were just guarding gold though; I suspect they were engaged in something the Government still does not want to acknowledge, though I have been unable to find out what. The weapons that I have described as being issued to the Auxiliary Units are much as I have described although the Lewis Gun may not have been, as this powerful weapon would not have fitted into their clandestine role.

As a side anecdote, in the late 1960s an older gentleman walked into the Army Recruiting Office in Preston and asked to see the Officer Commanding. When they met he asked when they were going to come and get "these damned guns" as he wanted to carry out building work on his garage. The Recruiting Office staff went with the man to his house and found that his garage had a false wall at the back, which concealed fifty Canadian Ross Rifles that had been stored for irregular forces during the war and had been forgotten about.

The government building known as 100 Parliament Street is the home of Her Majesty's Revenue and Customs and there is a fifth floor annex on the side overlooking Parliament Square in London. It is accessed by a door in the stair well and a narrow flight of stairs. There is also a rather good coffee shop on the ground floor.

In the story, Geordie refers to 'Crab Airlines'. The nickname that the British Army and Royal Navy use for the RAF is 'Crabs'. There are various explanations about how they got this nickname, some more polite than others.

The Hermitage in St Petersburg is a truly outstanding museum and holds the treasures of the rich and ancient Russian culture.

During the Spanish Civil War the Republican government did ship most, if not all, of the national gold reserves of Spain to Moscow. This gold was used to pay for the arms and equipment that Russia supplied to the Republican Army. By the end of the war Russia insisted that all the gold had been used up in payments and none came back. There is a strong suspicion in Spain even today that this might not have been a totally accurate accounting.

Richard Holmes, the historian, did lecture at the Royal Military Academy Sandhurst and was very popular there. He has narrated some fine historical TV programmes and written some very readable military history books. Sadly he is no longer with us but I recommend his books to you, particularly one called 'Redcoat' if you have an interest in the history of the British Army during the time when the musket and bayonet won battles.

The village of Benidoleig in Alicante province is real. As is the restaurant and hotel called 'El Cid' and I recommend a visit. At the time of writing it really is being run by Charlie and she is making a very good job of it.

There are a lot of place names in the area that start with "Beni". These are a throwback to the time when Spain was ruled by the Moors, as is the stone terracing still seen on many of the mountain slopes.

The George Hotel in Huntingdon was an old coaching inn and is now a modern comfortable hotel that retains many of its historical features. My children were told all about the ghost when we stayed there. There is also reputed to be a ghost in Hinchingbrooke House which is a very attractive building that was once owned by Oliver Cromwell's family and is now part of Hinchingbrooke School. It is used for the senior classes and is also used for wedding receptions, antique fairs and other events at the weekends.

The caves and caverns of the Hope Valley near Castleton in Derbyshire do exist and are well worth a visit. The commercialization of these caverns has been done sympathetically. The mineral known as 'Blue John' is found nowhere else in the world, it was mined by the Romans and mining continues on a small scale even today. It is still possible to buy small pieces of Blue John in the gift shops and some of them are very attractive. The Hope Valley and its show caves, plus the village of Castleton itself, are both very pleasant to visit.

The tides in Morecambe Bay are fast moving and there really are quicksand patches. It is possible to hire a specially trained guide who can lead parties across the sands in safety and it is possible to catch flatfish, known locally as 'Dabs', with your feet. It is definitely not safe to try to walk across without a guide and people drown every year through underestimating the speed and power of the tides. The train line does run around the bay, close to the water and when I was a boy the smoke of steam trains could be seen running around the head of the bay.

The village of South Cave exists and is near Hull in East Yorkshire. Cave Castle is an old building that is now a very comfortable hotel and golf complex in the heart of the village. The underground passage was found in 1866 and did lead to the parish church. There were Auxiliary Units operating in the area as I have described and Blackburn's, the aircraft factory, was in Brough and still is, though now under new management. The parish of South Cave appears in the Domesday Book in the year 1086 and Roman artifacts are sometimes found there, so this unassuming village has quite a history.

Fulwood Barracks in Preston is a Victorian built complex and is still in use at the time of writing.

Lancaster Castle is a prison at the time of writing but its days may be numbered as Her Majesty's Prison Service reorganises. It is a fascinating place to visit, although not open to the public at present for obvious reasons. The cells where the Pendle Witches were held are still there and are pretty grim. There is a gun tower in the middle of the courtyard which was increased in height so that cannon balls could reach the Lune River at the time of the Spanish Armada and the change in the stonework can still be seen.

The book "Raise the Titanic" is one from that most prolific of writers, Clive Cussler, whose inventiveness I envy and whose books I really enjoy.

The ancient burial sites known as barrows are to be found in many places on Salisbury plain and the British Army takes considerable pains to ensure they are not disturbed or damaged. The village of Tilshead really exists and is a very nice little village nestled in a shallow valley out on the plain with Westdown Camp on the low hill above it. When the weather conditions are right it is possible to stand in the high street and see the artillery shells passing over the hill behind the village. Sadly the story about the hidden crypt and the suspect grave are pure invention, though there is a small church there and the vicar does have to manage a group of parishes in these days of reduced congregations. The Rose and Crown is there and serves a nice pint of beer on a warm day.

Box Tunnel was designed and built by that great Victorian engineering genius Isambard Kingdom Brunel as part of the Great Western Railway. It is almost two miles long and runs beneath Box Hill. There are many rumours about what can be found in hidden tunnels under the hill including stories of captured UFOs being stored there or steam trains being kept as a strategic reserve for when the oil runs out and the diesels grind to a halt.

Far less fanciful are the real caverns that were excavated, under Box Hill, before and during World War 2. Massive ammunition depots were gouged out, as was a reserve aero engine factory that would have been brought into use had the nearby Bristol Aero Engine factory been destroyed by enemy bombing. Communications hubs were also built under there as was a narrow gauge railway to move ammunition supplies in and out. The entrance to one of these artificial caverns can be seen from the westbound train to the right of the tunnel entrance, though it is now mostly hidden by vegetation. Rudloe Manor sits on top of the hill and is still a Ministry of Defence site. It has been used by a number of 'lodger' units over the years; many of them involved in communication or security duties. I am reliably informed that the mound with the lift shaft does exist and it can be seen on aerial photographs that are available on the internet.

So there we have it, a mixture of fact from days gone by and speculation on my part. Did the British Government risk taking all their gold across the Atlantic and past the U Boats? Did they hide some within the UK just in case? Would the Auxiliary Units have been the people to entrust the gold to? Given the secretive nature of the British government on matters concerning the Auxiliary Units, even today, will we ever know?